MEANS AND MOTIVE

Addie studied the crime board. "I've just started, and already there seems to be more than enough of a motive for Nikki to have killed Chad." Addie's heart raced. "You know, Pippi"—she glanced down at her still-sleeping Yorkipoo and rolled her eyes—"never mind. If Chad treated Nikki horribly, there's a good chance he treated other people that way too. Maybe even the Elf. The first thing I have to do is find out more about Chad. There has to be another suspect in his past who would want to see him dead for the same reasons as Nikki might have. Maybe that someone committed murder when he or she was pushed too far."

She added, *Need to find out more about Chad*, and stabbed the tip of the marker at the end for emphasis. She circled *Nikki's ex*, *abusive*, *controlling*, and *manipulative* and drew a line to the *Motives* column with a question mark behind them. Addie started shuffling all the different angles, trying to find other motives for someone wanting Chad dead. . . .

Books by Lauren Elliott

Beyond the Page Bookstore Mysteries
MURDER BY THE BOOK
PROLOGUE TO MURDER
MURDER IN THE FIRST EDITION
PROOF OF MURDER
A PAGE MARKED FOR MURDER
UNDER THE COVER OF MURDER
TO THE TOME OF MURDER
A MARGIN FOR MURDER
DEDICATION TO MURDER
A LIMITED EDITION MURDER
EPILOGUE TO A CHRISTMAS MURDER

Crystals & CuriosiTEAS Mysteries
STEEPED IN SECRETS
MURDER IN A CUP
A SPIRITED BLEND

Published by Kensington Publishing Corp.

Epilogue
to a
Christmas
Murder

Lauren Elliott

Kensington Publishing Corp.
kensingtonbooks.com

KENSINGTON BOOKS are published by

Kensington Publishing Corp.
900 Third Avenue
New York, NY 10022

All Kensington titles, imprints, and distributed lines are available at special quantity discounts for bulk purchases for sales promotion, premiums, fundraising, educational, or institutional use.

Special book excerpts or customized printings can also be created to fit specific needs. For details, write or phone the office of the Kensington Sales Manager: Attn.: Sales Department. Kensington Publishing Corp., 900 Third Avenue, New York, NY 10022. Phone: 1-800-221-2647.

KENSINGTON and the KENSINGTON COZIES teapot logo Reg US Pat. & TM Off.

First Printing: October 2025

ISBN: 978-1-4967-5334-2
ISBN: 978-1-4967-5335-9 (ebook)

10 9 8 7 6 5 4 3 2 1

Printed in the United States of America

The authorized representative in the EU for product safety and compliance is eucomply OU, Parnu mnt 139b-14, Apt 123
Tallinn, Berlin 11317, hello@eucompliancepartner.com.

Epilogue
to a
Christmas
Murder

Chapter One

Addison Greyborne stared unseeing as she gazed into the bay window of Beyond the Page Books and Curios. Her mind drifted and swirled like the snow that piled up around her feet, and with the silence of the falling snow, each flake that fell on her cheeks awakened another memory of her last Christmas, the Christmas she'd spent in the sleepy little West Yorkshire village of Moorscrag.

As the snow and wind lapped at her cheeks, alternating images flashed through her mind's eye of that special place and the dear friends she'd made there. She rubbed at the pained spot in her chest, but the ache in her heart grew at one image in particular, and a sense of loss, along with all the haunting *what-ifs* that accompanied it.

Other images then rushed through her mind, overwhelming her. Each one pushed her deeper into a state that took her between a sense of loss and the apprehension of the homecoming she'd experienced when she'd returned from England. At the time, she hadn't been sure she could adjust to life back in Greyborne Harbor. She wasn't the same person she was when she left.

Now, as she stood in front of the window to the bookshop, she recalled the dread she'd experienced on the flight home, knowing that right down the street from her house was the house where her ex, Simon, and his first wife, Laurel, lived happily with their seventeen-year-old son, Mason. Little did she know on the return flight that Simon's forever-after—without her—wouldn't be the change in Greyborne Harbor that would cut her the deepest.

As Addie shuffled and stomped to keep the blood flowing in her freezing feet, the blanket of snow deafened her to everything except her own recollections, which rushed back on her like the erratic, swirling snow itself.

She'd known that when she returned home, she wasn't quite finished relinquishing her ghosts of the past. Even though, bit by bit, during her year in England, Addie had made great leaps forward in coming to terms with learning that not only Simon, but everyone else in her family she had known and trusted had kept the truth from her. The discovery about her grandmother Hattie not being who Addie had thought she was her entire life left Addie reeling. The sense of being lost and alone in the realization her whole life had been based on a lie. A knowledge that had left her floundering and disconnected from the Addie she'd once been.

She blinked to stem the tears burning behind her eyes as she mentally relived her homecoming this past summer, aware then that to truly become her new self, she still had one more layer of the old her to peel away. One more remnant of her past life needed to be laid to rest. Marc Chandler. A man who had never lied to her, never told her he was something he was not, a man she thought she'd loved at one time, would soon be wed. As much as she'd convinced herself she'd be okay with Marc making vows to another woman, when Marc and his betrothed said "I do" that summer day, Addie hadn't been prepared.

It had shaken her to her very core.

Not because she had any remnants of romantic feelings left toward him. No, those had been dealt with and played out long ago, and it was definitely not because she didn't want to see him happy. Her heartache had come with facing the fact that Marc, as her friend, and onetime love, was the one last connection she had to her old self. The person she had been in her old life—before everything changed for her.

The day when Marc took his wedding vows was the day the last little piece of her slipped away. It was final. The old Addie had gone. The part of her she'd clung to in order to feel like . . . well, to feel like the person she had been her whole life before she became someone else, had evaporated, leaving her feeling a shell of her former self.

A car horn blared in the background, bringing Addie back to reality. She shivered, but didn't go inside. Instead, she continued to watch the goings-on through the large picture window.

Paige Stringer, her assistant manager, answered the phone, and while Addie couldn't hear the conversation, Paige's smile indicated that she had everything well in hand.

Did Addie even belong here anymore?

She fought to embrace her current self and living situation, but she struggled to push away the enticing sense of the warmth and belonging she'd discovered in the sleepy little English village last year. Those memories sent her spiraling deeper into all the *what-ifs* she still harbored.

After all, Paige, in Addie's absence, had successfully run the bookshop and even after her return, Paige ran the bookstore and bookmobile service with expert precision. It seemed Addie's little protégé had surpassed the teacher.

Just as Nikki, the shop assistant and Addie's housemate, had run Addie's household and looked after Addie's community commitments with equal meticulousness. It all made Addie feel obsolete in her own life.

She sniffled and snuggled Pippi, her little Yorkipoo, tighter under her arm. Even after all these months back in Greyborne Harbor, she still had no idea who Addie Greyborne really was and where the new her belonged.

It was in melancholy times like these that Addie missed Catherine Lewis—or should she say, Catherine Vanguard now, after her marriage to Felix. The dashing globetrotter who had stolen away the only woman Addie had come to know as a mother figure. If her grandmother Hattie hadn't interfered in Addie's father's life all those years ago, when Addie wasn't much more than a toddler . . . after Addie's mother had died, Catherine would have ended up as Addie's stepmother. Even now, though, they had a special bond. At the moment Addie wasn't certain which one she was more upset with: Hattie, for not allowing her father's planned remarriage to go through, or Felix, for sweeping Catherine away. Addie only knew she needed a mother to talk to.

The door slammed open, and a little girl scampered out, holding her arms high above her head while she spun in circles and danced in the falling snow.

"Auntie Addie?"

"Yes?" Addie glanced down into the large, quizzical blue eyes of the little girl dancing like a snow fairy.

"Did you and Mommy make the display last night?" She pointed to the picture window.

Addie refocused her thoughts and glanced at Paige, who was frantically writing something on a pad of paper. "Does your mommy know you're out here, Emma?" Addie shifted Pippi in her arm, leaned down, and with her free hand finished zipping the little girl's coat up to her chin, pulling her collar to her ears and rosy-red cheeks. "Did you hear me?" Addie asked as Emma stared wide-eyed into the shop's window.

"I just came out for a minute." Emma jerked her chin toward the window.

Addie's brows shot up.

"I mean," Emma whispered, her tiny voice quivered, lacking its earlier defiance. "I couldn't see over the poster you put at the back, and I just wanted to see what was in the window display." Her big, round eyes looked tentatively up, and her little hand slipped into Addie's. "Your windows are always so pretty, and we came in the back door, so I just wanted to see it all."

Addie smiled and squeezed the girl's cold hand in hers. How could she stay annoyed with that beautiful little face? Addie glanced into the bookshop again at Paige still on the phone. "I guess we can look for a minute or two. But you're going to have to bundle up and keep these ice-cold hands in your pocket." She lifted Emma's hand to her face and blew warm breath on it. "Okay?"

"Okay." Emma slipped her hands inside her coat pocket but quickly withdrew her right hand and pointed. "Is that the same lighthouse you used a long time ago in the window?"

Addie let out a short laugh. "You have a good memory, my friend. Yes, your mommy and I found a string of mini lights and those tiny wreaths in an old Victorian Christmas village set we found in the storeroom. So, we wrapped them around the lighthouse and added the wreaths so that it looks just like the real one in the harbor."

"But there's no Santa sleigh full of presents out front of the real one, is there?" Emma asked, her voice reaching a fevered pitch of concern. "Aren't they afraid a really bad person would steal them?"

"You're right. The Santa sleigh will be set up in the lobby of the lighthouse museum, so it's snuggled in, all safe from any bad people, and the security guard can keep an eye on it."

"Then why do you have it outside of the building here?"

"It's not really meant to be a proper portrayal of the actual scene, it's . . ." Addie looked at the confusion in Emma's eyes. "Think of the window scene along with the selection of Christmas books more like an advertisement that's hopefully going to help the lighthouse museum's Twelve Days of Christmas charity fundraiser sell more tickets so they can reach their fundraising goal."

"But isn't that lying?"

"No, it's called a promotion. When people can visualize . . ." She glanced at Emma, who was waiting eagerly for the explanation. Addie shook her head humbly. This little eight-year-old girl certainly knew more than Addie had known when she was eight. "Then they are more likely to want to buy tickets, and then the raffle committee will make all the money they need for programming next year. I even heard," she said, grinning, and tapped Emma on the nose, "that one of those programs is an all-inclusive children's learning center in the museum. Wouldn't you like that?"

At Emma's head nod, Addie continued, explaining how it took her and Emma's mommy one full afternoon to wrap all the tiny boxes of presents in the Santa sleigh. They were meant to look like the contest gifts people would be trying to win in the twelve nightly raffle drawings leading up to Christmas Eve.

"So, you see," added Addie, "the window display is meant as a type of poster to make people want to buy raffle tickets—and all those Christmas books too." Addie gestured to the books in the window.

"Is that's what wrapped up in the sleigh?" Emma

asked, her fingers pointing to the books in the window exhibit.

"No, the huge sleigh in the lobby of the lighthouse museum is filled with all sorts of donated items from businesses in town." She leaned down and whispered, "I also hear there are lots of yummy, homemade goodies too."

"I hope I win! I love Christmas goodies." Emma smiled a toothy smile that Addie couldn't help but mirror.

"You'll probably have a pretty good chance if your mommy buys tickets. Every night for the twelve days leading up to Christmas Eve, one name will be drawn from a barrel containing all the names of people who bought tickets, and each day the person whose name was drawn will win that day's contents of Santa's sack. Each bag is marked Day One, Two, Three, etc., and the closer we get to Christmas Eve, the bigger and more valuable the items will get, leading up to the grand prize drawing, which has lots and lots of prizes and a free trip to Hawaii."

"What if I win that one?"

"Then you and your mommy will have an amazing time in Hawaii. Maybe you can pack me in your suitcase so I can come along?"

Emma giggled, but her face grew serious as she looked back into the window. "But if you're selling the books, how can you be putting them in the Santa sack too? Won't Santa be mad that you are selling the ones he's giving away?"

Addie looked about, hoping for rescue. She wasn't sure how to explain the whole situation to a child, and she hoped she wasn't going to slip up and say something that Emma wasn't ready to hear yet about Santa. "Your mommy and I picked out some other very special books that we knew Santa would love to have in the sleigh to give away with all the other gifts he's got for the winners."

Emma seemingly took that explanation in stride and pointed to the one left of the lighthouse. "What's so special about that one that it's on a bookstand?"

"That book is a newer edition, and it's just in the window for display, but the real one that we're going to donate for the Christmas Eve gala is coming all the way from England, sent here by my friend Mr. Reginald Pressman."

"Does that mean books from England are more special?" Emma asked.

"Oh, no, not necessarily. The book was written by an American author, but the one being sent from England is special because that author signed it many years ago. See where the wooden page marker is holding the book open to the title page, which says *The Four Million*? It contains a famous short story titled 'The Gift of the Magi.'"

Emma nodded.

"It's an extra-special story about two people who sell their most important personal possessions so they could get money to buy Christmas gifts for each other, and that makes them as wise and selfless as the Magi, the wise men who visited baby Jesus."

"Did the Magi write it?"

"No, it was written by an American author named O. Henry, and it was first published in a magazine called *New York World* in 1905."

"But that's a magazine, not a book."

"You're right, but the next year, the story was added into a book collection of stories by the same author titled *The Four Million,* and the copy I ordered to give away is far more valuable than the one in the window, because it's a 1906 first edition signed by O. Henry himself."

Emma's eyes widened. "Wait, does that mean you and my mommy are like the Magi—giving away your most cherished possessions so other people will be happy?"

"No," Addie said with a short laugh. "Come on, little one, we're both freezing. Let's go get some hot chocolate, okay?"

She ushered Emma back into the shop to warm up and drew in a breath, savoring the usual scent of old books and leather. But this time of year brought with it the delicious aromas of cinnamon sticks, spiced apples, and gingerbread from the potpourri dishes set out on the bookshelves throughout the shop. If she could only bottle the scent and sell it, she could retire a millionaire.

Paige was still on the phone, and by her stance and the stiffness in her shoulders, Addie sensed that the call she'd initially thought was going smoothly, was not going well.

"Let's go sit in the reading alcove in the back corner. I'll get our hot cocoa while you pick out a short story book. There are some classic Golden Books that just came in that would be good, so take a look at those."

"Those are for babies."

"My mistake. You're just growing up so fast I completely forgot you are eight years old now."

"That means I can pick anything I want, right?"

"Yes, but only from the children's section, and make sure it's a short book because the store opens in fifteen minutes." Addie laughed as Emma's little legs took her off in a run to the children's section by the back wall.

As soon as Addie set Pippi on the floor, she immediately went around the back of the counter to her bed. Addie poured both her and Emma a take-out cup of hot chocolate from the large urn on the counter. She glanced at Paige, who had now stepped to the far side of the bookshop and was engaged in a very animated discussion. As much as she was dying to know why her shop manager was in such a state, she knew that as soon as her friend was done, she'd verbally unload whatever it was she appeared to be so stressed about.

Addie took a seat in a leather chair, set the two cups on the side table, and waited for Emma to bring over a book. She hoped that Paige's mother, Martha Stringer, wasn't interfering again in Paige and Logan Ashmore's Christmas Day wedding.

"*Oomph!*" Addie gasped as a rambunctious eight-year-old raced around the end of the bookshelf and dropped into her lap in one whirling movement. "I see you found a book?"

"Yes." Emma's small voice squeaked with delight. "And look—" She shoved the book in Addie's face. "It's *The Four Million* just like the one in the window!"

"Yes, I see," said Addie with a laugh as she clasped the book and pushed it out from under her nose. "But I think this story could be a little too old for an eight-year-old. Perhaps I should help you find something different."

"But Auntie . . ." Emma's little chin quivered. "I want this one. I'm eight now, remember?"

"I suppose it would be okay, but if you can't understand it, then please let me know and we'll find something else." Addie knew she shouldn't give in so easily, but when Emma turned her big, round eyes on her, Addie's heart did everything a sucker of an auntie's would do. It melted, and she was putty in the little girl's hand. Oh well, it was an auntie's job to spoil a child, wasn't it?

Addie settled back in the large, cozy leather chair, and as Emma perched on her lap, she began reading.

"Emma," said Paige from above them, "what did I say about reading that much over your grade level? You know the rules. No middle-school books until you're at least in fifth grade."

"But Mommy—"

"No buts. Now, go put that book back, and let Addie and Mommy talk for a minute, okay, pumpkin?"

"O . . . k . . . a. . . . y, Mommy." She turned her blue, tear-filled eyes on Addie, gave her a shaky smile, hopped down, and then disappeared around the bookshelf corner.

"I'm so sorry, Paige, I—"

"No, it's me who should be apologizing." She flipped her recently cut short, bobbed blond hair from her eyes and blew at a stray strand. "I should have kept a better eye on her. I haven't even got the register set up or done a tour around the shop to pick up any stacks of books from the book club meeting last night. I still have to—"

"It's all right. At least you got the hot cocoa made,

and I'm here early. Because I was worried about the roads getting bad if the storm hits earlier than they thought it would. I can help with the rest of the opening." Addie glanced toward the window and gestured. "Besides, I don't see a line waiting to get in anyway, so relax. It's not urgent that we open precisely at nine." Addie placed her hands on Paige's shaking shoulders. "What in the world has you in such a state, though?"

"It's just that I'm a horrible person, and it seems I'm a horrible mother too. I saw Emma go outside, but I was too wrapped up—"

"You stop right there. You are definitely not a bad mother. She was fine. I was there—and you are not a bad person either. Who told you that you were? I'll set them straight." Addie huffed and brought her clenched fist up to her face, grinning.

"It's just that when our wedding planner called, I assumed Carol-Ann was calling to confirm more details. But instead, she was crying and told me that if my mother was going to go behind her back and continue to change all the arrangements we've made, she was going to quit. Then she said, 'No, Paige. I like you and Logan, but your mother has pushed it too far. I do quit.'"

Addie gasped.

"Then it took me over half an hour for me to try to talk her out of walking away from my wedding, that's supposed to happen in less than three weeks." Paige sniffled. "She still said no. Not as long as my mother was involved." Paige's sniffles turned to sobs bordering on hysterical.

"Oh no, my friend," Addie said, pulling a tissue out

from inside her sleeve, gulped back her chest pangs, and cradled Paige in her arms. Addie had been through this stage of wedding planning, first with the volatile lead-up to her best friend Serena Ludlow's wedding and keeping her from throwing in the towel at the eleventh-hour, and then her own—nearly—wedding, so she knew how unforeseen calamities could easily crop up. One thing she had learned through it all was that tissues were a must-have, especially three weeks before the big day, and it was her job as the maid of honor to keep them well stocked and handy.

Chapter Two

"It can't be that bad, can it?" Addie asked, patting Paige's back as her friend sobbed on her shoulder. "Why don't you let me talk to Carol-Ann. I'm sure we can fix this with her and get everything back on track."

"We can't. It's . . . it's wor-worse than that." Paige sniffled between sobs. "My mother has gone and changed the venues, the menu, the flowers, the—"

Addie gasped and held Paige at arm's length. "What do you mean, she changed everything? Can she do that? You've already paid deposits, haven't you?"

"Yes." Paige broke out in renewed sobs. "She took the refunded money and used it for *her* choice of venues."

"Without asking you?"

Paige nodded, wiped her nose with the tissue, and took a breath. "That's why Carol-Ann quit. She said first thing this morning she got emails from all the wedding vendors we'd booked telling her how sad they were to hear the event was cancelled, and they had transferred the majority of the deposits, less cancelation fees, back to the account they had on record."

Renewed tears flowed down Paige's scarlet cheeks. "That's my mother's credit card . . . she was paying for most of it . . ." She broke into another bout of sobbing. "Of course, Carol-Ann was confused and called me to find out if we had cancelled the whole wedding," Paige managed to sputter out between sobs.

"But you didn't, did you?"

"No, definitely not, and I called Mom right away and asked her what Carol-Ann was talking about, because we were going to lose all our vendors."

"And?" Addie waited until Paige got her bearings again.

"She said she had used the refunded money already to pay the deposits on a 'proper' wedding venue and reception area that would cost less than the church and the Grey Gull Inn."

The pressure in Addie's head grew with each word Paige spoke. It didn't matter if Martha was paying for it or not. How dare she derail Paige's big day without even discussing it with her—and with only three weeks until the wedding?

Addie opened her mouth to have her say about Martha Stringer's actions and to tell Paige not to worry—that Addie would march next door to the bakery and give Paige's mother a piece of her mind—but two big blue eyes filled with tears and fear, stared up at her from around the corner of the bookshelf.

Addie snapped her mouth closed and looked at Paige, gesturing her head toward Emma, standing behind her.

Paige swiped at her own tear-covered cheeks and swung around. "Are you ready to put up the Open sign?"

"Are you and Logan not getting married?" Emma asked, her voice as small as she had become as she shrank against the bookshelf.

"Oh no, honey, that's not what happened at all." Paige sank to her knees, took the little girl's hands in hers, and started to explain what had happened as best she could to an eight-year-old.

Addie marveled how Paige didn't make her mother out to be the bad guy in the story but indicated that it was all just a misunderstanding with Emma's grandmother.

Addie jumped at a rap on the front door. She turned and saw four ladies waiting not so patiently for the shop to open and glanced at the clock. It was a quarter past nine. She gave Paige a reassuring squeeze on the shoulder and smiled at Emma as she passed them and hurried to open the door.

The morning flew by, with the constant flow of people getting a start on their Christmas shopping as they tried to beat the impending storm, and between the customers and making sure Pippi got out occasionally to relieve herself, Addie forgot all about the trials Paige was experiencing until she looked up from the cash register and stared into a pair of faded-blue eyes.

"Martha!" Addie closed the till and noted the woman had no books to pay for in her hands. "How can I help you?"

"Since Emma's off school until after the holidays, I told Paige I'd pick her up at noon and take Emma to lunch to give her a break, but I can't find either of them anywhere." She waved her hand wildly in a circle. "Tell me that I didn't misunderstand, and Paige took the day off too." Her eyes widened. "You're not working alone today, are you? Where is that Nikki person?" Her gloved hand went to her lips. "My goodness, I do hope she hasn't gone off the road somewhere. The roads are horrible today."

"Nikki is fine. She'll be in at one, but . . ." Addie swallowed hard as she took a second to scan for listening ears. Judging by the empty shop, she realized it must be the usual noon hour lull. "I would like to talk to you for a—"

"Maybe Paige is busy in the storeroom, then."

"Yeah, that must be where—but—"

"Never mind." Martha waved. "Just tell her I was in and to meet me at Mario's Ristorante on Main Street at three o'clock sharp for a menu sampling." She clutched her handbag to her chest and walked away from the counter. "And tell her to drive carefully because the snow started and the roads look slick," she said, calling over her shoulder.

"Wait!" said Addie, giving the shop another quick glance around. If she was going to confront the woman about Paige and Logan's wedding, this might be the best time before the woman could do any more damage. "Can we talk for a minute?"

Martha turned her now-not-so-friendly gaze on Addie. "If you are going to tell me to back off and stop interfering in my baby girl's wedding, I'll have none of it." She wagged her finger, and her eyes filled with resentment. "*I'm* the one paying for this wedding, and *I* will be the one to say who will come and who will not. Were you aware they invited—"

"No, but the guest list is only one of the things I wanted to—"

"Never mind, then," Martha said snappishly, then pulled herself to her full yet diminutive height at Addie's shoulder. "Since it's *my* money, I will decide who will be invited and who won't, where it will be held, and what we will eat, not some upstart Carol-Ann Bingham, who fancies herself a . . . what does she call herself? Oh right, a *wedding planner*, whatever that is, and a very expensive one at that. Have you seen what her retainer fee alone is? I can't imagine what her final bill will be," she huffed.

"Yes, but aren't they planning to pay you back?"

"I'll believe it when I see it. Until then it's my dollar," Martha scoffed.

Addie gulped and tried to rearrange her thoughts. She had known that Martha's often-prickly personality wouldn't make bringing up Paige's wedding easy, and she had suspected she might not embrace the discussion wholeheartedly, but Addie hadn't been prepared for her near-violent outburst. "It's just that . . ." She slowly rounded the counter toward Martha, afraid she'd startle the woman into another tirade. "These are plans that have been in place for months now, and—"

"I'm aware." Martha harrumphed and crossed her ample arms over her heaving chest.

Addie took a deep breath. "And . . . they are what Paige and Logan want. They're the ones who actually made the plans; the wedding planner only—"

"Stop right there!" Martha held up her hand. "I know full well that what was booked is *not* the wedding of Paige's dreams. Heavens, she's talked about her dream wedding since she was six years old and the first time I took her and her sisters to Mario's." She uncrossed her arms, leaned forward, and glared at Addie. "So, you tell me. Who knows her better? The mother who bore and raised her, or some newcomer who has bamboozled my daughter into thinking she should be married at the largest church in Greyborne Harbor and hold a huge reception at the Grey Gull Inn and inviting everyone in town at *my* expense!" Her voice rose to a screech. "At least when you were going to hold yours there, you had the decency only to book the top two floors, not the entire restaurant. Unlike this wedding planner, Carol-Ann *Bingham*," she spat out her last name. "Who seems to think I have unlimited funds to pay all willy-nilly for all the wasteful extravagance that I know my daughter doesn't really want."

"But it's not wasteful if it is what Paige wants. People change. Paige has changed, Martha. She certainly isn't that little, wide-eyed six-year-old girl anymore. She's grown, and her dreams have grown, and—"

Martha's hand flew up, stemming Addie's argument. "If you'll excuse me, I have a lot more to do in order to give my baby the wedding of *her* dreams."

"Are they *her* dreams, Martha, or are they yours?" The words tumbled out of Addie's mouth harsher and faster than she could mentally check them, and she stared at Martha in shock.

Martha scowled furiously at her, then swung around, sending the overhead doorbells into a chaotic jangle at her departure.

"What have I done?" Addie grabbed the edge of the counter to steady herself and sat down hard on one of the stools.

"Wow, you were great. Thanks for trying," Paige meekly said from behind her.

Addie spun the stool around and looked at Paige. "I'm afraid I just made things worse for you."

"No, what you said was perfect. Now it will get her thinking, and after she does, she'll see that you were right. I have grown up, and this is still her dream, but not mine."

Addie stood and placed her hands gently on Paige's shoulders. "But you didn't see the look on her face when she left. I think I really hurt her."

"Granted, your tone was a bit harsh, but the words were perfect."

"That's what my grandmo—er, my aunt Hattie used to tell me when I was growing up. 'It's not what you say, Addie dearest, it's how you say it.' I thought I'd learned my lesson, but I'm afraid I just made things worse for you and Logan. I'm sor—"

"Don't you dare apologize. Everything will be fine, and I'm grateful you were looking out for me. Now that it's been said, Mom will come around, you'll see." She wrapped her arms around Addie.

"As your maid of honor, aren't I supposed to be comforting you, not the other way around?" Addie said with a short laugh when Paige released her from the bear hug.

"Come on, you know we are here to pick each other up. That's what friends do, right?"

"Right," said Addie, smiling and gazing out the window. Her smile faded. "By the look of it out there, we might just have a whole afternoon to keep each other perked up." Addie gestured to the scene unfolding outside. Snow was falling so thickly that Addie could barely make out the park entrance across the street. "If the wind picks up, we're in for quite the nor'easter."

Paige glanced out and sighed. "I know they said it was going to snow, but an all-out whiteout is not what I expected to see today."

"Me neither." Addie walked to the bay window and glanced right and left. "The street is empty, so it's looking like it definitely will be a long afternoon."

Paige slipped to her side and took a quick glance out. "Yeah, it's pretty wild out there, isn't it?" She took out her phone and started scrolling. "Yikes, there's a weather warning now. It says a major storm is churning its way up the coast and bringing high winds and snow, with the worst of it to hit the Pen Hollow Peninsula, Greyborne Harbor, and Salem areas."

"Yay! Lucky us." Addie frowned. "Where is Emma?"

"Don't worry. She's safe and sound in the back. I found some scraps from our decorating work the other day, gave her a bottle of glue and a sheet of construction paper, and told her to go to town and make Grandma a nice Christmas picture to put on her fridge."

Addie raised a questioning brow.

"I might be mad at my mother, but it doesn't involve Emma. She adores the old battle-ax. I'm not sure why, though—"

"Probably because she smells like cookies."

"I know, she does, doesn't she?" said Paige, chuckling. "Anyway, Emma feels bad that we're mad at Grandma, and she wanted to make something nice for her." Paige shrugged. "What was I supposed to do, say no, tell her to stay away from the awful woman who is ruining my life? I can't do that, no matter what I think. Emma still loves her, and she loves Emma." Paige looked helplessly at Addie.

"It's tough, I know," Addie said with a weak smile. "But you're right. You should never put your differences between—"

The door flew open with a *bang* against the doorstop, and the wind spewed snow all over the entrance, sending the overhead bells into a frenzied dance.

A man wearing a black hat and coat stumbled through, turned, then heaved against the door to close it. "I'm sorry about that, but it's really kicking up out there."

Addie drew in a sharp gasp. "It can't be?" she said under her breath.

Paige looked curiously at her.

The man removed his fedora, raised his head, and gazed at Addie, his fog-gray eyes shimmering in the overhead lights. "Miss Greyborne, it's so nice to see you again."

Chapter Three

"De . . . Detective Inspector Parker? What are you doing here?" Addie sucked in a gulp of air in an attempt to force down the unexpected lump that left her breathless.

Noah unbuttoned his black wool trench coat. "I flew into Boston because I thought I might take a side trip to drop this off before I get a flight to my final destination, New York City." He pulled out a brown paper–wrapped parcel from an inside coat pocket and held it out.

The melody of his genteel, upper-crust London accent immediately took Addie back to last Christmas, and those special memories rushed back, crushing her heart. Willing her face not to betray her tumultuous thoughts, she crossed the floor, silently cursing the unsteadiness of her legs, and took the package from his hand. "What's this?"

"You did order a book from Reginald Pressman, did you not?"

"Did I know you were bringing this?"

He grinned sheepishly. "Surprise!"

She stared blankly at him, trying to compute why he was standing in front of her. In her shop. In Greyborne Harbor. It didn't make sense. "Um . . . well, it is good to see you again and . . . well . . . totally unexpected, of course," she said with a nervous laugh. "I, um . . . well—"

As she gazed at him, she couldn't shake the memory of how they'd first met and her first impression of him. Even now, her fists clenched as she remembered his infuriating manner toward her, and how she'd thought him a despicable person.

He must have read her thoughts, because a knowing glint sparkled in his eyes and a soft smile touched his lips. Addie's heart knocked against her rib cage at that smile and the knowledge that she'd pegged him wrong from the start. It hadn't taken her long to go from loathing the man to finding him utterly enticing. Noah Parker was officially the first and only person of her acquaintance that inspired a constant pendulum of emotion in her.

His gaze shifted from her eyes to her lips and then back again. All of Addie's *what-ifs* and the pain that came with them rushed through her, causing her breath to catch in her throat.

"Oh dear, I feel I've made you uncomfortable," Noah said. "I do apologize. Now that I have discharged my duties for our friend Reginald, I'll take my leave." He put his hat on and turned toward the door.

"No!" cried Addie, stepping toward him. "You've

just surprised me, that's all. Please, forgive my rudeness, come in and sit. Can I get you a coffee or a hot chocolate?" she asked, gesturing to the urn and drip coffeemaker on the far end of the Victorian-style sales counter.

He glanced out the window. "It does look like this might not be quite the time to head back out on the motorway, so . . . why not? Thank you." He smiled, removed his hat again, and looked from a silent Addie to a spellbound Paige. "Now, since this is my first trip to America, do I help myself, or do you—"

"Our hostess seems to have forgotten her manners today. Let me reintroduce myself." Paige gave Addie a sideways half smile and held out her hand to DI Parker in greeting. "I don't know if you remember me, but I'm Paige Stringer. I met you last year in England and I'll be happy to prepare your beverage of choice."

"It's very nice to see you again, Miss Stringer, but please call me Noah."

"Then you must call me Paige. We Americans aren't used to such formalities, anyway."

"That's right, and you'll have to forgive me, Inspector Parker." Addie unglued her gaze from him and regained her voice. "I'm just so surprised to see you here."

"I'm not here in the capacity of an inspector, so please, Noah is fine, really. To be honest, I wasn't certain what kind of greeting I was going to receive. The offer of a hot beverage before heading back out is perfect. Thank you," he said with a smile, then turned to Paige. "Black coffee would be lovely, and thank you."

Addie smiled shyly at him and turned her attention

to the package. She laid it on the counter and removed the brown paper wrapping, revealing a red cloth cover with "O. Henry, *The Four Million*" set in gold, gilded lettering. "This is very nice." She traced the title with her finger. "And in just as good condition as I remember it being when we found it in Second Chance Books and Bindery."

"Brilliant. I'm certain Reginald will be thrilled to hear that you approve."

Addie looked at him curiously. "That's the second time you've referred to Mr. Pressman as 'Reginald.' I worked for him for over a year, and I never had the nerve to call him anything other than by his formal name."

Noah shrugged as he set his coffee mug on the counter. "What can I say? After I moved to Moorscrag, I became a regular customer, and he and I became mates, I suppose."

"Hmm." Addie eyed him. "I had heard you moved to a cottage on Moorscrag Lane, but I had no idea that you were a voracious reader too. You are full of surprises, aren't you, Inspector?" Addie wryly grinned as she picked up the cup Paige had set down in front of her, eyeing him over the rim as she took a sip.

His face flushed, and he turned toward the window, taking a drink of his coffee.

Addie glanced over at Paige, who was grinning like a Cheshire cat.

"What?" Addie mouthed.

Paige flung the back of her hand across her forehead and crumpled her knees, feigning a swoon. Addie swatted at her and choked on her coffee.

Noah swiveled around on the stool, his eyes filled with alarm.

"I'm fine." Addie waved off his concern. "I just need to take smaller sips of hot coffee."

He nodded and took his phone out of the pocket of his coat, lying across the stool beside him. Tapped in something, then began scrolling. "Forgive me, but I'm just checking the driving report, as it does look somewhat nastier out there than when I arrived," he said distractedly. "And . . . it's not looking good," he added without glancing up from his phone. "It appears the roads to Boston are closed, as is the airport. Could either of you be so kind as to recommend a top-notch hotel or B&B where I might stay for the night?"

"Addie would be happy to help you, wouldn't you?" Paige said quickly and pulled Addie to her side. "My daughter's in the back room crafting, and I really should check on her, so . . . ." Paige backed away with a grin on her pixie-like face, and with fingers crossed, she headed to the back room, giggling as she went.

Noah smiled, hinting that he'd caught on to Paige's antics, and pinned Addie with an encouraging gaze.

Addie swallowed hard, trying to corral the sensation of hundreds of butterflies swirling in her chest. She'd forgotten the power of his striking eyes and how the gray hue could change so suddenly depending on how the light hit them. "I can help you find lodging." She smiled reassuringly and tapped in a number on her phone.

"Hi, Lillian. Addie Greyborne here. I was—Yes, yes, it's been a while. I'm fine, and yes, I did enjoy my sabbatical in England." She rolled her eyes at Noah, who accompanied his mouthing the word 'sabbatical' with air quotes. "I'm calling to see if a . . . friend?" She looked at Noah, who returned a smile. "Could book a—Yes, tonight. Oh, the entire hotel is full? . . . Yes, yes, the storm, of course. Do you know, or have you heard if anyone has an available room?" She shrugged helplessly at Noah. "Okay, thanks anyway, Lillian, and no, I won't be a stranger. See you soon. Bye."

Addie frowned and scrolled through her contact list. "Don't worry, there are some more places I can try."

"Don't go to any trouble for me. I can sleep in the hire car. The seats go all the way back. I'll be fine."

"You will not sleep in a rental car, or any other car for that matter. Not in this weather. You'll freeze to death. If you have to . . ." She swallowed, her thoughts wavering between what she knew would be the right thing to do and all the what-ifs that looped through her mind. "If you have to, you could stay with—"

The ring from her phone drowned out the words she was about to utter, and she quickly pressed Accept Call.

"Good afternoon, Addie Greyborne speaking." She was well aware her voice sounded unusually cheerful in her relief that they were interrupted before she'd invited Noah to stay at her house and commit what could be a friendship-ending move.

She had what her aunt Hattie would have called a 'wee bit of a crush,' that was for certain, which would be fine if he felt the same way. But what if he wasn't as enamored with her or wasn't ready to move forward because the ghost of his late wife still haunted him, like her late fiancé, David, used to haunt her? What if the whole experience of him being her houseguest turned out to be awkward? She inwardly shivered. No, no more what-ifs. She wasn't willing to face those or any from her past. She simply needed to find him someplace else to stay.

"Beyond the Page Books and Curios, how can I help you? . . . Hi, Lillian." She gave Noah a confused glance. "Yes, we're still looking. I was just about to call . . . The Greyborne Point B&B? That's fantastic news. Thank you. I'll call Bin right away. Thank you so, so much . . . yes . . . yes, thanks, bye."

"Lillian said Bin Thomas, one of the sisters who owns a B&B, called her to let her know that if anyone needed a room for the night, they'd had a couple of cancellations. Apparently, some of their original guests had to cancel due to the roads." Addie grinned and tapped in the B&B's phone number.

A few minutes later, Addie gave Noah the address to the Greyborne Point B&B and watched with a sinking sensation as he input the address into Google Maps. This could be it. The last time she'd ever see him.

"It's been a pleasure seeing you again, Addie." Noah eased into his coat and placed his fedora on his head.

Not knowing what to say without making a fool of herself, she reciprocated the smile he gave her and watched him walk out her door—and possibly her life.

Addie sat down hard on a stool and took the first deep breath she'd had since he'd walked in. She looked around the vacant bookstore. There wasn't a soul around to verify that what had happened really *did* happen, and for a split second, she wondered if maybe it had been a dream.

"Where is he?" Paige asked from behind her.

Addie jerked and swiveled around.

Paige stood on tiptoes, scanning the shop as if he might be hiding somewhere.

"Then he really was here?" Addie asked.

Paige chuckled. "No, you didn't imagine it. Although it's too bad he's gone. I could have listened to him talk all day, but Emma needed help, and . . . well, it's too bad I missed him."

"He's not gone."

"Yikes." Paige threw her hand over her mouth and glanced quickly around. "I hope he didn't hear me," she whispered.

"No, he's gone from the bookstore"—Addie sighed, and couldn't help the *and out of my life* thought from intruding—"but not Greyborne Harbor. I—"

"You did it, then. You invited him to stay at your place."

"No, I don't know him well enough to offer my guest room. I found a room for him at the sisters' B&B."

"That's too bad."

"No." Addie shook her head. "It's not, is it? I mean, we hardly know each other."

"What do you mean you 'hardly know each other'? You solved a murder with that man."

"Yes, but . . ." Addie's raw emotions toward Noah were too new for her to share openly with Paige just now. As much as she trusted her assistant, she hardly trusted herself with these new sensations. So, instead of telling Paige her new truth, she went with an old one, one that Paige would believe. "Remember how infuriating he can be? What if he was like that as my houseguest, and I ended up—"

"Ended up what? Having the same feelings you developed for him when you got to know him better? Come on, Addie. His feelings are clear by the way he looks at you—and the simple fact that he drove out of his way on icy winter roads to deliver a book, of all things, to you when arrangements had already been made for a courier. It's *your* feelings now that you have to figure out."

Addie shook her head. She had underestimated her friend . . . again. "I have no clue what you're talking about."

Paige *tsk*ed, went behind the counter, and picked up the landline phone. "Sure, you don't." Her grin was anything but reassuring. "Wouldn't it be faster to discover all that about him *if* he was staying in your guest room?"

"You're not calling the B&B to cancel his room, are you?" Flustered, Addie reached for the phone.

"No, silly," said Paige with a short laugh. "But I should. You missed a golden opportunity. I'm calling Nikki to cancel her this afternoon, because by the look of it out there, we won't be needing a third staffer to come in."

Addie gazed out the window. All she could think about as she pressed her forehead to the cold window glass and watched the snow whirling across the street was whether Noah had made it safely down the hill to the B&B on the harbor. Then she shook her head. *Silly girl. He was a Detective Chief Inspector in London. He can survive the roads in Greyborne Harbor.* "You really think I should have offered him a room at my house?"

"Yes, you have a built-in chaperone with Nikki still living there, in case you were worried what people might think. Not that I think you should give two figs what people think. It's the twenty-first century. Nobody cares anymore anyhow."

Addie snorted. "Even if I cared what people think, they already think the worst of me for running away from my problems and spending a year in England instead of coming back after my two-week vacation and dealing with it all then."

"*Pfft*, what do they know? Besides, the people who know the situation understand why you did what you did. It was your version of that movie *Eat, Pray, Love.* None of those people saw you after Simon broke your heart over and over in the weeks that followed your planned wedding day. Then to top it off, finding out you weren't who you thought you were your whole life." Paige squeezed Addie's shoulder. "I can't imagine what you were going through, and I'm your friend, so clearly neither could a town full of acquaintances and strangers."

Addie blinked back a sudden onslaught of tears. She would not cry. Not anymore. But Paige was right. Beyond the suffering of a broken heart, no one had truly understood her feelings of being lost and confused over who she was when she'd discovered that her great-aunt was really her grandmother and the person she'd loved as her Gran had been her aunt. She'd known in that moment that she'd been lied to her whole life by everyone she trusted the most.

Addie hung her head. "But even after all these months, there are a few who still roll their eyes when they see me, and I can hear them whispering about me when I pass. They say things like, 'It must be nice to be a rich Greyborne and able to run away from your problems,' and—"

"No." Paige continued her rant. "They are not you, and you did what you needed to do for you so you could heal. Now you're back, and you are a different person, and if that person wants to invite a man she met in England to stay at her house, let them . . . let them go suck eggs or something!"

"Paige Stringer!" Addie laughed. "I have never heard you get so bent out of shape over anything like that before."

"Well, it bugs me. Who do these people think they are to tell you how you should or should not grieve? The emotional police of the world? My mother even understood, and she's the most judgmental person I know."

"Speaking of your mother . . ." Addie winced, waiting for the explosion that might follow. "What are we going to do about her cancelling everything?"

Chapter Four

"If you're going to meet your mom at three, you probably should head out soon, because the roads are only getting worse." Addie scowled at the swirling snow outside the window.

"I don't want to meet her."

"I know you don't," Addie said softly. "But you have to. You need to confront her about cancelling your reservations and forcing you to go with someone you don't want or take a risk of not having *any* food at whatever low-cost venue she booked for the reception. Maybe if you plead your case to her, you can still call your vendors back and pick up your bookings again, but if you wait much longer, who knows?"

"I know, I know, I know." Paige made her way to the bay window and stared out onto the empty, snow-covered road. "Bill is closing the bakery early because they've had about as many customers this afternoon as we've had, and he's going to take Emma home with him. I guess as soon as she's gone, I'll go meet Mom." She glanced at Addie beside her. "Wish me luck in changing her mind and me not having to run away and elope."

"Let's hope it doesn't come to that. You've waited forever for Logan to propose, and you should have the wedding that you both want." Addie ushered Paige over to a chair in a reading nook, and after settling her friend, took the seat next to her. "I know Logan meant the best for all of you by waiting to get his lieutenant position and the accompanying salary increase before he officially proposed—"

"Even though I told him over and over that the money wasn't important, I only wanted him."

"Yeah, but he's stubborn," chuckled Addie.

"He sure is, but remember, him wanting to wait was because he knew my life hadn't been easy, and he wanted me to feel safe and somewhat financially secure with him and he felt the promotion finally gave us that." Paige swiped at the tears trickling down her cheeks.

"Exactly!" said Addie. "He only ever thought about you and Emma, and now that he's achieved that stability, you guys can finally move forward and build your lives as a family. So, wouldn't the Christmas Day wedding of your dreams be a whole lot better than an impersonal civil ceremony with a justice of the peace?"

"But don't forget we planned on saving for another year before getting married until Mom said we'd waited long enough, and insisted on helping us pay for. And to be honest, I was tired of waiting so it was me who convinced Logan she was doing it out of the goodness of her heart because she wanted us to be able to get on with our lives and build our family." Paige sniffled. "But now, I see that same, seemingly good-hearted woman is showing her true colors and trying to plan the wedding *she* never had. She's ruining everything for us, and darn it. I want my wedding, but if I can't have it, then like it or not, we'll elope."

"Awe, sweetie. She'll come around, you'll see," Addie said, wrapping her arms around Paige as she sobbed.

"Mom," Emma called from the back room. "Grampa Bill's here."

"Okay, darling, I'll be right there." Paige sniffled and swiped her cheeks with a tissue Addie handed her from the stash up her sleeve.

"My grandma used to store tissues in her cleavage. I'm glad you're not giving me tissues from *there*." She softly chuckled, dabbed her eyes and nose, then hurried to the back. She called out a quick goodbye a few moments later.

"Good . . . luck," Addie ended on a whisper when the heavy back door banged shut, and that was that. She was off too.

Addie was glad Old Bill Unger had become part of Paige and Emma's family. It might have taken Martha and him nearly fifty years to find one another again after being high school sweethearts, but he treated all five of Martha's girls and their children as though they were his own.

When Addie returned from England, it was reassuring to find Martha and Bill's relationship was stronger than ever. They both behaved like love-struck teen-agers, and considering Addie had only ever known the pricklier side of a very unhappy woman, it was refresh-ing. That was, until recently. Now it seemed the closer Paige's wedding drew, Martha's past heartaches with Paige's father revealed the old, crustier side of Martha that Addie knew all too well, and it broke her heart.

"I think we should close a bit early, too, Pippi," Addie said, peeking over the counter at her little friend curled up, her tail touching her little black nose. "Give me a minute to call the lighthouse museum to alleviate Deanna's fears about the featured book not arriving in time for the gala auction. I'll let her know I will drop it and all the book donations off after the storm passes, and then we can head home before it gets any worse out there, okay?"

Pippi groaned, got up, shook herself, and slunk around the end of the counter, stretched and yawned, then sat back on her haunches, staring bleary-eyed at Addie.

"I'm sorry, madam, did I wake you from your sleep?" Pippi yipped.

"Okay, then, let's get you home. I feel exactly like you do when it's this cold and snowy. I just want to curl up and sleep all day too. Let me make the call first."

"Well, that's not what I expected. I don't think Deanna Jackson has looked out a window recently." Addie stared at her phone after hanging up and shook her head at the museum curator's lack of common sense. "Can you believe, Pippi, that she told me to drop all the books off on my way home today because they're finishing putting the bags together for the daily draws? I bet her staff is thrilled about having to work in this storm when they know they should be hunkered down nice and safe at home." Addie scooped Pippi up in her arms, snuggled her close, and kissed the top of her head. "Okay, I guess we have one stop to make, and then we can head home."

Addie gasped when the frosty air bit into her lungs, and she buried her face in her coat collar as she made her way down the back steps through the drifted snow. But one peek at the snowdrifts piled up past the windows of her MINI, she knew they wouldn't be going anywhere for a while. She braced against the wind and made her way back up and into her shop, the door closing with a *bang* behind her.

"Here we are again." Addie set Pippi in her carrier case on the floor.

Pippi's little head poked through the round opening at the end of the bag, her puppy-dog eyes beseeching Addie.

"Believe me, my friend, you're better off in here while I clean off Miss Mini. The poor old gal has been struggling lately. Fingers crossed she has one more winter left in her." Addie pulled her scarf up to her eyes, braced herself, and headed back out into the storm. Fifteen minutes later, Addie, snow-covered and shivering, stumbled back through the door.

"It . . . it se . . . seems our dear friend is dead . . . deader than a doornail," Addie stuttered between chattering teeth. "I'll . . . I'll have to call the gar . . . garage, or we'll be sleeping here tonight, little one." She removed one glove, clamped it between her teeth to quell the chattering, then unzipped Pippi from the carrier bag.

After fishing her phone out of her coat pocket, she looked up every mechanic in town, only to be informed by overwhelmed-sounding people that there was at least a three- to four-hour wait for a tow truck.

She tapped Recent Calls, then pressed Speaker, and with shivering hands, set the phone on the small desk while she rubbed her arms up and down, trying to get her blood circulating again. "Hi, Deanna, it's Addie. I'm sorry, but my car won't start, and I won't be able to get out of here for at least a few hours."

"Sorry about that," Deanna said, her voice echoing through the small speaker. "No worries. We have a board of directors meeting tonight, so I'll be at the museum until late. Just drop your donations off once your car is back on the road."

Addie scowled at her phone after hanging up. "Silly woman. Still having a board meeting in this weather?" She patted Pippi's head. "Well, what are we waiting for? Might as well use our time wisely."

For the next few hours, she busied herself by cleaning up the front of the shop and the back room, grateful that she, unlike some other people, was at least warm and cozy inside while she waited for a boost, and not sitting in a freezing car on the roadside. She shivered at the thought, recalling how cold and snowy she'd gotten in her short foray into the elements earlier.

Four hours after making her initial calls for help,

Addie waved goodbye to the tow-truck driver who'd finally managed to work his way down his lengthy list of stranded drivers.

"All right, little one," Addie said, zipping Pippi back into her carrier. "I hope you know our little detour is not my doing. I want nothing more now than to get the both of us home safe and snuggled up by the fire with a hot dinner and a cup of hot cocoa."

Pippi let out a soft whimper.

"I know, right? I still can't believe Deanna's holding a meeting tonight, of all things. I bet she hasn't poked her head outside the museum once today." Addie scoffed and picked up the carrier. "I'm pretty sure if she had, she would have told me to go directly home and cancelled that board meeting. No one should be out on the roads on a night like this."

Pippi whined from inside her carrier.

"I know, but as far as I know, Deanna is a reasonable woman, and her feeling the pressure of the raffle starting next week and the gala on Christmas Eve is the only logical explanation for her being too busy to keep an eye on the weather."

As Addie headed to the museum, the MINI tossed from side to side on the uneven ruts created by other erratic drivers traveling down the hill toward the harbor. Addie's white-knuckle grip on the steering wheel cramped her fingers, and numbness crept into her hands.

"Almost there," she murmured under her breath as she tried to keep her focus on the road ahead, even though the wipers struggled under the weight of the snow and barely kept the windshield clear enough for her to see out. She pulled hard on the steering wheel as she bounced over a deep furrow, then lurched her way into the parking lot of the nautical museum located in the old lighthouse-keeper's cottage at the base. At least she hoped she was in the lot and not on the lawn. Addie hissed out a breath when she finally came to a full stop, glad she'd made it in one piece.

She glanced out the side window at the snowbanks around the museum entrance and shivered. "To make it worse, look at this, Pippi." Addie exhaled. "It's so freaking cold, I can see my breath. I think even Miss Mini's heater is frozen. Come on, let's get inside and warm up." She grabbed the doggy carrier and the tote bag containing the book donations, shouldered them awkwardly as she braced against the biting wind, and waded through knee-deep snow to the main door of the lighthouse museum.

"Why didn't I just stand my ground and tell her I'd bring them by another day?" she grumbled and opened the door with her hip.

By the time she stepped into the lobby, she was chilled clear to the bone, and fiery sensations crept over her numbed cheeks. "We sure aren't in England anymore, are we?" She looked down at the carrier, where Pippi had buried her head deep inside her warm blanket and let out a soft *yip*.

"I feel the same." Addie banged snow off her boots, removed her gloves, and scanned the lobby.

Her heavy heart lifted at the sight. The entire lobby had been decorated like a scene out of a storybook. It was filled with ornately decorated Christmas trees placed throughout, creating a glimmering winter wonderland forest. Santa's sleigh was front and center, with

an assortment of carved, whimsical woodland lawn or-
naments surrounding it.

"Beautiful," she whispered.

Pippi stuck her nose through the carrier's opening,
whined her approval, then pulled her head back inside.

"Now, let's go find Deanna so we can get home,
shall we?" Addie walked around the sleigh and paused
when she got to the back side, where large boxes filled
with an assortment of local business donations waited
to be sorted and put into Christmas sacks. "I guess I
can see now why Deanna insisted I bring the books by
tonight. It appears, storm or not, there is still work to
be done, and they are just starting to fill the daily prize
sacks. Looks like our books are here just in the nick of
time."

Being the reason the volunteers were delayed in filling the sacks sat harder on her shoulders than any drive
on snowy roads ever could, and she was grateful for
Noah Parker's timely hand-delivered contribution.

What a day it had been, and how perfect an ending.
She smiled and casually perused some of the items in
the boxes, spotting a pair of red-and-white mittens
poking out of the top of one of the boxes.

Martha Stringer had shown her that exact same set
the week before, when she'd also revealed that she was
donating a cake of the winner's choice and a bakery
gift certificate. Addie picked up the soft, thick mittens
and turned them over in her hand. In this frigid weather, she needed something to keep her fingers together to help warm each other. Gloves just didn't cut
it. She returned them to the box, then drew out an ex-
quisite baby's patchwork quilt.

"Oh, Pippi, look. Wouldn't this just be the perfect Christmas gift for Serena and Zach's baby, Belle?"

She glanced from box to box, wishing she could win them all with the raffle tickets she'd purchased. "Pippi, look! Here's a toy train set that little Ollie would just love. And these dolls? There's one brunette and one blond that would be perfect for little Addie and for Emma. Oh, look at this. If I'm not mistaken, these are hand-painted antique plaster owl bookends. Wouldn't Paige just love to wake up Christmas morning and find these beauties under her tree?"

Addie grinned as she stood upright and stretched out her back. "I could do all my Christmas shopping right here tonight," she said wistfully. "But I'm going to have to take my chances like everyone else, I guess, and this isn't getting our donations to Deanna, is it?"

Smiling, she headed to the staircase leading up to the offices, but she stopped at a scraping sound behind her. With one foot hovering over the step, she slowly turned around, held her breath, and cocked her head, listening closer. When she didn't hear anything else, she decided it must have been the wind brushing a tree branch against the shutters and took the next step up.

A *bang* echoed through the lobby. "Dang it!" followed a muffled whisper.

"Is someone there?" Addie called, scanning the lobby.

"Just me." A short, round-faced man wearing an elf costume, complete with upturned toes on the shoes, appeared from behind one of the ornamental trees.

"You must be the one in charge of packing the Santa sacks for the giveaways," Addie said, grinning as she walked toward him, her hand outstretched.

He hesitantly accepted her handshake in his gloved hand and nodded shyly.

"I'm Addie Greyborne, and I can't believe my timing in bringing my donation in." She patted the large tote bag hanging under her arm. "As a matter of fact, I was just on my way upstairs to find Deanna to give them to her."

"You were?"

"Yes, and I was so afraid the rare book I ordered from England wouldn't be here in time, but thankfully a friend was coming over on holiday and . . ." Addie eyed the small man, whose look was fluctuating between confusion and elation with every word she said. "I'm sorry, you probably aren't interested in hearing all this, so let me just run upstairs and find Deanna, and then you can get back to work filling the Santa sacks." She started back to the stairs.

"Wait a moment, Miss Greyborne," he called. "I'm one of Deanna's event assistants, and I really do have a lot of work ahead of me tonight. Plus, Deanna has already headed home due to the weather. She lives outside of town, you know."

"Yeah, I seem to recall she lives north of town or something, doesn't she?"

"Yes, way out on Home Road." He stepped forward, wringing his hands. "I live close by and can walk, so that's why she left me here tonight alone to start packing the sacks. To save you a trip back, why don't you leave your donations with me, and then I'll pack them up with the other bagged items? That way we can both get home earlier tonight, because this storm only sounds like it's getting worse, and it's not going anywhere soon."

"That's kind of you, especially as all I want to do is go home, put my feet up, and roast in front of a blazing fire." She set Pippi's carrier down and was about to do the same with the bag of books, but paused. "What about the book for the auction, though? It doesn't go into any of Santa's sacks, so should I just go up and put it on Deanna's desk?"

The elf widened his eyes, grinned, pulled a key ring out of a pocket in his elf costume, and dangled it in front of his face. "I have the keys to the secure case allocated for it, so I'll lock it up after I've finished here."

Addie glanced at the donation items still in boxes, then looked back at the elf. "Tell you what, why don't I give you a hand? I can help you pack the bags, and then I can give you a ride home after we're done for the night. It's so bad out there, even walking might be treacherous."

"Um . . . sure, if you want to." He looked at the items still in the sleigh. "What we need first is more boxes to put the donations in that are still in the sleigh, so we can sort them into piles to figure out which daily prize sacks they get put into."

"Or . . ." Addie eyed the hodgepodge of items already in the boxes. "We could just spread everything out on the floor and sort it all that way."

"Ah . . . no, that won't work. This floor hasn't been cleaned yet today, and we can't take the chance of the prizes getting dirty, so . . ." He glanced upstairs. "Deanna was most insistent on me taking them all upstairs to the board room and spreading them around on the table to sort them out."

"That makes sense. If I were lucky enough to win a prize bag, I'd be unhappy to find the items covered with dirty snow grime. Like those beautiful mittens." She sighed. "What I wouldn't give to win those. I'm telling you, gloves sure aren't worth the money anymore with this weather. Gotta keep the fingers together so they can help keep each other warm and . . ." She looked at his bewildered expression and laughed. "I'd say it's not just my fingers affected by the cold. Point me in the direction of where I can find more boxes. Then we can start hauling these things upstairs."

"Go through those doors on the right into the museum and turn left. Take that corridor all the way down to the end, and you'll find a storeroom. If the door is locked, go to the information desk in the museum, and in the top right drawer behind the counter is another ring of keys. There are about a dozen keys on it, so you'll have to try each one, as I don't remember which one works. Sorry." He shrugged.

"Okay." Addie grinned and tried to recall his rapid barrage of directions, then she handed him her tote bag filled with the book donations, and with Pippi in tow, went off in search of boxes.

Upon reaching the storeroom, she tried the door handle. "It's locked, Pippi!" She banged her hand on the door. "Why didn't I just pick up the keys back in the gift shop before making this trek? At this rate, it's going to be midnight before we get home," she grumbled, then marched back down the hallway to the gift shop and the key ring.

* * *

"I can't believe we didn't find even one empty box in the entire storeroom. Do you think I got his directions wrong?" she asked, glancing down at Pippi, who stuck her head out of the opening of her carrier.

"Miss Greyborne, what are you doing back here?" Trevor Brown, the assistant curator of the museum, trotted down the back staircase.

Addie's hand flew to her chest. "I'm sorry. I thought everyone had gone for the night," she said, still trying to put her heart back in its place.

"No, we're just finishing up a board meeting." Trevor gestured to the stairs behind him. "But this is a staff area only, and it's after hours. What are you doing here?"

"Forgive me for being back here, but the event planner sent me on a quest to find boxes. There weren't any in the storeroom. Maybe you can tell me where I can find some? Then I can get back to assisting him with packing up the donations and getting them sorted into their Santa sacks."

"But the sacks have all been sorted," Trevor said, confusion filling his eyes. "For the most part, anyway, as we're waiting on a few last-minute donations, like your books, which I'm assuming perhaps is what brought you here tonight?"

"Yes, Deanna asked me to drop them off tonight, but . . ." Addie furrowed her brow. "I just saw the sleigh, and the prizes are all in boxes, not sacks."

"No, impossible. I myself worked with the volunteers all afternoon to sort and bag them, except, of course, for the food donations that we stored in the kitchen and your books, of course. You did say you had one for each giveaway and a special one for the auction at the gala, correct?"

"Yes, but I just left the event assistant, and he sent me looking for boxes so we—"

"You must have misunderstood. I have no idea who you're talking about."

"He was short and had a very round face and was wearing an elf costume. It even had the little turned-up toes on the shoes with a jingle bell on each of them."

"I haven't a clue what you're talking about." Trevor started toward the main lobby.

Addie followed and stopped short in the doorway. She couldn't believe her eyes. The sleigh was empty, and the donations and boxes were gone, right along with the man in the elf costume.

"He must have taken all the donations upstairs to the board room. Come on, we can ask him, then you'll see who I'm talking about," Addie said, turning for the stairs.

"What part of us being in a board meeting all evening didn't you understand? There is no elf upstairs! I have to find Deanna—now!" snapped Trevor as he shakily took his cell phone out of his back pocket and began dialing.

"The elf said she'd gone home hours ago," Addie weakly explained. Her gut churned with apprehension.

"No, she didn't. The board meeting, remember? She just stepped out for a few . . ." He cocked his head and listened on his cell.

Heels clicked on the floor as a tall, coiffured, blond-haired woman came around the corner of the staircase.

He glanced up and shoved his phone in his pocket. "Deanna darling, there you are. As you can see, we have a bit of an issue." He gestured over his shoulder toward the empty sleigh.

Deanna looked past Trevor, her face turning deathly gray. "Where are all the Santa sacks the volunteers put in the sleigh earlier?"

A sick sensation gurgled in Addie's stomach. Deanna Jackson had requested Addie drop the books off with *her* when Addie arrived. The elf had convinced her, however, to leave the book donations with him, and he had even managed to convince Addie that Deanna was gone for the day.

Addie could barely bring herself to look at the woman, who was so pale Addie feared she'd fall over. Clearly, the elf had lied to her, as Deanna Jackson was right in front of her and had been in the building the entire time. Her queasy sensation got worse with the realization that he'd also taken *The Four Million*.

Nausea turned into anger at the realization that the little elf had hoodwinked her just by dangling a key ring in her face and telling her he would lock it up in a secure case. She'd trusted him simply because she didn't want to have to make a second trip on icy roads.

Addie filled Deanna in on what had happened as Trevor stood silent, shaking his head.

"Where is Karl Rutherford, the security guard?" Deanna's gaze searched the lobby. "Why didn't he stop this man?"

"I haven't seen him," Trevor said. "I didn't even know he was working tonight."

"I didn't, either," Addie replied. "I never saw him at

all when I came in. The only one here was the man in the elf costume."

"Karl was here at five when we closed because I spoke to him." Deanna pulled out her phone. "I'd better call the police. I have to report the robbery. Trevor, while I'm talking to them, can you go up and tell the committee members what's happened and ask them to start looking for Karl . . . Yes, this is Deanna Jackson, curator at the lighthouse museum. I'd like to report a robbery and the disappearance of my security guard . . . Yes, I'll hold, thank you, sergeant . . ."

As Deanna paced the lobby, her heels clicking on the floor, Addie's heart pounded erratically. Why, oh why had her gut instincts chosen to fail her tonight?

Chapter Five

In a bid to release some of the pent-up anxiety swirling in Addie's stomach over her poor judgment, she walked to a window facing the parking lot and peered out. What she was looking for she didn't know, but she needed to look at something other than the empty Santa sleigh. All that met her gaze was a snow-filled parking lot and her MINI, nearly completely lost under a wind drifted pile. Deanna had hung up from talking with the police, but behind Addie the woman's high-pitched voice and the *clippity-clip* of her heels continued to echo throughout the lighthouse museum lobby as she inspected the damage and shouted directives to board members in their search for Karl.

"Trevor," Addie said, "do you think there's any chance that Karl went home because he was worried about the roads?" She gestured to the wind-driven snow hitting the window.

"Not Karl, at least, not without telling someone." Trevor shook his head adamantly. "He's worked here for over twenty years, and he's the most loyal, dependable employee we've ever had." He stroked his graying goatee, his eyes darting around the lobby. He headed toward the decorated tree forest behind the sleigh. "Karl, are you back here?" he called, disappearing into the Christmas forest. "Karl, can you hear me?" The trees shook frantically as he made his way around each one.

Addie glanced over at Deanna still pacing, clutching her phone in her hand. Needing to do something, Addie rushed back into the main part of the museum, echoing Trevor's pleas for an answer. She was met by the same silence. Echoes of other people searching for Karl reverberated through the museum until Addie was tempted to put her hands to her ears.

Not knowing what areas had been searched and which ones hadn't, she made her way down the corridor the elf had told her to follow. A storage closet was the perfect place to store . . . things—Addie shivered at the thought of what she might find—and even though she'd been in there earlier, she'd been searching for boxes, not security guards.

On her way, as Addie passed the gift shop, she stopped at a scraping sound. She cocked her head. The sound repeated. She hadn't been mistaken. Yes, the sound was coming from inside the gift shop. She moved toward the closed door and pressed her ear against the door glass. Unless rats or mice had suddenly developed rhythm, there was no mistaking the beat she heard for anything other than human noise. She crossed her fingers and pushed the door open.

"Karl, are you in here?" She cocked her head and listened closer. "Karl, is that you?" A *bang* came loud and clear from behind the counter. Addie scanned the back side of the sales desk. "Karl, can you hear me?"

A muffled noise that might have been a groan sounded again.

Addie cupped her hand around her ear. "Karl?"

The sound came again, but louder.

Addie couldn't believe it. The noise was coming from the inside of what looked like a narrow broom closet behind the desk. She pulled the handle and gritted her teeth. It wouldn't budge. She tugged harder, and just as she was on the verge of giving up and running for help, she saw a yellow piece of wood wedged into the bottom of the frame. She dislodged it with her foot, and the door swung open.

A hefty man, bound and gagged, tumbled out onto the floor at her feet.

"Karl," Addie gasped, dropping to her knees. "Are you okay?"

"H . . . e . . . lp me," was all he managed to hoarsely murmur before passing out.

"Karl?" she cried out and shook his shoulders.

She placed her fingers along his jugular vein. His pulse beat rapidly and weakly against her fingertips. His large barrel chest moved with shallow breaths.

Addie fished her phone out of the back pocket of her jeans and called for an ambulance. After giving the pertinent information, she hung up and yelled for help from the rest of the search party.

* * *

Even though the emergency crews had long since turned off the sirens to their vehicles, through the windows the dizzying flashes of blue and red lights still filled the museum's entrance as paramedics rolled Karl toward the door on a gurney.

One of them turned to Addie giving her a small smile. "He's lucky you found him when you did. Thanks to you, he's alive but just barely, and had it been much longer, who knows? Especially since he appears to have sustained a bad head injury."

"Given the condition he's in," said Addie staring down at the ashen face of the unconscious security guard. "I can't believe he came to long enough to make his presence known."

"Lucky he did, or there might have been a different outcome." The paramedic shrugged as they wheeled Karl out the door.

A blast of cold wind blew into the museum, and Addie shivered, not with the cold, since adrenaline still coursed through her body, but at the prospect of answering another round of questions since the senior police officer had arrived. What more could she say? How foolish she felt for believing an odd little elf, and how she had done nothing but mentally berate herself all evening? She glanced over at her friend Lieutenant Jerry Fowley, held her head high, and trudged over to him, ready to recite everything she had already told the initial officer responding to the emergency call.

"I know it's late, Addie, and I appreciate you sticking around to answer questions." He opened up his notebook and primed his pen. "Now, did you recognize this man dressed as an elf?"

She shored herself up, pushed away her gnawing hunger and overall exhaustion, and reminded herself that Jerry was a friend and only doing his job as the senior officer on the scene. "No, Jerry, as I already told Deputy Jacobs, I have no idea who the man wearing the elf costume was."

Jerry studied her, his brown eyes narrowing. "Are you absolutely sure, Addie, that you've never seen him before?"

"No, I haven't. He's never been into the bookshop, and I've never seen him around town. Look, I'm tired. Can I go now? Pippi and I are both hungry, she needs to go out, and I need to put my feet up and have a cup of tea."

"I suppose the chief wouldn't mind," he said, tapping his pen on his notebook. "Yes, that's fine, but you know the drill. Don't go leaving town any time soon, in case we have more questions, all right?"

Addie restrained the smile his botched attempt at mimicking Marc's scolding voice brought to her lips. "No worries. By the look of the snow outside the window, I'll be lucky to make it home."

"I could have one of the deputies drive you?"

"No, that's fine. I'll take it easy. Thanks anyway, and have a good night, Jerry. I hope you can find a lead on this elf somewhere out there." She waved her hand toward the window, knowing full well that the relentless snow had erased any trace of the man and his getaway vehicle.

Addie bundled herself up, shouldered Pippi in her carrier, and pushed out into the snowstorm. Her shoulders reflexively shrugged, and by the time she got to her car, she felt like a turtle hiding away from danger. After starting the engine to let it warm up and running the windshield wipers to clear the snow, she glanced across the parking lot at the Greyborne Point B&B. For a fleeting second, Addie played with the idea of stopping in to tell Noah Parker what had happened.

With the number of crime scenes she'd stumbled upon through the years, and how she'd been a sounding board for her father when he had worked as an NYPD detective, she'd grown accustomed to decompressing or brainstorming with someone in her circle in the aftermath of a crime. She missed the days when Marc would be one of the first responding officers and they'd sit for hours, discussing every aspect of the incident.

She put her MINI into drive. It was time she got real and accepted that the members of her circle were all moving on with their lives. Everyone, that was, except her. Life wasn't the same, and those days were in the past. Besides, Noah was here on holiday, not to play detective with her. She took one more look at the piling snow, and she knew she'd be lucky to make it home anyway. She was not in the mood for Jerry's I-told-you-so looks if he had to send someone out later to rescue her.

Addie's car bumped and lurched over the snow-covered ruts the police cars had left in the parking lot and eased her way onto Marine Drive. She paused at the bottom of the driveway leading up to the B&B. There was only a dim light coming from what she knew to be the upstairs hallway. What if she knocked and wasn't a welcome visitor?

Not having the energy tonight to deal with additional emotional damage, she pressed on the accelerator and crawled to the next corner, but she hit an icy patch and careened widely as she turned left onto Birch Road toward Main Street and the road home. Once her heart rate settled down, she glanced in the back seat at Pippi, who was staring at her with judgmental puppy-dog eyes. "I know, I know, you don't have to remind me. We should have been home hours ago."

The next morning, Addie roused herself from bed and cringed when she read the clock. "Come on, lazy bones. It's quarter to nine. We gotta get a move on." Addie slipped her feet into her slippers and trudged to the window. "It looks like the storm's passed." She looked at her little furry friend still curled up on the bed. "It left mounds of snow in its wake, so I think you'll enjoy your morning backyard play." She laughed and gave Pippi a scratch behind the ear as she passed on her way to the bathroom.

After Addie had washed and dressed, she listened at Nikki's door for any signs of her morning stirrings. When she heard none, Addie reluctantly removed her hand from the doorknob, deciding it would be kinder to fill Nikki in about last night's misadventures when her housemate came into the bookstore later. As much as she was dying to share her story with someone, waking Nikki up now in order to relay it didn't seem

any more appropriate than her barging in on Nikki last
night would have been. Like the old saying goes, let
sleeping dogs and babies lie.

Addie turned and traipsed downstairs to let Pippi
out for her morning constitutional and a quick romp in
the snow. She couldn't help but chuckle at the little dog
happily scurrying up and down the high drifts of snow.
Caught up in the moment, she rested her shoulder against
the doorjamb and watched the playful pup, recalling
her own fond memories of playing in the snow as a child.
Still smiling, Addie let Pippi play while she packed up
some food for her furry friend, then grabbed her coat,
gloves, and Pippi's carrier. Finally, after some cajoling
and flat-out bribery with a treat, Addie got Pippi back
in the house and into her carrier, and within moments
they were out the door.

"Look what you've done, Pippi," Addie teased as
she maneuvered her MINI through snowdrifts, crossing her fingers she wouldn't get stuck. "The sky might
be a brilliant shade of blue now, but with your outdoor
antics, we're late, and all our customers will be seeing
red as they wait in a line to get into the shop."

Pippi yipped her disagreement, pulled her head in
like a turtle, and snuggled into her carrier.

After a difficult and at times treacherous drive, due
to heaps of snow on the roads that hadn't been cleared
yet and the jarring, icy ruts left by the morning traffic,
all Addie could think of as she parked at the back of the
shop was coffee—dark, aromatic coffee. She stumbled
her way through the snowbanks, zigzagged her way up
the icy snow-covered stairs, and nearly fell through the
back door of Beyond the Page Books and Curios.

Elation bubbled up inside her that she'd made it safely, and she could all but taste the luscious, perfect first cup of the day as she tore her gloves off. Her numb fingers fumbled with the alarm, alerting her to the fact that if she wasn't careful, she'd accidentally set her own alarm off.

When no alarm sounded, signaling she'd finally gotten the correct code in, Addie set her coat and gloves down, let Pippi out of her carrier, and made her way to the front of the shop. She dropped a pod in the coffeemaker, unlocked the door, and turned the sign to Open. She couldn't decide whether to be elated or disappointed that a line of people wasn't scowling at her from the other side of the front door.

"Looks like we beat the rush, Pippi." She filled Pippi's food dish behind the desk, poured a touch of cream into her coffee mug, took a deep satisfying sip, and shivered. "It's freezing in here, don't you think?" She glanced down at her shivering little Yorkipoo.

"I should have packed your doggie sweater, but I didn't think it'd be this cold in the shop." Addie hugged her arms around Pippi and checked the thermostat. "No wonder you're shivering. It's forty-five degrees in here."

She tapped the thermostat, hoping it would quickly rise to a comfortable seventy-two. She tapped it again. No change. She tapped it again, willing it to obey. The number "45" glared back at her.

She snuggled Pippi closer. "I really should have brought your sweater. Do you think we have time to go back home and get it?" But the thought of traveling the roads she came in on again didn't sit well in her gut.

On the off chance the thermostat had finally complied with her wishes for warmth, she checked it again. "Forty-three? It went down two degrees? I can see my breath!"

Addie grabbed her handbag, dug around for her phone, and after fishing it out, crossed her fingers that the bill she was about to accrue didn't ding her budget too much. When Martha's furnace at the bakery had stopped working a few years ago, not only did she have to close for a couple of days, but the bill Martha had received left the woman speechless, which never happened. A wonky furnace was not something Addie had accounted for at this time of year. Before she called Martha for the HVAC repairman's number, Addie crossed her fingers again, in the hopes it was only a small parts issue and would be cheap and easy to fix. She couldn't close down. Not for a day, much less two or more. It was only two weeks till Christmas, her busiest time of the year.

At the least, Martha could tell her who to call because she didn't have a clue, ever since the local handyman Brian, whom she used to call for these sorts of things, had packed up and moved to Salem while she was away in England.

The shop door's bells tinkled out their greeting.

"I'll be with you in a moment," she called without looking up as she started to tap in the bakery's phone number.

"Shall I just sit and wait at the counter, then?"

Addie looked up. "Noah?"

A voice sailed through her phone, but she clicked off the call. She was pretty certain she'd get an earful from Martha for hanging up on her. But Addie didn't care. Not when Noah stood before her, a smile on his face and his fog-gray gaze burning into hers. Both things she thought she'd never see again after he'd walked off into the storm the day before.

"You came back," she whispered, more to herself than to him.

Chapter Six

Noah cocked his head, his smile slipping slightly. "Of course I came back. You didn't think I'd leave Greyborne Harbor without seeing you again, did you?"

Addie crossed her arms and pinched her elbow. No, she wasn't dreaming, which meant she hadn't dreamt about him being here before either. Noah Parker really was in her shop in Greyborne Harbor, USA.

It was all real, and if Noah Parker hadn't been a figment of her imagination, then the elf-thief and Addie's unwitting part in the theft of all the town business's donations, including the priceless book, was also not a fever dream.

All night she'd tossed and turned, replaying the details of how she'd unknowingly aided in the robbery and the shocking discovery of a severely injured Karl, tumbling out of a broom closet at her feet. As she'd lain in bed, she'd hoped against all hope that it was all a crazy, half-awake/half-asleep dream, like the ones she sometimes had. But that meant if it was all a crazy dream, then Noah hadn't made a stop in Greyborne Harbor to drop off a rare book either—a rare book she no longer had possession of because she'd handed it over to a rotund elf.

"Addie?" Noah's voice came to her as if through a tunnel.

No, she didn't have the book. She didn't have any of the donated books. Santa's sleigh was empty, and the charity drive and gala were doomed, all because of her. Her head felt light, and she clutched the counter to keep herself upright.

"Addie?" Noah's warm hands clutched her shoulders, and he guided her to a leather chair. "Here, sit. You don't look so good."

Addie peered up at him, a retort on the rudeness of saying such a thing to a woman flittering on her tongue, but she couldn't get a word out when she saw the concern in his eyes. Yes, the man was here in the flesh, holding her shoulders and looking at her as if he cared. He was in her bookshop, not thousands of miles away in West Yorkshire.

Whether it was the warmth of his hands or his calming presence, her anxiety eased, and before she could contain it, a soft moan escaped her lips.

"Are you all right?"

"Yes." She shook her head.

He grinned and gently squeezed her shoulders before releasing her and settling in a chair next to her.

"Your words say yes, but your head says no. Would you like me to get you some water, or with the temperature in this room, a hot cocoa?"

She reciprocated his smile and ignored the butterflies swirling in her chest. What was going on? Why was she acting like a thirteen-year-old with her first crush? There was a time when she'd thought this man insufferable, but as he sat across from her, his face a portrait of concern and genuine caring, she no longer could ignore her heart's mutinous pounding.

Addie met his gaze and chuckled. "You must think me batty, don't you? Blame it on my lack of sleep last night."

Laugh lines crinkled next to his eyes. "I would never insinuate that a woman was batty. I have too much of a sense of self-preservation." He avoided her playful swat. "Tell me something," he said, slowly scanning the shop.

"With the day I had yesterday, you might want to be careful with that request. I have a lot to say. But if you're feeling strong, ask away."

"Is it always so cold in the shops here in America?" He pulled his coat collar up around his ears.

"Cold? Oh, right. I'm sorry. I was in the middle of calling about my broken furnace and . . . then you walked back into my lif—my shop."

A tiny frown creased his forehead. "I know a gentleman should never say this to a lady, so apologies beforehand, but you don't look so good. Are you sure I can't help you, get you something, call somebody?"

"I'm fine, really. I just had a tough day yesterday,

and then it doesn't help that I drove on questionable roads to get here, only to find it freezing in here today of all days. The coldest day we've had in years, according to the Weather Channel, that is."

Noah stood, took off his coat, and started rolling up his sleeves. "Point me in the right direction . . . Addie?"

Addie blinked and raised her gaze from his bare, defined forearms to his gray eyes. However, the shift in her gaze did nothing to alleviate the tightness in her chest, made worse by the same butterflies she'd silently cursed earlier. A nervous laugh escaped her, and she stared in shock at the twinkle in his eyes and cheeky grin on his lips.

In the moment, she felt as inept and out of place as her middle-school self did at her first school dance with her first crush. Then a wave of panic rushed through her. If this was the new Addie, the one to rise from the ashes of her past, she wasn't on board at all with this bumbling, awkward off-kilter woman.

"Addie?" Noah's voice brought her back to the present.

No, she had to get it together. She refused to be controlled by her past. She was her future, and she would no longer let fear over someone breaking her heart again rule her decisions. She straightened her shoulders, sat up straighter, and gestured to his bare forearms. "I thought you were freezing?"

"I am, which is why I'm asking where your furnace is. I'll see if I can fix it."

Addie stared up at him, trying to figure out the man

before her. He was a walking enigma, and that attracted her more than she cared to admit.

"You know how to fix furnaces?"

"My late wife always said I was handy to have around." He attempted a smile, but it didn't quite reach his eyes.

After they'd made a tentative connection in England, Noah had confided in her that his wife had been murdered, but since he never elaborated, she had no idea what the circumstances surrounding her death were. Most important was the murderer ever caught, and had he laid her ghost to rest, or was he still haunted by every remembrance of her, as she had been by David's memory for so long?

His eyes shimmered in the sunlight and mesmerized her, reminding her of how they'd captured her on the first day they met on the moors of Yorkshire. A dead body had lain between them then, but that was before he'd spoken to her and ruined everything about that moment. As they say, you only get one chance to make a first impression, and his had irritated her clear through her skin to her bones. Now she couldn't take her eyes off this man, who was still one big question mark, a puzzle that, in Addie's mind, needed to be solved. Then all the what-ifs she'd struggled with since they'd met came crashing back over her, crushing her with their weight.

Noah sat again and clutched her hands in his. "Truly, Addie, are you okay?" He rubbed her hands in his. "Of course, you're not feeling well. Your hands are like blocks of ice."

"I'm fine." She released her hands from his and waved off his look of concern. "I just didn't get much sleep last night and . . ." Hot tears seeped down her cheeks.

He dug around in his coat pockets and offered her a freshly ironed handkerchief.

"Thank you," she whispered, dabbing at her eyes and her nose. "I'm afraid we didn't get a chance to talk much yesterday, and . . ." She dropped her gaze. "How was your night at the bed-and-breakfast? Was it okay? Comfortable?"

"Yes, it was most comfortable. The two ladies who operate it are very charming and seemed most anxious to please." His eyes twinkled.

"Oh dear, I forgot to warn you about them." She recalled that Simon had had similar experiences with the sisters. "They have a weakness for good-looking, younger men, but they really are harmless."

"I thought so, and I went out of my way to make them feel as cherished as they made me and another not-so-tolerant gentleman feel." The laugh lines around his eyes crinkled, and a playful grin played across his lips. "So, you think I'm good-looking, do you?"

Heat burned on Addie's cheeks as she opened her mouth to respond.

His smile softened. "You don't have to answer that. I do have my dignity to keep intact. What's left of it, anyway." He rubbed his hands together, cupped them, and blew into them. "So, back to the original question I asked you. Where's your furnace?" He laughed at her quirked eyebrow. "Look, I don't promise to know anything about American heating systems, but like I said, I was known for being handy, and, really, how different can a British system be from an American one? I promise to try not to break anything further. What brand is your furnace?"

She hopped up and went to the filing cabinet behind the sales counter. After digging around, she unearthed the owner's manual and brought it back to him. "Here you go."

He fished out his phone. "Give me a few moments to watch a few YouTube videos on this furnace type, and then we'll go tinkering with the real thing."

"Would you like some coffee?"

"More beautiful words have never been spoken." He smiled up at her, kicking her heart into overdrive, before turning his attention to his screen.

Addie made his coffee and brought it back just as he shoved his phone back into his pocket.

He took a tentative sip and sighed. "You are a lifesaver. Now, I think I've done enough research to not break anything. So, lead the way?" He held out a smooth, unblemished hand.

Addie studied his palm. It was clear from the lack of calluses that it had been a while since he'd held a tool. "Look, I appreciate the offer, but I think a professional would be the best option."

He *tsk*ed. "Remember, I'm England's best handyman. Some say I'm a jack-of-all-trades—"

"And an expert at none?" Addie smiled and led the

way to the utility room. "Speaking of England, you mentioned yesterday that you were spending the holidays in New York City. Do you have family there?"

"No. No, I don't," he said softly, and his confident stride lessened. "It's just someplace where I have always wanted to spend Christmas, see it all lit up like it is in all those holiday movies." He halted and gazed into her eyes. "Actually"—his voice wavered—"it was a place my late wife always wanted me to take her for Christmas, and I never did."

He broke his gaze from her and glanced out the bay window. "I'm quite certain the roads will open up soon and . . . then I can be on my way, don't you think?" he asked without looking at her.

Addie wasn't sure if it was the empty way in which he said it or the sudden shift from playful banter to talking about his late wife that brought tears to her eyes. She brushed them quickly away. She wouldn't let him see her cry.

"Yes," she said, her voice cracking. "I'm sure the roads will be open very soon, and then you can be on your way." Her voice trailed to a whisper.

"Yes, on my way," he said in a bemused voice.

Addie scrunched her forehead and studied the back of Noah Parker. There had been a time when he hadn't been willing to give her the time of day, but now he appeared to be torn about leaving her.

Quit making assumptions!

Noah turned abruptly, taking Addie off guard.

"Do you find it hard?" he asked. "This time of

year . . . without your fiancé?" Heartbreak etched fine lines around his mouth and eyes.

Addie's heart sank, not only in pain for past losses, his and hers, but because he might not be on the last leg of his journey in dealing with his wife's death. They were like two ships passing in the night. While she was finally moving to the safety of a harbor of acceptance, she sensed he was still being tossed and turned by waves of grief. A state she knew too well.

She pressed her lips firmly together and nodded. "You remember me talking about David?"

After she'd inserted herself in his murder inquiry last year, Noah had taken a deep dive into her background. He'd learned all about David and had expressed a kind of kinship between him and Addie due to their past loved ones' deaths.

"I remember everything you say, Addie."

Addie's brain short-circuited. She knew what she should say, what she should do, but his previous words about his late wife didn't match the warmth coming from his eyes as he gazed down at her. The biting pain of her fingernails into her palms grounded her. She put on her most winning smile. "Can I get that in writing?"

He chuckled, and the sadness that had crept across his face earlier vanished. He pointed toward the utility room door. "Shall we commence with the furnace-fixing? If we wait too long, your little dog will be a pupsicle."

"That was a horrible joke," said Addie with a short laugh.

Pippi, whom Addie had forgotten to worry about in the hubbub of Noah Parker, yipped at Addie's feet.

"Your dog doesn't seem to think so." Noah bent down and scratched behind the little dog's ears. "Your owner is a difficult audience."

Addie scoffed. "No, I just know a good joke when I hear one." She winked and opened the utility room door. "Your furnace adventure awaits. I'm going to get a refill of coffee. Come on, Pippi."

Pippi looked up at her, turned back to Noah, and then pitter-pattered after him.

"Traitor," she hissed to the dog's fluffy tail.

After making her coffee, she traipsed back to the utility room in time to watch Noah fiddling with the furnace panel, Pippi at his feet. "Looks like you have a helpful partner."

"She's offering me moral support." Noah paused in opening the front panel and patted Pippi's head.

Addie hid her smile behind her coffee cup. "Did you hear what happened last night?"

"No, I didn't hear anything about last night." He hissed in pain as the front panel snapped back into place, pinching his finger.

"You okay?" Addie asked, taking a step forward.

He shook his finger and nodded. "All part of the experience." He tackled the front panel again and soon had it off, revealing the furnace's inner workings. "You could entertain me with your tales of last night's adventures while I see what I can do here."

"It all started with an elf who hoodwinked me into helping him commit theft."

At his quirked eyebrow, she proceeded to tell him about her experiences at the lighthouse museum.

"You found the security guard?"

She nodded.

"That must have been horrible." He jerked his hand back, swore, and studied his finger again before plopping it in his mouth for a second. "American furnaces are feistier than English ones, and I also think this was installed soon after the Revolutionary War."

Addie laughed, relieved to have a reason to do so after telling her harrowing story of the night before. "You're probably not too far off. But, yeah, it was such a relief when we found out that Karl was only knocked out and not . . . dead."

"I imagine it was." He paused in his tinkering and gazed up at her, a mischievous twinkle in his eyes. "It seems to me, Addie, that bodies seem to find you wherever you are, don't they?"

Addie chuckled. "Well, I like to think all of us are blessed in some way. Some people are blessed with natural beauty; others have a knack for art. Some have a green thumb. Some are even born to be able to walk and chew gum at the same time without tripping." She shook her head regretfully. "Sadly, the star I was born under forgot to gift me with any of those talents, and instead, it gave me the talent of finding trouble, usually in the form of a body."

"I disagree." His lips curved in a cheeky grin.

"With what part? Compared to my friend Serena, who can walk out of the house in under two minutes flat and look gorgeous, this was the work of a full fifteen." She grinned and motioned her hands from her ponytail and down her cardigan and blue jeans–clad body, then flushed at Noah's appreciative gaze. She ignored it—and her goose bumps. "As for my art, once, during a heated game of Pictionary, Paige mistook my stick-figure drawing of a man for a cow—and you were witness to my less-than-graceful moments in England."

"And?" His body vibrated with restrained laughter.

"And what?"

"The green thumb part?" He gestured to the foliage of a plant in the shop, barely visible from their vantage point in the utility room. "Looks like you've got a green thumb, after all."

Addie snorted, stalked over to the plant, grabbed it, brought it back, and set it on the floor next to him with a *thump*. A cloud of dust erupted from the fake leaves, and she sneezed.

"Bless you." He handed her another handkerchief from his pocket.

She eyed his pockets. "First of all, do you have an endless supply of those, like a clown does, and secondly"—she pointed at the plant—"I can't even keep a fake plant in the prime of its life." She dabbed at her watery eyes but paused at the strange sound coming from Noah, a sound she had never heard from the man. She eyed him and then gaped at him in mock indignation. "Are you laughing at the fate of my poor plant?"

A full-throttled laugh erupted from his chest, and he stood up, bringing her plant with him. "Your plant's in good company, then. A coworker once gifted me with a succulent. I researched how to keep one alive, and I was so proud of myself for apparently doing just that. Several months later, though, my coworker stopped by for a cuppa, and when she saw me water it, she asked me what in the world I was doing. When I told her I'd managed to keep the dumb thing alive, she laughed so hard I thought she was going to hyperventilate." He leaned closer and dropped his voice, his warm, minty breath wafting over Addie's cheek. "Turns out she'd given me a fake plant, knowing full well I'd kill a real one."

A beat of silence pulsed in the air before both Addie and Noah fell into a fit of laughter, one they didn't come out of until his hand fell on top of hers, bringing her to her senses. Reluctantly, she pulled her hand out from under his and wiped her eyes. "That's a good one, Noah. I bet you didn't live that one down."

"No, in fact, a week later, when I arrived at work, there were so many fake succulents in my office I couldn't get to my desk." He glanced at her hand resting on his hip, and a sad smile flittered across his mouth, but it was replaced so soon with a grand one that Addie figured she'd missed the flicker of regret on his lips.

"So, Addie, does the local constabulary have any leads on who might have committed the theft and assault?" He handed her back her plant and continued tinkering with the furnace.

It was back to shoptalk, then? Addie inwardly sighed. "The police didn't have any leads last night, but they were hopeful that when the security guard woke up, he might be able to give them more information."

"I take it you haven't heard anything today on the matter, then?"

Addie shook her head. "Despite what you might think, I do not have a direct line to the police station, and I'm not generally kept in the loop with their crime-solving efforts."

"Lucky them." He grinned and concentrated on the furnace.

The doorbells jingling in a frenzy had Addie snapping her mouth shut on an equally tongue-in-cheek, British retort. She angled her head to see the front door and smiled at the redheaded whirlwind calling for her.

"Back here." Addie waved her to the back room.

"Addie, did you hear?" Serena removed her gloves, and her eyes widened when she looked down and spotted Noah on his knees in front of the furnace. "Inspector Parker? What on earth are you doing down there, first of all, and in Greyborne Harbor, second of all?"

"Mrs. Ludlow, isn't it?" Noah stood, brushed his hands on his pants, and held his hand out. "How lovely to see you again."

"Addie didn't tell me you were planning to visit." Serena shivered and pulled her gloves back on. "Why is it as cold in here as it is out there?" She glanced at Noah's exposed forearms, the screwdriver clutched in his hand, and then at the open furnace. "Never mind. I'm still waiting to hear how you came to be here, Inspector? Are you following an international criminal from England, who happens to reside in Greyborne Harbor?"

Noah let out a short laugh and shared a look with Addie.

Serena's eyes widened. "I'm right, aren't I? You're here on an undercover mission, and it has something to do with that man's body they discovered on the rocks below the lighthouse this morning, doesn't it?"

Chapter Seven

"What?" Addie said. "What man did they find below the lighthouse?"

"I don't know who he is, and by the sound of it, the police don't know yet either. I heard he was unrecognizable because of the waves smashing him against the rocks, and they—"

"Who told you all this?"

"Marc did, when I dropped by the police station on my way to work."

"He just came out and told *you* about the body?"

"Not exactly told me. I overheard it when I was standing at the desk waiting to give him the tea blend I made up for Whitney to help with her morning sickness." A sharp gasp escaped Addie's throat at the same time as one erupted from Serena—who instantly clasped her hand over her mouth. "You didn't hear that from me. They weren't ready to tell anyone yet, and they only told me because she wanted to know if there was anything herbal she could safely take," she whispered.

"Whitney is pregnant?" It felt as if the floor evaporated from under Addie, and she reached out to steady herself on the furnace.

Noah tilted his head, his face a mask of concern.

This was all too much information for one morning. On top of the events of last night, a broken furnace, and an English policeman who starred in all the *what-if* fantasies she'd had since leaving England, Addie didn't need the discovery that Marc's wife was pregnant too. Not only that, but there was a dead man near the lighthouse who could very well be the elf thief, which meant all the donations he'd stolen had most likely gone over the cliff with him, to be lost forever in the unforgiving winter sea. She was tempted to ask Serena for some of the tea she'd made for Whitney, as her stomach was sloshing with queasiness.

"When is she due?" Addie forced a steadiness into her voice.

"In about six months." Serena smiled at Noah. "Marc is my brother, the chief of police, and Whitney is his wife. They got married in late July. That's why Addie had to get back from England when she did."

"I see," said Noah, looking at Addie. "I take it you and Whitney are good mates, then?"

"Not really. We're more like acquaintances, recent ones at that."

"I see. So, it's you and Marc who are good friends?"

"Addie was going to be my sister-in-law at one time until . . . well, she met Simon, and then that all went sideways and—"

"Serena, remember, Noah is here on holiday, so I don't think we need to bore him with a rundown of all our past . . . connections, do you?"

Serena shot her an apologetic look. "No, no, he doesn't need that. Sorry." Her cheeks rosied, bringing out her emotional tell—a mottled facial complexion.

"Especially," continued Addie, "since he was kind enough to make a stop on his way to New York City to bring me the book I had specially ordered from Mr. Pressman. I mean," she said, flustered by her immediate lashing out at her best friend. She softened her tone. "I just wouldn't want to bore him with the goings-on of our little town when he's here for such a short time."

Noah shivered and scowled at the still-broken furnace. "I, for one, am interested in hearing about the body they discovered. This is a small town, so I do hope it wasn't a mate of yours?"

At the mention of "mates"—an expression she hadn't heard since she was in England—Addie refocused her thoughts from Marc being a father in only six months to the present day and the death of someone in town she possibly knew. "I doubt it"—she frowned—"but I could be wrong. You'd think, though, that if it was someone who was known to the community, battered by waves or not, there would be one or two identifying markers, like clothing or a wedding ring?"

"Yeah, but . . . I guess we'll just have to wait for

more information, until they know for sure, right?" A combination of hope and dread filled Serena's big brown eyes.

"I wonder if it was your elf thief from last night," said Noah, playing with the screwdriver in his hands. "When I was driving to the bed-and-breakfast yesterday, I missed the right turn into their drive because of the bad visibility, and I turned around in the lighthouse car park. The museum doesn't look very far from the cliff edge."

"Just a minute here." Serena held her hands up. "What 'elf thief' from last night?"

"I would think you'd have heard about the whole episode when you were at the station," Addie said.

"Not a word about any elf thief."

"That's interesting that there was no mention of it," said Noah. "The museum car park is right off the main doors, and in the storm last night, it would have been easy for anyone to get turned around and head in the direction of the cliff instead of the road." Noah played his finger over his chin. "Unless, of course, there's a good reason for the constables not to suspect this body was that of the thief, that is."

"You're right!" Addie said. "I wonder if—"

"Can we take a beat here?" said Serena, giving a time-out signal. "What. Elf. Thief?"

"I'm sorry." Addie winced. "I haven't had time to tell you of my misadventures last night at the lighthouse museum." Addie motioned for Serena and Noah to take a seat in some worn-out chairs Addie had hidden away in the utility room and proceeded to fill

Serena in on the elf thief and Karl's unfortunate incident. "So, you see, it makes sense to us that the fellow they found was the same man who stole the Twelve Days of Christmas raffle donations."

"I think you'd better tell Marc all that, because I never heard a word about anyone wearing an elf suit."

"You're right," said Addie. "He might not have read last night's reports yet. If so, he's probably not aware or he might not have had time to put two and two together, especially since he wasn't the responding senior officer at the scene." Addie reached for her cell phone but stilled when Noah's hand covered hers.

She looked questioningly at him.

"I think the chief of police knows what he's doing, don't you?"

Addie's face burned, and she slipped her hand from his. "It's just that it makes perfect sense that, with the robbery happening only feet away and the storm last night, the thief would become disoriented in his haste to get away and go off in the wrong direction."

Noah looked at Serena. "Did you overhear anything about a vehicle, car or lorry, being found at the base of the cliff?"

"No, nothing. I only heard about the man's body."

"There you go." He smiled reassuringly at Addie. "If it was the elf thief, he would have had to have had transportation of some kind. I doubt he loaded up all the gifts you described in one sack and simply escaped with it over his shoulder. No sign of vehicle wreckage in the area around the body means the victim was most likely on foot, and therefore not your elf thief."

"You're right again. The elf would have to have had a large car or a truck."

"Or Santa was his accomplice and waiting on the rooftop for him," Serena said jokingly.

"It's more likely," Addie said with an involuntary eye roll, "that the poor man was someone on foot who got confused, lost his bearings in the storm, and unwittingly went over the cliff side, but," she added pensively, "it does seem a little coincidental that a man turns up dead just steps away from where a robbery had just taken place, don't you think?"

"I thought you didn't believe in coincidences," said Serena.

"I don't, which is why I'm grasping for answers, I suppose."

"I agree it is odd, and it does bear looking into," said Noah. "However, since neither you nor I are on the payroll of the Greyborne Harbor Police Department, and we don't have access to the same information they have, we should let them get on with their work, don't you think?"

"Those words sound vaguely familiar to me." Shrugged Addie nonchalantly.

"That doesn't surprise me because I doubt I'm the only one who's ever said them to you." He gave her a knowing look accompanied by a smile that completely enveloped his face, one that brought back memories of Moorscrag and all the what-ifs that could have been if she'd changed her mind and stayed after that last night in the pub.

With Noah's gaze still locked on her, Addie became uncomfortably aware that the heat rising from under her collar generated by his intuitive words and entrancing smile had spread upward over her now flaming cheeks.

Serena modestly looked away and checked her phone. "Yikes!" she cried. "It's well past ten. I'd better get to the tea shop. I promised Elle I'd be in first thing to make up the special-blend orders for the week."

"Aren't you still supposed to be on maternity leave?" asked Addie, fighting to keep her voice steady while she tried to recover from her latest influx of emotions. "Isn't that why you promoted Elle from shop assistant to assistant manager?"

"Yes, but I'm getting so bored at home. Plus, I want to keep my hand in the daily goings-on of my shop, so I'm starting off with a few hours one day a week."

"How in the world do you get bored with twin preschoolers and a new baby?"

"'Bored' wasn't the best word. It's more like my sanity desperately needs some quiet, alone, adulting time. My best memories of running my tea shop are the hours I'd spend alone locked in the back room with my herbs and plants, creating delicious brews. I miss the peace and quiet of that, I guess. I love my husband and my kids, but it's a loud, busy house now, and I need some downtime." She shrugged. "Speaking of peace and quiet, it's eerily silent in here. Where are Paige and Nikki this morning?"

"Paige is off with her mother right now, trying to avoid a family feud over her mom's recent changes to all of her wedding plans. And since the roads still aren't great, I doubt we'll be busy in the store today. I suggested she ask Nikki, as one of her bridesmaids, to go along to make sure murder charges aren't laid against either her or her mom before the afternoon is over."

"I wondered how long it would take until Martha interfered with all the plans you guys made." Serena shook her head and chuckled glumly. "But I gotta run. I only have my mom's babysitting services until noon, when Belle's next feeding is due." She glanced at Noah. "She was named for the bluebells on the moors. It was so beautiful when I was there last spring." She closed her eyes and sighed wistfully, only to snap them open moments later. "I gotta run. It was nice to see you again, Inspector—"

"Noah, please."

"Noah." She nodded in acknowledgment then turned to Addie. "And I'll talk to *you* later, because I'm sure we have *lots* of catching up to do." Serena flashed Noah an innocent smile and then gave Addie an impish grin. Her not-so-restrained giggles could be heard over the tinkling of the doorbells when she left.

Addie glanced at Noah, who was fiddling with the screwdriver again. While he wasn't laughing, there was a soft smile on his face and an amused sparkle in his eyes.

"You'll have to excuse Serena," said Addie. "She does tend to get carried away and create more of a situation than there really is."

"I remember well." He smiled. "I take it she's a new mum?"

"She has three-year-old twins and a two-month-old baby girl."

"Then she is busy, and I can fully understand her need for solitude, even though temporary." The earlier sparkle diminished in his eyes, and he dropped his gaze to his cup of coffee on a box next to the furnace. "Any chance I could have another? This one is as cold as the air in here."

Chapter Eight

Addie's chest squeezed at the pensive look that came across Noah's face. She couldn't help but wonder if the comments he made about children came from his own experiences. Children were something he'd never mentioned, but it was a strong possibility he had a few since he'd been married. If that was the case, though, it was curious that none of her English friends had ever mentioned anything about children being part of his life in Moorscrag. One thing she did know for sure was that—children or no children—his breath was visible when he talked.

"I'm so sorry. We got caught up in Serena's news about the dead body, and we distracted you. But seriously, I can call a repairman." She eyed the furnace and the screwdriver in Noah's hand.

"Give me a few more minutes to try all the tips and tricks I have up my handyman sleeve."

"While you do that, I'll make you a fresh cup."

Moments later, she returned, a steaming coffee cup in hand. "How's it going? Are you sure you don't want me to call? My business neighbor, Martha, knows a great repairman."

Noah quit tinkering with the furnace and looked up at her. "Before you go spending the money on an expensive emergency, let me do all I can, okay? I swear, if it's more than a minor adjustment, I won't touch it, and I'll leave it to the professionals."

"Deal. With the awful weather keeping customers away, I need all the money-saving options I can come up with."

"I'm certain you aren't the only shopkeeper in town who is feeling the ill effects of the recent storm." He glanced at the furnace. "Do you have a torch and a piece of sandpaper, by any chance?"

"Be right back. I know I have a flashlight, but the sandpaper might be a little harder to unearth." Addie backed out of the small furnace room, turned and headed into the bookshop storeroom, pulled open a desk drawer, and retrieved the flashlight she kept there. After rifling through another drawer where she stored miscellaneous crafting materials Emma used when biding her time in the back room while waiting for Paige, Addie triumphantly pulled out a small piece of sandpaper, walked back to the utility area, and handed it to Noah.

"Much obliged." He took the items from her with a smile. "If my one last trick doesn't work, I'm afraid I've failed you."

"Don't worry about it. I was going to call anyway before you offered to help." Addie waved away his concern. "I've got some paperwork to do. I'll leave you to it."

She headed to the front counter and applied herself to reconciling receipts from the previous business days. An echo of *clink*s and *clank*s of metal on metal, a few curses, and soft scraping noises came from the back. A screeching whine was soon followed by the familiar humming *purr* of the old furnace's fan reverberating throughout the shop.

Addie blew out a sigh of relief, raced to the back room, and stood at the utility area doorway. "You did it!" She gave him a thumbs-up.

"Yes," he said, tossing his grimy hands up in a conceding gesture.

"I seem to have, but it was nothing, really. I should have checked the igniter rod first. It's showing a fair bit of corrosion. I gave it a good scrape to clean it off so that it could ignite and the fuel could burn."

"But that's it? The furnace is safe to use now?"

"Yes," he said rising to his feet. "I should admit though that this happens a lot back in the UK with oil furnaces. I feel stupid for not checking for that issue right away, but at least I got some good conversation and two cups of coffee out of the deal." He set the flashlight, screwdriver, and sandpaper in her waiting hand. "Now, can you point me in the direction of the closest hand soap and sink, and then may I impose on you one last time for a third cup of your splendid coffee before I head out on the motorway?"

"Well, as your first one turned cold before you could drink it, this would technically be only your second cup of coffee."

"I like the way you think." He grinned. "My heart thanks you for saving it from too much caffeine."

"*You* saved me from freezing to death, as well as a huge HVAC bill, so I'm just returning the favor," she said, stepping back and motioning to the door to the left of the utility area.

Noah followed her directions and slipped around the corner into the restroom, leaving the door open to wash his hands.

Addie looked on noting that every movement he made appeared to be methodical and intentional leaving nothing to chance. It made her think that it must have taken him well out of his comfort zone to make a stop in Greyborne Harbor when he knew a storm was brewing. However, as he methodically dried his hands on a paper hand towel, Addie wondered if getting stranded, even overnight, had been his initial intention. As he appeared to be in no hurry to leave, even though the highways were now deemed safe for travel.

When Noah was sufficiently satisfied with the cleanliness of his hands they returned to the storefront. Addie dropped another pod into the coffeemaker, keeping her eye on him as he perused the bookshelf beside the counter. Although it was clear the inspector was in no hurry to get back on the road, the reason for his delay escaped her. Was it because he wanted to spend more time with her? If so, why not just come right out and say so? She recalled that last night in the pub in England, and it had taken Mickey, the wobbly-eyed village drunk, to explain to Addie that Noah was trying to ask her out in his roundabout, inept way.

Addie scowled at the burbling machine as it hissed out a stream of coffee. Or, as she truly didn't understand the enigma of a man skimming his fingers over her books, it was more likely that he was delaying his departure after the news of a mysterious death. As an officer of the law and one who lived for the pursuit of justice, he probably wanted to stick around to learn the outcome and whether or not there was a connection to the robbery. Heck, she couldn't blame him if he did because she wanted to find that out too.

"I never asked you," she said over her shoulder, "are you meeting family or friends in New York for the holidays?"

"No."

"No to family or no to friends?" she asked, setting a mug on the counter in front of him. "Coffee's ready."

"No to you, as you *did* ask me that already." He faintly smiled and took a seat at the counter. "It's a bucket-list trip, and there's no rush. I'm quite certain the landmarks of New York will still be in place whenever I get there." He sipped his coffee but avoided looking at her.

Addie inwardly berated herself at her temporary mental lapse. "You're right, I did ask already. Sorry, I've been so distracted that I've even forgotten what I had for breakfast." Her stomach joined in the conversation, and she smiled apologetically. "Actually, I think I completely forgot to *eat* breakfast today."

The jangling of the doorbells interrupted what Noah was about to say, and Addie smiled at Jerry standing in the doorway alcove.

"Good morning, Lieutenant Fowley. What can I do for you on this very cold and snowy morning?"

"Just here to ask you more follow-up questions from last night."

"Yes, of course. Just be aware that I didn't get much sleep after that experience, and I don't recall anything else from what I already told you last night, but you can go ahead and ask again if you need to."

"I know it was an upsetting incident for you, and I'm sorry you had to go through that." He glanced at Noah, then looked back at Addie. "Could we please talk in private?" He jerked his head toward the back room.

"We can talk here. This is a . . . a . . . friend from Yorkshire." She motioned toward Noah. "Detective Inspector Noah Parker, this is my friend, Lieutenant Jerry Fowley."

"You're an inspector?" Jerry grinned and reached out his hand in greeting. "I'm honored to meet a fellow law enforcement officer, and an inspector detective to boot. Isn't that something? So, what brings you across the pond to these parts?"

"I brought our friend here a book she ordered, as I was heading to New York City for the holidays anyway." He smiled at Addie.

Addie ignored the warmth growing in her chest with his smile and did her best to come off as cool and collected. "He did me a favor, except it was the book that was supposed to be auctioned off at the Christmas Eve gala. Apparently it was one of the items stolen last night."

"That's what I came to ask you about," Jerry said. "Do you have descriptions or anything about the books you gave to the elf? We'll need that so we can send out a warning to booksellers in the state to be on the lookout for them."

"I can get that information to you, but it will take some time. I'll just drop it off at the station, okay?"

"Sounds good, and thank you. Well, that's all for now, I guess, unless you, Inspector, have any insights into this robbery."

Noah grinned at Addie. "I would love to chime in, but I think our friend here is champing at the bit to tell you herself."

"Can you tell us if you've made any connections between the dead man and the elf thief?" asked Addie.

"You know I can't discuss details about an ongoing investigation with you," Jerry said.

"I don't want the details." Addie gave him her best impression of puppy-dog eyes. "I only want to know if the body is that of the elf thief, because I'm just sick with the thought that a man I had a conversation with ended up going over the cliff and getting . . ." She swallowed at the bile rising in her throat. "Well, you know."

"May I remind you, this man you had a conversation with was also a thief—one who deprived the museum of the ability to raise much-needed funds?"

"Yes, but—"

"Let me put your mind at rest, then. We compared the body we found to your description of the thief last night, and I can tell you. It's not the same man."

"But don't you think it's a strange coincidence that a man died just yards away from where a robbery took place? So, how can you be sure it's not the same man?"

Jerry drew in a slow, thoughtful breath. "Because that's what we do. We make comparisons and examine evidence, and the evidence in this case tells us they are not the same person."

"But how can you be sure, especially if the body had been battered against the rocks as badly as I was . . ."

"As you were *what*, Addie?" Jerry's forehead creased.

She glanced at Noah, who shrugged, leaving her to deal with the doo-doo she'd stepped in. "N . . . n . . . nothing."

"Have you been talking to that redheaded friend of yours? You know, the same one I saw around the office this morning?"

Addie winced and softly smiled.

"She is the chief's sister," Jerry went on. "So, I can't fault her too much, but let's just say there was no sign of any vehicle on the rocks, which the thief would have needed to escape with the amount of merchandise he took. You told me last night there were a half-dozen cars in the parking lot, but you never mentioned seeing a truck, right?"

"But it was freezing and snowing, and I was in a hurry, so I might have just missed noticing one," Addie said.

"There's no evidence of any vehicle on the rocks, and nothing that resembled any of the donations described on the list we got from the museum. Also, the man you described doesn't match the description of the body type or size, and most important, there was no sign of any jingle bells on elf-toed shoes."

"Be that as it may, doesn't it seem like too much of a coincidence?"

"Perhaps." Jerry sighed.

"Could he have been an accomplice?" Noah asked.

"I suppose," Jerry said.

"Yes, Noah's right. The dead man could be the elf's accomp—"

"I assure you, Addie, if there is *any* connection, we will find it," Jerry interrupted.

"Yes, of course you will," she murmured.

"I don't want you to get reprimanded by the powers that be, if you know who I mean, so please keep your nose out of this, okay?"

Addie scowled at him and gave a mock salute. "Absolutely. Heard you loud and clear."

"Good." Jerry eyed her. "Unless, of course, you want the chief's sermon?" He tipped his cap at Noah. "Inspector, it was a pleasure meeting you."

After Jerry left and a beat of silence passed, a cheeky grin played over Noah's lips.

"What?" Addie asked.

"It's just that he said the same—" Noah snapped his mouth shut. "Nothing." The corners of his mouth twitched, and laughter danced in his eyes.

"Good. I knew you were too smart to finish that sentence." Her own smile won out, and she bit her bottom lip to keep her grin from growing.

"When I passed the tea shop this morning," he said, with a cheery lift to his voice that matched the still playful glint in his eyes, "I noticed a sign advertising Cornish pasties. Are they any good?"

"Yes," said Addie, taken aback by the sudden change of topic, "and you'd be hard pressed to find any better outside of Cornwall."

"That's a bold statement, considering delicious pasties can be found in most counties in the UK."

"I know, but those aren't from an authentic Cornish recipe, handed down through the generations by one of the top bakers in Cornwall, are they?" Addie challenged.

"Do you mean that baker who works next door?"

"No, but Serena and her husband, Zach, were on a tour of England for their honeymoon a few years ago. She got to talking to the owner of a shop there, they hit it off, and the woman taught her the secrets to making the best pasties in all of England. Apparently, this woman is an award-winning pasty maker."

"I'd love a bit of home about now." He glanced up at the clock. "It's coming on twelve, and as I've heard your stomach rumble for a while now, I think we're both famished. Could I tempt you with one?"

"That would be nice, but I eat them all the time. Besides, I brought a lunch with me, knowing there was no one to cover the lunch hour here at the shop. You go ahead, though. It's a lovely tea shop, and it might just give you that taste of home you need right now," she said with a knowing smile.

Chapter Nine

Noah gathered his coat and gloves and rushed out the door with a grateful smile on his lips. From the look of excitement in his eyes, Addie figured a good old Cornish pasty would fix his homesickness. She recalled her first few days in England and the similar effect a sign for authentic American hamburgers had on her. She had snatched at anything to deal with the culture shock, and she suspected it was much like that for Noah.

Who was she kidding? It was only the other day she was standing in the snow, staring at a Victorian village scene in a window display, shedding tears over the home in England where she'd left her heart. She pushed the images of Moorscrag from her mind, reminding herself that she *was* home.

The door banged open, and Addie jumped.

"Oops, sorry," said Serena, shoving her back against

the door to close it. "It's really blowing out there, and the wind just grabbed it. No new snow, but the gale-force winds are sure stirring up what we do have." She stamped her boots on the mat, tilted her head from side to side, slid one glove off, and touched her cheeks. "It's warm in here now, though," she said, slipping off her other glove. "So, your inspector didn't break the furnace even more?" she said with a saucy grin.

"He's hardly *my* inspector." Addie waved away Serena's comment. "Noah's a miracle worker."

"That's why he's sitting in the tea shop with a look of self-satisfaction all over his face."

"I think it's more like a Cornish pasty giving him that look. If I were to guess, I think he's experiencing a little bit of homesickness right now," Addie said.

"How long has he been here?"

"Just a couple of days."

"He doesn't strike me as the type to get all gloomy about home in such a short period of time."

"No, but I remember my first few days over there, and it's . . . it's a culture shock, especially this time of year. The holiday season makes people think of missed family and friends more, I suppose."

"You're probably right, but are you certain he's only been here a few days? Maybe I hit the nail on the head when I said something about him being here on a secret mission." Serena leaned closer and whispered, "Maybe he's been following that man they found on the rocks for months." Her eyes grew large, and her face paled as she stood straight up. "Maybe *he* pushed the man off the cliff. You did say he stayed right across the road at the bed-and-breakfast last night, right?"

"Don't be silly, Serena." Addie's laugh evaporated when she saw the serious look on her friend's face. "He's a police inspector, for goodness' sake. Not an international hit man!"

"How do you know for sure? Remember last year how he tried to stop us from looking into the death of that poor woman and—"

Addie held her hand up. "That murderer was apprehended, and it was *not* DI Parker. Besides, he would have had to have been in Moorscrag at some point in the last week for Mr. Pressman to have given him the book he brought me."

"He could have found out you needed the book, flew back to get it, and then used it as a good alibi for being here when he killed the man. Marc would surely look at his plane ticket and figure he couldn't be a suspect because he only arrived—"

"What on earth are you talking on about?"

"It's possible."

"Maybe in a spy movie, but not in real life," Addie said.

"It was the plot in a book Zach is reading."

"There you go. Not real life."

"Then, why is he still here? Ask yourself that," Serena said with a look of smug satisfaction.

"Because of the storm."

Serena pointed toward the window. "I don't see any storm today, do you? Yet there he is, sitting in my tea shop. It's past noon, and he's still eating his lunch when he"—she hooked air quotes—"*supposedly* has a flight to catch to New York?"

"Maybe his flight isn't until later?"

"Or maybe there is another reason he's hanging around, and if he's not a trained assassin building an alibi, that must mean he's staying to be with you."

"Don't be silly. We could barely tolerate each other last year, remember?" Addie waved off Serena's catlike grin and feigned sorting sales receipts. The problem was, there weren't any for the morning, and it was clear she was just shuffling blank papers.

Serena reached across the counter and placed her hand over Addie's. "You know you have never been able to keep anything from me. I've noticed you go off dreamily into space at least once a day since you came back, and whenever his name comes up, you turn fifty shades of red. Something changed between you and him after Paige and I left, didn't it?"

Addie shook her head, keeping her gaze averted.

"Don't try and tell me that. I know all the signs of a woman in love—"

"I'm not in love! I'm just *curious*, that's all."

"I know I have been busy since you came home," said Serena, "and I haven't been the best friend you needed, especially when I made such a fuss about making sure you did come back, but—"

"That wasn't your fault. Your dad was recovering from his surgery, you just found out you were pregnant again, Marc was getting married, and . . . and it was just a crazy time. Since then, you've been a bit busy bringing a new life into the world and caring for your family." Addie squeezed Serena's hand. "You have been the very best friend I could ever have." Tears burned behind Addie's eyes, but her smile was filled with all the warmth and love she felt for her friend.

"We just haven't had the time to really sit and talk about *feelings* much since I came back."

"Do you want to talk about it now?"

Addie glanced at the clock. "It might be better later. I expect Noah will be back any minute . . ."

Serena's eyes narrowed.

"But just so you don't think I'm brushing you off right now, let's just say that our first impression of a stuffy, upper-crust Englishman, devoid of any emotion or genuine concern, was false." Addie shook her head, shame heating her cheeks. "Remember how we did anything we could to avoid dealing with him?"

Serena nodded.

"One night he came to my cottage and asked for my advice on something about the case. We had a long chat, and through that experience I learned that my assumptions of him had been completely wrong." Addie fiddled with the blank papers. "On the last night I was there, my friends in the village held a going-away party for me at the pub. He showed up, but he had no idea I was leaving the next day . . ."

Serena leaned forward. "What? What happened?"

"He said a few things that made me wonder what would happen if I stayed."

"Like what? What did he say?"

If the situation hadn't conjured up such painful memories, Addie would have laughed at the fully engrossed expression on Serena's face as she hung on every word Addie uttered. "That's not important, but now, sometimes when I think about him, I regret not having taken the time to explore a relationship to see if it went anywhere. I've just been torn, that's all."

"Then you should be thrilled that he doesn't seem to be in a hurry to leave. Be happy that the man you haven't been able to stop daydreaming about is right here in your bookstore in the States."

"I am happy."

"Then you should tell your face." Serena circled her hand at Addie's face.

"It's just that . . ."

"Just that what? You're still not over getting your heart broken by Simon?"

"No, it's not that. I am ready to move forward, but I don't know if Noah is ready yet."

"What do you mean?"

"One of the reasons we bonded that night while we were working in my cottage was that he told me he had performed a background check on me because, and I quote, 'I figured there must be something in your background that could tell me why you're the most incorrigible person I have ever met, and I discovered it wasn't the only time you interfered in a police investigation' unquote. He also knew about my father being a detective and about"—she cast her eyes downward— "David being murdered, and he said he understood how I felt."

"What did he mean, he understood?"

"His wife had been murdered too."

"I see."

"Yes, it was like we belonged to a small but select club after that. We had something in common that not everyone else understands: a murdered spouse, or soon-to-be spouse, and how it affects everything in our lives as we try to move on and make a future without the ones who were snatched away from us."

"That's a club I definitely don't ever want to be a member of."

"And I hope you never are, but I don't think that he's ready to really move on."

"Why? Does he constantly talk about his wife?"

"No, hardly ever, but his Christmas trip to New York is a checkmark off *her* bucket list. I get the impression that he feels guilty for not taking her before she . . . died."

"That's the thing, isn't it? She didn't just die. It's not like she had been sick or anything. She was murdered, and there is no way for anyone to prepare for that," Serena hoarsely whispered.

"No, there isn't. So, if this trip is about her and fulfilling a promise to her, then he's not ready for a new relationship yet, and I'm not ready for another heartbreak."

"You weren't ready for Marc when he came along, and you thought you were. Who knows? Maybe Noah will surprise you too?"

"Yes, there was Marc," said Addie, gazing at the door, memories of him barging through it, either to scold her or to collaborate with her, swirling through her head. She plopped a pod in the coffeemaker. "But you remember how that turned out. Let's face it, Marc was bad timing on my part. I couldn't put all my ghosts to rest then. Maybe if we had met a few years later, who knows? Now we'll never know. Time has moved us both on. I'm afraid Noah's ghosts still play a big part in his life, like they did in mine back then, and I don't want to end up being the one he pushes away, like I did to Marc."

The outer door from the alleyway into the back room banged.

"Addie!" Paige frantically yelled. "You aren't going to believe what happened at the dress fitting just now." Panting, Paige scurried out of the back room, her open coat flapping wildly as she ran toward Addie.

"You're as white as the snow! You'd better sit down," said Serena, taking Paige by the shoulders and ushering her to a stool.

"Is it your mother?" asked Addie.

Paige emphatically shook her head as she struggled to catch her breath. "Sorry," she wheezed, "I ran all the way from the dress shop."

"Try to stay calm. Now, take a deep breath and tell us what happened," Addie said.

"Okay," Paige croaked and patted her heaving chest. "The . . . the police have just taken Nikki in for questioning about a . . . a dead body they found."

Chapter Ten

"Whose body, and why would Nikki know anything about it?" asked Addie.

"Her ex-husband's," Paige said.

"You're kidding, right?" Serena asked.

Paige shook her head.

"Then it's not going to take Marc very long to figure out Nikki couldn't know anything about Chad's death," said Serena. "He knows she hasn't been back to Chicago since she left that monster of a man." She shivered.

"That's the thing," said Paige. "His body was discovered on the rocks below the lighthouse."

"What?" cried Serena, as she grabbed for the counter. "You're saying my cousin's ex-husband was *here* in Greyborne Harbor, and it was *his* body that was found early this morning?"

Addie took one look at Serena's drawn face and grabbed her shoulders, helping her navigate her way onto the stool beside Paige's. "Take a breath, Serena. Don't worry. I'm sure there must be some explanation. As soon as they start questioning Nikki, they'll figure out she doesn't know anything about his being in town, let alone having anything to do with his death, especially since it's been so long since she's seen him."

Serena took a few deep breaths. "You're right, and Marc knows that whatever Chad did or got himself tangled up in after she left, whether it was drugs, alcohol, or gambling debts, she would know nothing about it now, and it wouldn't have anything to do with her."

"Drink this," said Addie, handing Serena her own freshly brewed cup of coffee. "You look like you need a jolt of caffeine to get your blood moving again. Sit and focus on your breathing. Slowly in and out, that's it."

Serena nodded in appreciation and took the cup from her hand, then sighed and closed her eyes for a bit. After a few moments, eyes still shut, Serena said, "If I recall, Chad's drinking was part of the problem back then, not his only one, but he got worse the more he drank. It wouldn't surprise me if that's why he took a tumble off the cliff." She opened her eyes, raised her cup to her lips, and paused, looking at Addie over the rim. "It's too bad, of course, that he died, but as he very nearly killed Nikki more than once, I guess it's karma or something," she added quietly, taking a sip.

Addie silently contemplated the notion of karma. While she didn't necessarily believe in it, she did believe in natural consequences. And, of all people— from the stories Nikki had told since Addie had met her, hired her, and then become her housemate—Chad had many natural consequences coming his way.

Serena started to take another sip, but then stopped and set her cup on the counter. "What I'd like to know is where Marc got the idea of dragging his own cousin down to the police station to inform her of Chad's death. How could he possibly think that was even a good idea in the first place? She must have been humiliated. I know I was when he dragged me away once and stuffed me in the back of his police car."

"That's the thing," said Paige. "It wasn't Marc. It was Jerry."

"There you go," said Addie. "Marc might have sent Jerry to get her so he could tell her personally and privately about Chad, and to calm her fears by letting her know she doesn't have to worry about him showing up on her doorstep anymore."

"I don't think that's the case," said Paige. "When Jerry came in, he told her right off that her ex was dead."

"Jerry told her, not Marc?" Serena asked.

Paige nodded her head.

"So much for my theory, then." Addie frowned. "What exactly did he say to her?"

"He said, and I hope I'm quoting him correctly, 'Nikki Harrison, I regret to inform you that the body of your ex-husband, Chad Sanders, was discovered early this morning on the rocks below the lighthouse.' Nikki said, 'That's impossible. He lives and works in Chicago.' Jerry then said, 'We have it on good authority that he was staying here in town and had been for at least a week, and we have a few questions we'd like to ask you.' Nikki said, 'I don't know anything about him being here,' and Jerry touched his hand to his hand-cuffs on his utility belt, real threatening-like, and said, 'Miss Harrison, if you could please come with us,' and then they took her away."

"Chad's been in town for a week?" asked Addie.

"Yes, but Jerry made it sound like it could have been longer. At least, that's what I got out of it when he said *at least* a week."

"That means he was stalking her." Serena pushed her coffee cup away and rose to her feet. "I have to go. I need to pop in the shop to let them know I won't be back, and then I gotta go tell Mom we have a mole in the family. Obviously, someone told Chad where Nikki was living, and it sure wasn't me or Marc." Serena grabbed her coat and hurried out the door, shoving her arms into the sleeves as she went.

"It wouldn't have been Janis, either," said Paige sullenly. "Her mom's the one who managed to finally convince Nikki that she was going to have to leave him. Her life depended on it, because he wasn't ever going to change, and Serena and Marc's parents then took her in when she did leave. I sure hope Serena settles down before she says something to her mom she can't take back, causing a rift between them."

Addie studied Paige's taut face and squeezed her hand. "Speaking of moms, how did the dress fitting go with *your* mom?"

"Ah"—Paige waved her off—"there's a lot of tension between us, but I decided that if putting up with her taking over the wedding planning makes her happy, then I don't care anymore, as long as by Christmas Day evening, Logan and I are married. That's what's important. Not how we got there."

"Good attitude." Addie smiled. "Does that mean you're finished for the day and back here or . . . ?"

"No." Paige glanced up at the clock. "I left Mom at the dress shop. I have to get back. We were just starting on the final fitting for her mother-of-the-bride dress when Jerry came in and arrested Nikki."

"Wait. You said she was taken in for questioning. You never said she was arrested."

"Questioning, arrested, is there a difference?" called Paige over her shoulder as she hurried toward the back exit.

"Yes, there is!" hollered Addie to the bang of the rear door as it closed. "A big difference."

She gazed around the empty store while shuffling the blank papers on the counter and then tucked them back into a drawer, not knowing what else to do as she'd done all her work in the morning. She walked over to a shelf and pulled off a copy of Charles Dickens's *A Christmas Carol*, then settled into a leather chair and quickly lost herself in Dickens's Victorian world until the front door opened, sending the bells jingling and cold wind scurrying across the floor and up her legs.

She jumped, shivered, and then laughed at the sight of Noah not able to stop the smile that crept across her lips when a pair of luminous gray eyes set on hers. "That'll teach me to read about the ghost of Christmas past when I'm supposed to be working," she said, still chuckling as she closed the book. "So, how was your pasty?"

"Splendid, simply splendid, and thank you for pointing me in the direction of SerenaTEA. It's a most charming little tea shop." Noah's heartfelt smile showed his genuine happiness as he took a seat in the neighboring leather chair. "You can let your mate, Serena, know that I just had the best cuppa since I left the UK. All in all, my little sojourn to your neighborhood tea shop was exactly what was called for today."

"Let's hope that little pick-me-up will help you make it through the next leg of your Christmas journey." She played with the pages of her book, not daring to look at him. "Then, when you get to New York"— she hesitantly glanced up—"I'm pretty sure you'll find tons of traditional-style English tea shops that will bring you the same comfort as Serena's did for the duration of your stay."

He eyed the book clutched in her hands and gave her a wry smile. "Actually . . ." His gaze traveled her face, from her eyes, down her nose, to her lips, and back up her left cheek to her eyes again. "I was thinking of staying here another day." He gestured to the window. "It seems the coastal road to the motorway has iced over, with the windblown snow across the roadway making travel from Greyborne Harbor to the main motorway not recommended."

The blood rushing to her head deafened her to all but his words swirling around in her mind. "Do . . . do they still have a room available at the B&B, or do you need to make other arrangements?" asked Addie, mentally crossing her fingers for him to say he needed to stay with her. She scolded the prim, proper, and rather Victorian part of her that reared its morals, and she scoffed down at the book in her hands.

Her scoff must have been verbal, as well, because Noah cocked his head and studied her, a soft smile on his lips.

She pointed to her throat and cleared it for good measure. "Something in my throat."

"Hate when that happens." But the twinkle in his eyes proved he knew she meant something other than what she was actually saying. "To answer your question, the visitors who had booked in for the holidays are in the same situation as I am, but on the other end and can't get here. Which means, the ladies are more than happy to have me stay on until their reserved guests arrive."

"That's . . . that's wonderful," said Addie, catching herself wavering somewhere between disappointment and relief. "I'm sure the sisters prefer having a paying guest over having another empty room over the holidays."

"I'm certain they do, but I must admit . . ." His cheeks rosied, and he ran a finger between his neck and shirt collar. "That's not the only reason I have decided to delay my departure for New York."

"It's not?" Addie struggled to keep her voice cool and nonchalant.

"No, I just overheard one of the servers in the tea shop telling Serena that she had a mobile call from her boyfriend, who apparently works as a police deputy?"

"Yes, that would be Elle Hollingsworth, Paige's best friend. She's been dating a deputy for a few years now."

"All I can say is this young Elle person had a lot to say about a certain situation."

"If you're questioning her credibility, she's a reliable source and knows a lot of what's going on in the police station."

Noah arched a brow.

"Her boyfriend overshares everything with her, to Marc's displeasure."

"Yes, that does tend to happen with couples, and yes, I suppose I was curious to know if she's credible because she had something very interesting to say."

"Was it about the Christmas thief? Do they know who it was?"

He shook his head.

"Then what?"

Noah glanced over his shoulder, leaned closer, and dropped his voice. "She told Serena her boyfriend had to cancel their dinner date tonight because he has to work late on a"—he took another quick look around and whispered—"a murder investigation."

"Murder?"

Noah nodded.

"Are you sure she said 'murder'?"

"Positive. I was only a few feet away, and as far as I know, there's only been one body found in Greyborne Harbor recently. She must have been talking about the body on the rocks, and they discovered evidence of foul play."

"But that man couldn't have been murdered." Addie quickly replayed her conversation with Paige earlier. There'd been no reference to murder, only that Chad was dead.

"Unless you have bodies dropping from the sky here in your quaint little village, I'd say you have a murder victim, not an unfortunate accident."

"But . . ." Addie took a deep breath and centered her thoughts. "I was told that the police identified the man as Chad Sanders. He was the ex-husband of Nikki, my shop assistant and roommate. We only thought that the police wanted to talk to her."

"I'm sorry." Noah reached over and gently squeezed her hand. "I had no idea you knew him."

"I didn't, and he wasn't a welcome guest in town, because Nikki had left him years ago—and for good reason. She's not a murderer, though."

"You said they took her in to talk to her?"

Addie nodded.

"Don't worry. That's totally normal for her to be questioned in this circumstance, as she knew him and had a connection to him."

"True, but Paige also threw out the word 'arrested' on her way out, and she failed to qualify whether she was actually arrested or just taken in for questioning." Addie wished she'd run after Paige and asked which it was.

"That's a different story, then." Noah held his hands up in a helpless gesture. "But I'm just the messenger here. I don't know the story or the particulars of the case, but I thought you might be interested in hearing the latest."

"I'm sorry, you're right." Addie sighed, stood, and placed Dickens's story back on the shelves. She was done with ghosts. "But just so we're clear and you don't get any wrong signals from what others might say, as much as my housemate might have wanted that man dead over the years, she would never ever take it upon herself to make that happen." Addie shook her head. "No, she would never. There has to be another explanation."

"There is always the possibility it is exactly what we initially thought—that this bloke's death was, in fact, connected to the robbery." He smiled softly. "Remember, both of these investigations are in the early stages. Your mate Marc wasn't even aware this morning the man they found had been murdered. At the time, it was ruled an accident and was not your elf thief."

"You're right. I'm assuming the preliminary coroner's report proves Chad was murdered. The police will have to take a closer look at my theory to see if there are any links to the two crimes."

"That also means that until some evidence is found that can link the murder and the robbery, if there is any, the police will now be forced to dissect every aspect of your housemate's life until the case is solved. So, we need to find that link. I trust your gut, and if you say your housemate didn't do it, we need to find out who did."

"You're right." She glanced up at the clock. "Could you stay for a few minutes and look after Pippi and the shop—" Addie stopped mid-stride when she saw the glimmer of excitement fade in Noah's eyes. It was clear the detective inspector loved the thrill of the chase—including investigating a murder. She, too, had grown to accept that fact about herself since murders seemed to follow her wherever she went. "Never mind," she said. "How does a quick stop at my house before a tour of the local police station sound?"

Chapter Eleven

"I'll just be a minute," said Addie, ducking into the back seat to retrieve Pippi in her dog carrier.

"This is your house?" Noah scanned the three-story, ornate Queen Anne from the car. "I had no idea you were a woman of such means."

"It was an inheritance. Trust me, on what I take in at the bookshop, I never would have been able to afford this and all that came with it." She chuckled, closed the door with her hip, and made the cautionary trek up the slippery, double-wide front steps to the covered porch. She fished her house key out of her pocket, inserted it into the lock, and poked her head inside. "Nikki, are you home?"

The ticking of the large grandfather clock in the living room to her left was the only answer.

Addie tapped the code into the alarm system by the door and released Pippi from her carrier. "Okay, little one, I'm sorry, but you're going to have to stay here for a while. I shouldn't be long, but I need to find out if Auntie Nikki's okay and figure out if there's any way I can help her. There's plenty of kibble and water left in your bowls in the kitchen. Love you." She rubbed Pippi's head, reset the alarm, locked the door, and hurried as fast as she dared back to the car.

"Brrrrr!" She shivered as she climbed in and fastened her seat belt. "The storm might have passed, but I sure can see why the roads and surfaces are icing over. I think it was a good call you made about not heading out on the highway today." She involuntarily shivered again as she turned around on the driveway and they headed for the police station.

"Can you tell me about this inheritance that appears to have left you with one of the largest homes I have yet to see in Greyborne Harbor, or is it something you don't want to talk about?"

"There's not much to say. A relative died and left me her family home—I mean, the Greyborne family home, as you might have guessed by the town name, and—"

Her beloved red-and-white MINI Cooper's rear end swung widely from side to side on an icy patch, and Addie fought to keep it steady on the steep decline of Oak Street. Addie pushed her conversation and the presence of Noah to the side and concentrated on keeping her car on the road instead of in the ditch. She just needed to get to the bottom of the hill without damaging her car or worse. She shivered again, her teeth grating painfully against each other.

"I suppose," said Noah, his tone irritatingly calm,

"that you could have done worse than inheriting a property in Greyborne Harbor."

Addie scowled, unsure what he meant, and flicked a glance at him.

The car's back end began to fishtail, and she tightened her grip on the steering wheel. She hoped they would be able to come to a full stop when they hit the ice patch at the intersection and sighed in relief when they did. After catching her breath, Addie glanced over at Noah. From his laid-back body language, it was clear he truly had no idea how close they'd come to total annihilation—or, at the very least, a smashed bumper.

"Yes . . . I suppose I could have."

"I imagine that your standing in the community is highly regarded because of your family link to the town."

"Believe me, I personally played no part in the town's history."

"Surely, you must be an esteemed member of the community, though. Take that bloke back up on the hill who was clearing snow off his truck. When we passed and he saw you, he smiled and waved. It made me think you must know all your neighbors, or you're in very high standing in the community and garner their reverence."

"'Reverence'? You do know you're not in England anymore, don't you? This is the colonies, and we do not worship people, except pop stars and some actors. No, my aunt—I mean, grandmother—is the person in my family who was highly regarded, because of what she did for the community, and not because of her name."

"My apologies. I've only ever known a society based on a hierarchal and peerage system, although that is slowly changing in the UK too."

She turned her face away because she knew the bloke he was talking about. Simon was a topic she really didn't care to sit at the stop sign and chat about. She pressed down on the accelerator and turned onto the main road toward the center of town. She hoped that when she and Noah had passed by him, Simon had noticed Addie wasn't alone in the car and felt a little pang of what she did every time she passed his house and saw him and Laurel together.

"I don't know many of the townspeople, and I'm certainly not in as high of a standing as my grandmother was. As a matter of fact, it wasn't too many years ago they tried to run me out of town because they said I brought a criminal element with me when I relocated here."

"You did?" He stretched and nestled into his seat with an amused expression in his eyes. "Could it have had anything to do with all the murderers who seem to drop their victims at your feet?"

"I think you're just jealous of my talent. Heck, if victims consistently dropped at your feet, it'd make your job easier, wouldn't it? Envy does not look good on you, Inspector Parker. If you're lucky, perhaps I could teach you how to be a calamity magnet like my- self and—" Her car tires hit another patch of ice, send- ing the back of the car into a swing.

"I wasn't aware I'd be getting a lesson right away." Noah chuckled and released his grip on the handle above the door when the car stopped swerving. "I think you missed one of your greatest talents, though."

"And which one is that?"

"Your knack for creating difficult situations."

"Yes, but I've found the best lessons are learned on the job." She glanced in the rearview mirror and thanked her stars that at least that intersection had been recently salted.

Silence dominated the car, and out of her peripheral vision Addie saw Noah frequently glance over at her. She assumed it was because he was burning with unanswered questions since she hadn't elaborated on anything. He was a curious man by nature and trade. But Addie forged ahead, and concentrated on the road, avoiding icy patches and other vehicles swerving to avoid the ones in their path. It wasn't that she didn't want to share with him the past details of her life, but driving in hazardous road conditions was not the time or place for such a heart-to-heart talk.

Besides, she had to focus on what was currently going on. Her past, at the moment, didn't matter. What mattered was that Nikki had been arrested, and Addie needed to know why.

As they neared the police station, Addie glanced at Noah. "Do me a favor, when we get to the police station, don't mention anything about the murder. Let me make casual inquiries about the robbery first, and we'll wait and see if the conversation ends up tying the two incidents together."

Noah's luminous eyes darkened, and a frown replaced his earlier easy smile.

"What?" she asked, pulling into the public parking lot beside the sandstone municipal building, and turned off the car.

"I'm not sure if you're aware, Miss Greyborne, but this is *not* my first investigation."

"I wasn't implying that it was."

"Weren't you?"

Now she remembered why Noah and she had butted heads on more than one occasion back in England. "No, I said what I did because I know these people and have worked with them, and there is a specific way to deal with Marc Chandler."

"Is this the same Marc Chandler who is Serena's brother and whom you were going to marry at one time?" By the sparkle that had returned to his eyes, he was clearly amused as he started to get out of the passenger door.

"Yes," Addie said as she pushed her door open and got out. "As a matter of fact, it is." She slammed her door and glared at him over the roof of the MINI.

Noah won the staring contest, when Addie turned away and trekked through the snowdrifts to the sidewalk, not bothering to wait for the annoying British man slogging through the drifts behind her.

"Like that gentleman who waved at you, whom you chose to ignore up on your road? Simon, I believe, is his name."

Addie stopped short and turned. "How did you know it was Simon?"

"You told me."

"When?"

"Just now," he said with a teasing wink, then joined her on the cleared sidewalk.

"Cheeky," she sputtered, noting that he was good at his job and reminding herself never to doubt or under-estimate him again. Turning on her boot heel, Addie marched up the wide steps to the police station and flung the door open so hard it banged on the doorstop. "And I'll have you know that it wasn't a matter of *choosing* to ignore him. I was a bit busy trying to keep us alive on the drive down the hill," she snapped.

The five people sitting on the plastic waiting room chairs turned and stared at her.

"Sorry." She cringed, ignored Noah's grin, and walked over to the reception counter, where Noah—still with an amused gleam in his eyes—gave her a nudge when the desk sergeant asked her a question.

"Sorry, what was that?" Addie asked.

"What can I do for you today?" repeated the young officer.

Addie eyed the young man and wondered if it was bring-your-son-to-work day or if she was really getting that old. "Sorry, I was lost in my own little world there." She shored herself up in an attempt to make her seem more authoritative than she felt. "I would like to see Chief Chandler."

Noah gave her arm a nudge.

"Please." She smiled.

"May I ask what you need to see the chief about?"

"It's about a . . . a robbery."

The officer sat upright and leaned forward. "Is this a

current robbery?" he asked in a low voice. "Like, is it going on right now?" He glanced around the waiting room and pulled a yellow notepad closer to him.

"No, no, nothing like that. It happened last night."

"I see." The young officer's face relaxed. "Are you the victim, then?"

"Yes and no."

Confusion filled his dark brown eyes. "Which one is it?"

"I was there."

"I see." He nodded, eyeing Addie suspiciously. "Could I have your name, please?" He poised his pen over the notepad.

"It's Addie, Addie Greyborne."

"Addie Greyborne," he said, making note. "Please take a seat, don't leave, and don't go anywhere," he said nervously. "I'll be right back." The young officer stood up, backed toward the door beside the desk, and knocked, keeping his eyes steadfastly on Addie the entire time.

"Come in!" boomed a voice through the closed door.

The young deputy took one last look at Addie and Noah, then slipped inside.

"He thinks you did it, and you're here to confess."

"Why would he think that?"

"Not many people come into a police station and announce they were at a robbery the previous night without further information about how they were involved."

"Well, Marc knows I wasn't the thief."

"If he's read the report, that is." He glanced at the area behind the desk. "I wouldn't be surprised if your mate Marc is on the phone now asking for backup in the waiting room because that officer told him a desperate robber had just walked in."

"You've got to be kidding, right?" she said, along with giving an involuntary eye roll. "I must have missed the part where you told me you were also a murder-mystery writer."

"I'm just saying, you never know how people will take things in this day and age."

"Whatever. Then we might as well do as we're told while we wait for the armed officers to show up and drag me away."

Noah's amused, lopsided smile disappeared from his lips.

"I'm sorry. I didn't mean to sound snappy," Addie said. "It's just that I have no idea who that desk sergeant is, and he doesn't know me, because so much has changed, yet nothing at all really has in the year and a half since I've been in here." She took in the drab walls and the plastic chairs.

"There's no need to apologize. I, too, know what it's like trying to live in a world where you don't quite feel like you fit anymore."

All the air left Addie's lungs, and she coughed to hide the effect his words caused. She eyed him, trying to see his earlier cheeky side, but only sincerity flickered in his gaze. She couldn't discuss this with him now, not in the police station, not with Marc just on the other side of the wall. "I still fit in this place," Addie lied.

Noah led her to two empty chairs, sat next to her, and took her hand in his, giving it a reassuring squeeze.

"Perhaps things have changed more than you want to admit."

His last words stung because he was right, and as much as she'd tried to hide from the truth since coming back, she knew she couldn't ignore it any longer. Nothing was—or would ever be—the same. She and Marc would never be what they once were, and now he had a baby on the way. Would they even ever get back to being friends? They had barely spoken since his wedding, and even then, it was only fleeting, superficial conversation.

Addie mindlessly tapped her foot to the rhythm of the clock ticking away the seconds and contemplated how she fit into her new life, with her old friends making new connections and starting new journeys without her.

As she took another scan of the room, she knew one thing for certain. Nothing at the police station, besides the new deputy, had changed. It had been a long time since she'd sat in this waiting room, yet somehow it seemed like just yesterday. The same posters were on the walls; the same faded paint color gave the room a drab, unwelcoming aura; and the same awful chairs made visitors wait in pensive, uncomfortable silence. Addie squirmed in her seat. *Really, they couldn't have replaced these chairs in a year and a half?*

She shifted onto her hip and gave Noah an awkward smile. "Sorry about this wait."

Marc's office door opened, and Addie jumped to her feet, but hope faded when the desk sergeant came out, closed the door, looked at Addie, and shrugged.

"I can't believe this," she said, sitting back down.

"I really thought if I didn't mention the"—she looked about her and dropped her voice—"dead guy, he'd see us right away."

"Especially when the young officer told him he had a robber out in the waiting room, right?" Noah grinned, stretched out his long legs, crossed his ankles, and pulled his cell phone out of his jacket pocket. "We're not the only people who are waiting to speak to the chief, by the looks of it. You might as well get comfortable," he said, scrolling through his phone.

"I just thought that since I gave a statement last night, he might have another question or two about the robbery and would want to see me. Then I could slip in something about Chad's body and ask what he thought killed him. Then, bam, we're talking about the murder." She glanced toward the clock, then at her phone.

"What's that saying about best-laid plans and all?"

"*Pfft!*" Addie settled back to play a game on her phone, something she rarely had time to do. Even with the distraction, time felt as though it was standing still, and she shifted on the hard chair. As an edgy feeling surged through her, she glanced up and saw Marc standing in his office door frame, staring at her.

He took a deep breath and waved them into his office. After the door closed behind them, Marc sat behind the desk and motioned to the two chairs across from him. "Addie"—he said her name as if it exhausted him—"have a seat, and . . . ?" He looked questioningly at Noah.

"Noah, Noah Parker." Noah held out his hand in greeting.

Marc studied him as he shook his hand. "I take it by

the accent that you're a friend of Addie's from England?"

"'Friend'?" He flashed a side glance at Addie, his crooked smile broadening. "I'd say we are—"

"We have a good working relationship," added Addie quickly.

"Are you the fellow she worked for at the bookshop in Yorkshire?"

"That would be Reginald Pressman. No, I'm more like the detective inspector who became associated with Miss Greyborne when—"

"Don't tell me, when she invited herself to become a part of your investigation into that murder?"

"I see you know her well, then?"

"Yes, yes, I do." Marc gave Addie a lopsided smile, which barely made up for the way he'd said her name earlier, then he focused on Noah. "I heard about you through my sister, Serena, actually. But I only recalled your name just now. I understand she had the honor of making your acquaintance when she went over to rescue this one." He gestured to Addie.

"In my experience," said Noah, a note of protectiveness in his tone, "Addie is more than capable of taking care of herself, and she definitely requires no rescuing."

"I agree. Please, don't get me wrong. Addie has proven on many occasions she's more than capable of getting herself out of sticky situations. However, I've discovered over the years that she often needs rescuing from herself." He winked at her.

Addie bristled. "Excuse me, gentlemen. I'm right here, so stop talking over me like I'm not."

"Sorry," said Marc.

"Yes, my apologies," added Noah.

Addie wanted nothing more than to wipe the grins off both their faces. "No one needed to rescue me. It was a murder that *we*"—she waggled her thumb between her and Noah—"solved together, by the way."

Marc sat back and folded his arms across his chest. "That sounds like a story I'd like to hear more about." He quietly chuckled. "Are you telling me, Noah, that it's not just my investigations she invites herself into?"

"It seems not, and from what I read about her on-line"—Noah dropped his voice—"Addie here seems to have a habit of tripping over bodies. It does make one wonder if she is truly as innocent in the crimes as she presents herself to be."

"Like a professional patient who makes herself sick in order to get medical attention?" asked Marc.

"Or the firefighter who commits arson so he can appear to be the hero in the situation when it's eventually put out," said Noah.

Marc leaned closer and pinned his eyes on Addie. "Or the amateur sleuth who builds her reputation on solving a murder she committed in order to—"

"Or," Addie interrupted as she scooted to the edge of her seat, resting her elbows on her knees, "maybe the nurse who puts her patients' lives at risk so she can save them and be lauded as a medical superstar." She blew theatrically on her fingernails, polished them on her sleeve, and grinned at the gaping faces of Marc and Noah. "What? You thought I didn't know what you two were doing?"

Noah's captivating smile warmed Addie from head to toe.

"It seems that this band of brothers not only includes a Brit and an American, but a civilian as well." Noah stuck his hand out and shook Addie's. "Welcome aboard." He seemed to hold her hand a moment longer than necessary and only broke contact when Marc cleared his throat.

Flustered at the attention and Noah's warm hand engulfing hers, Addie bought some time by studying the room as the men traded war stories. The same clock ticked away on the wall above the file cabinet behind his desk. She played her fingers over the aged wooden arms of the chair that had always been hers. From her vantage point, she could see the dent he'd put in the filing cabinet when he'd caught her going through a file once.

She didn't need to be indulging such thoughts. Done with memory lane, she cut short Marc's retellings of her 'involvement' in a case. "If you're done spreading misinformation about me, I have a few questions for you."

"You have questions for me?" Marc fumbled with a stack of papers in front of him and straightened his shoulders. His eyes darkened, and there was that telltale tic in his jaw that told her she might have pushed too far, too fast. "I believe I'm the chief of police here, and I should be the one asking questions, or did you take and pass the police academy course while you were away?"

"I think what my *friend* here is trying to say," added

Noah quickly, "is that she was involved in the robbery at the lighthouse museum last night, and she was wondering if you have any leads in that case."

"That's it? That's the case you're in here about?"

"Yes. That's the one. Why? Is there another one I should be asking about?" she said, feigning innocence.

"Not one I am at liberty to discuss," he said, pushing the papers to the side.

"Does the robbery have anything to do with the man whose body was discovered on the rocks below the lighthouse?"

"Addie," Noah chided. "So much for it casually coming up in the conversation."

"Well . . ." She shrugged helplessly.

"It's all right, Noah. Word is going to get around soon enough." Marc's shoulders drooped, and he sat back, scrubbing his hands through his thick chestnut-brown hair. "I've had to recuse myself from that case. Therefore, I am not privy to any of the evidence they've gathered. So, you see, Miss Marple, it's not because I won't tell you anything—especially since I know you'll eventually worm the details out of someone anyway— it's because I can't. I have no idea what's going on."

"Did you recuse yourself because the victim was identified as Chad Sanders, Nikki's ex?"

He blew out a deep breath and sighed. "Tell me how you knew about that? No, wait! *Don't* tell me, because then I would have to arrest the person who told you, and if it's who I think it is, I don't want to have to visit *both* my cousin and my sister in their respective jail cells.

And now, if you'll excuse me, I'm late for a meeting with the DA. I'm sure you can see yourselves out." Marc grabbed a file folder from his desk and headed toward the door, then stopped and turned. "Inspector, I do hope you enjoy your stay in Greyborne Harbor. My department would be gratefully obliged if you could please remind the young Miss Marple here that you are on vacation, not on a working holiday."

He flashed Addie a cautionary look as he left.

Chapter Twelve

Addie pulled out of the police station parking lot, drove around the corner, and dropped Noah off at his rental car parked on the street by the bookshop. She then ran into the shop, closed up for the day, and drove as fast as the icy roads would allow in order for her to get home to Pippi, who had been left alone longer than she'd planned. By now, the poor thing must be pacing the floor, anxious to go out to do her business.

As Addie turned into her driveway, she hesitated at the sight of Serena's Jeep Wrangler parked outside her house and glanced at the dash clock. "It's dinnertime. You're never here at dinnertime. What about the family?" Addie muttered turning off the car, jumped out, and raced up the steps.

"What's wrong?" she cried out when she burst through the front door.

"We're in here," called Serena from the living room, to her left.

Addie poked her head around the door frame of the French pocket door. Serena sat cross-legged in a chair by the fireplace, and Nikki, on the sofa with her feet up on the coffee table, casually twirled tresses of her long cinnamon-red hair around her finger.

"Is everything okay?" Addie hesitantly asked.

"Better than ever," said Nikki, her attention focused on her phone screen. "It says on this website that Chad had recently filed the documents necessary to make his sporting goods business into a franchise."

"Which means what?" asked Serena, studying Nikki over the rim of her teacup.

Addie kicked off her boots, dropped her coat on the arm of the sofa, and sat. "He was going to sell the rights for other people to use his name and business plan."

"Yes," Nikki said, "but they would have to pay him money, lots and lots of money, to use his business model, his products, and his trademarked brand name. They pay annual royalties, too, which means he was expanding quickly and about to become very rich." She lowered her phone.

"Can you take over that plan now?" asked Serena. "You were part owner of the business, weren't you?"

"No, in order to be free of him, or so I thought at the time, he made me sign an affidavit that was filed as an addendum along with the divorce papers. It stated that I agreed to the dissolving of our business partnership along with the marriage, and that I had no further interest in his business holdings."

"That's too bad," said Serena. "But now that he's dead, who gets his businesses and the rights to that franchise thingy?"

"That's a good question," said Nikki. "As far as I know, he had no living family members, so unless he had a girlfriend and made her the beneficiary, I have no idea." She shrugged. "But it's funny, I guess, because before I left, right after he opened his third location in the Chicago area, he had talked about offering franchise opportunities for his stores. At the time, I saw it as a reflection of his very inflated ego. He had this image of himself as a power mogul in the sporting goods industry."

"But wasn't he too much of a control freak to do something like that?" asked Serena.

"Yeah, at least that's what I thought at the time. I never thought he'd actually trust anyone when it came to his business ideas and finances, which, by law, he would have had to open up for review in order to become an accredited franchiser." Nikki shrugged. "I guess he eventually did. Who knew?" She shook her head and went back to reading her screen.

"So, what happened today, Nikki?" asked Addie. "All I heard was that you were at the dress shop on Main Street with Paige and Martha, then Jerry came in and arrested you."

"I wasn't arrested. They only wanted to ask me some routine questions because I'm his ex-wife and all."

"What questions could you have possibly answered?" asked Serena. "It's been a few years since you've even seen Chad, hasn't it?"

Nikki laid her phone beside her on the sofa, but remained silent.

"You didn't know Chad was in town, did you?" asked Serena, narrowing her eyes and studying her cousin's slender face. "Did you?" she repeated when Nikki looked away without answering.

"No, I haven't seen him since, you know, when I left him . . . Anyone want more tea? Yikes, forgive me, Addie, you don't even have any. I'll get you a cup now." Nikki stood and hurried toward the kitchen.

"That was weird," said Addie. "You don't think she knew he was in town, do you?"

"No . . . I don't think so. She would have told Marc for sure. She was always afraid Chad would figure out where she was living now, even though everyone told him they had no idea where she was."

"And you don't think he ever figured it out because so much of her family lived here?"

"No, my mom made a point of spreading the rumor that Nikki had moved to Australia, where another cousin of ours lives. Nikki was terrified that he'd find out the truth and come here after her. You know she had to change her phone number and email address last year because he kept sending her horrible messages and leaving threatening voice mails. So, no," she said hesitantly, "I'm pretty sure she didn't know he was here."

"You don't sound a hundred percent sure."

"I'm not, when I think about it. She hasn't been herself these last few days, and now it makes me wonder . . ."

*   *   *

Addie tossed and turned for the second night in a row, unable to get to sleep with Serena's words playing over in her head. By 4 a.m., she sat up, punched the pillow, and then threw it across the room, sending Pippi spinning in dazed circles. The little dog soon found a more congenial corner of the bed to settle into, then quickly went back to sleep.

"That's it!" she called out. "Hear me, universe . . . In my next life, I want to come back as a dog!" She heaved the duvet over her face.

By morning, it was all Addie could do to ready herself for a day of maneuvering knee-high snowdrifts, slogging down slushy sidewalks, and then making nice to overly cheery Christmas shoppers. The thought of the long day ahead of her felt like more than she'd be able to cope with.

When she arrived at her parking stall behind Beyond the Page, she was astonished to find that her spot had been cleared of all the snow. After wrestling out of her coat, hat, and gloves in the back room, she stared at a fresh, steaming cup of coffee with her name printed on it sitting on her desk.

"Paige?" she called.

No answer.

She poked her head out the door and scanned the front of the store. Noah sat at the counter, drinking from a paper cup and having what appeared to be a lighthearted and jovial conversation with Paige.

"Good morning." Addie approached the front counter and looked curiously from one to the other.

"Good morning," said Noah, raising his cup in greeting.

Paige grinned at Addie.

"I was just telling Paige about my latest experience with the sisters at the bed-and-breakfast last night."

Paige cleared her throat. "You remember how gaga they were whenever Si—well, whenever"—she dropped her voice—"Dr. Emerson came in here?"

"It's okay, Paige, you can say Simon's name."

"It sounds like they are even more man-crazy over Noah, if that's even possible."

"In their defense," Noah said, "they have been perfectly charming hostesses. They just take their hostessing a little to the extreme with a few of their guests. But I must say, they are taking *great* care in providing myself and Mr. Greg Carpenter with the very, very best of what their little B&B has to offer." His cheeky smile turned to a full-throated laugh, and he sputtered his coffee.

Paige handed him a tissue and began laughing hysterically, tears running down her face.

Addie eyed the pair skeptically as there appeared to be an inside joke between the two of them, and she was lost. "Do I dare ask what services they are providing to you?"

"The . . ." Noah shook his head while he tried to fight the laughter that had overtaken him. "The . . ." He struggled to compose himself, but then snorted when Paige did too.

"Bev," Paige sputtered out, "actually started to cut his meat up for him last night at dinner." Her words came in a rush between her bouts of laughter.

"She did what?" Addie asked. "Cut your meat? Like a mother might do for a small child?"

"Yes!" Noah gasped, trying to catch his breath. "Exactly like that!"

Addie tried to suppress her own giggling fit at the image in her head, but also ended up bursting into loud laughter.

"It was all rather unsettling at first." Noah wiped his eyes.

"I bet it was," Addie coughed out in her fading laughter. "I had no idea they even offered a dinner option."

"It seems that when the weather turns bad, they do offer extra meals, as most of their guests are on the more elderly side. That way their guests don't have to go out into bad weather or drive on less-than-desirable roads. They can just purchase luncheon and dinner meals at an additional cost. Last night, the Swiss steak sounded good, so I thought I'd give it a go."

"And was it so tough you had trouble cutting it?" Addie asked questioningly, trying to understand what had transpired to bring on their fits of laughter.

"I hadn't even tried yet. The taller of the sisters—"

"That would be Bev," Addie put in.

"Bev, brought it to the table where Mr. Carpenter and I were dining, and the shorter one—"

"Bin."

"She rushed over and started to cut it up for him." Paige laughed. "I can just picture Bin bent over Noah's plate, cutting the meat into little, itty-bitty pieces like I used to do with Emma."

"Then she tried to feed me . . ." Noah burst into deep, hearty laughter and wrapped his arms around his middle in an attempt to catch his breath.

"She didn't!?" Addie gaped at him.

"Trust me, she was mid-airplane before I came out of my shock and stopped her from plunging the fork in my mouth."

Addie fell into another fit of laughter. Tears streaked down each of their faces, along with the occasional hiccup, which made them all laugh even harder.

A throat cleared behind them, and Addie jumped. "Marc?" She gasped to catch her breath, but snorted instead.

"Looks like I missed a good joke."

"What can we do for you this morning?" Addie asked, attempting to compose herself and put her business face back on. Only barely winning the struggle, she gave him a quick once-over and was as equally surprised by the blue jeans–clad legs and snow boots he was wearing. Nothing about him screamed police-issue attire. "I didn't know you took weekdays off?"

"Not generally," he replied, glancing at Noah. "Can we talk?"

"Me?" Noah pointed his finger at his chest. "You want to talk to me?"

"Yeah, if you have a minute."

"Ahh . . . sure," said Noah, glancing questioningly at Addie as he got up from the stool. "Did you want to go outside, Marc?" he asked, reaching for his coat on the stool beside him.

"I'm sure Addie wouldn't mind if we stepped into the back room, would you?" Marc glanced at her.

"No, sure, go ahead." Addie shrugged and gestured to the back at the same time as Marc and Noah headed in that direction.

"I wonder what's going on," said Paige, as Marc closed the door behind them.

"Yes, it does seem all cloak-and-dagger-ish, doesn't it?" Addie eyed the door they had disappeared through. "Marc only met Noah yesterday. What in the world would he have to talk to him about that requires them being out of our earshot?"

"Should we?"

"We should. Could you hand me that empty water glass from under the counter?"

"I guess there's one advantage to not cleaning up after a shift." Paige snickered. "I'm not sure how well it would have gone over for us to interrupt their little whatever-it-is to ask to come in and get a glass."

"We'd be busted for sure," Addie whispered as they tiptoed like 007 agents toward the door that led to the back room.

Addie grinned mischievously, held the glass against the door, then placed her ear over the rim to hear what was being said on the other side.

"Anything?" Paige whispered.

Addie shook her head, then moved the glass over a touch on the door, narrowing her eyes as she concentrated.

"Now?" asked Paige.

Addie shook her head and moved the glass again. Unexpectedly, the door moved away from her, and she stumbled forward, stopped only by hands that caught her before she hit the floor.

She awkwardly looked up at her savior and uncomfortably smiled her gratitude at Marc as she tried to regain her footing.

"No problem," said Marc, depositing Addie into Noah's arms. "Noah, I think I'll leave you to explain," he said and walked toward the front door.

By the time Addie had gotten her feet under her, Marc was gone. "What was that all about?"

Noah looked as pleased as Martha's cat did when he dropped a mouse offering at her feet.

"I didn't expect such a grand welcome, but thank you anyway." Noah smiled as his arms tightened around her.

"You're as batty as Marc is right now." She couldn't think straight with Noah's arms holding her, so she pushed away from his chest. "What's going on?"

Noah grinned and puffed out his chest. "Say hello to the district attorney's latest *possible*, specially appointed police consultant."

Chapter Thirteen

Addie eyed Noah. "Did you say the DA's 'specially appointed police consultant'?"

"What I said was *possible* consultant."

"Either you are or you aren't, right?"

"Technically, yes. However, it won't be officially confirmed until I meet with the DA himself. He has to speak with my chief superintendent in West Yorkshire, and then if they both agree with Marc's recommendation"—he rubbed his hands together—"then Bob's your uncle, and I'm . . ." Unease reflected in his eyes. "Sorry, I'm not bragging. I'm just excited to be an official part of the team. You okay with that?"

"I really don't get a say, do I? I'm just surprised, that's all." A bitter taste of jealousy coated her tongue, and at Paige's elbow nudge, Addie forced a smile she didn't feel.

"Think of it this way. Since Nikki is your friend and

colleague, it'll be great for someone other than a lieutenant to be in line to investigate the case. As I understand it, there is mounting evidence against her, making her the prime suspect, at least so far."

"You're kidding!" Paige exclaimed.

"I would never kid about someone being possibly implicated as a murder suspect, no matter who they are," Noah said gently.

"No, of course, you wouldn't." Paige lowered her head.

Addie gave Paige's shoulder a reassuring squeeze, then turned her attention back to Noah. "Don't get me wrong, I'm thrilled that you're being considered. I . . . I wasn't certain I had heard right, but I guess it makes sense. Jerry is a good officer, but as far as I know, he's never had to lead a murder investigation by himself. He'll probably need some direction, and so I'm glad it could be you doing the leading in this case. You'll find Jerry a great asset to the investigation team, though. I know Marc always did."

"That's the thing. My understanding from Marc was that Jerry has been reassigned to the elf robbery."

"I thought Marc was leading that investigation?"

Noah shrugged. "I guess Marc has been put on forced leave until the whole matter involving his close family member has been resolved."

"The DA forced him out and now wants to replace him with you?"

"In a manner of speaking, yes, but it wasn't the DA's idea. It seemed to have sprung from the concerns the mayor had about Marc remaining on the job in any capacity through all this. It sounds as though the mayor had concerns about Marc's ability to remain neutral in the murder investigation if he was still around the station and had access to police resources."

"He should know better than that. Marc has had to recuse himself from cases before, and there was never a question of a conflict of interest."

"Apparently things are different now." He shrugged. "It seems it's an election year, and the mayor wants a quick conviction."

"So he wants to railroad Nikki, and he's afraid that if Marc is involved in any way, that won't happen."

"Aren't you forgetting who the DA is thinking of putting in charge in Marc's place?" Paige grinned slyly, wrapping a short blond curl around her finger.

Addie chuckled. "You're right, and who better than an ex–Metropolitan Police Department chief inspector and current detective inspector with the West Yorkshire Police Department? Besides, the DA also knows the mayor and how he operates, so I'm fairly certain he will be taking Marc's recommendation of you very seriously."

"Nothing's official yet," Noah reminded her. "I've only been asked to go and meet with the DA."

"That's just a formality. You're a shoo-in. Do you see how great this is, though? It's perfect. The mayor, who has been a thorn in Marc's side for years, is finally going to get bested by Marc—and he's not even working the case!" Addie's laughter sent her honey-brown ponytail swinging wildly.

Noah grinned. "I take it you approve now?"

"Yes, I do. Its wonderful news!"

The best part was that it meant Noah would be staying in Greyborne Harbor longer. She hoped her giddiness with this news didn't show on her face.

Noah eyed her as though he could read her mind. His eyes sparkled as he made a sweeping bowing motion. "Now, *milady*, I must take my leave. I must head over to the station and hopefully pass my job interview. Then they can brief me on what evidence they have to charge your friend Miss Nikki Harrison with first-degree murder."

"Wait—are you saying that Nikki has already been arrested for murder, not just been taken in for more questioning?"

"It was my understanding from Marc that the DA felt they had all the evidence they needed for an arrest warrant. I believe a judge was expected to sign off on it right away, and then officers would head to her home and take her into custody."

"When?"

"Now, I presume."

"Now?" Addie's eyes flew wide open. "Her house is my house. I should be there—she was still in bed when I left. She was so exhausted after what they put her through yesterday . . ." She looked at Paige. "I have to go so I can be there for Nikki. Can you watch Pippi and cover the store for me?"

Paige nodded, and Addie grabbed her coat off the coatrack and bolted for the back door.

"Wait, Addie!" yelled Noah. "It's probably too late because . . ."

Addie didn't stop to hear the rest, and the door slammed shut behind her, blocking out his final words.

"It's never too late to do what is right," she muttered,

then drove away bouncing over the snow furrows in the alley. She raced as fast as the snow-rutted road would allow her to go, and soon she burst through her front door, calling for Nikki. When there was no answer, she realized it *was* too late. Nikki had already been taken into custody.

She whipped out her phone and punched in Serena's number. "Hey, did you know Nikki was going to be arrested for murder this morning? . . . No, I'll go to the station. You call Marc to see what he knows . . . okay, okay, but just so you know, he was taken off the case . . . no, he's on forced leave . . ." She held the phone away from her ear when Serena started furiously ranting. "Yes, yes, okay . . . then just find out what he does know." Addie clicked off, hopped back in her MINI, and raced to the police station.

She arrived at the front steps seconds after DA Jeff Wilson did—he was being rushed up the stairs by a member of his security team. Biding her time, Addie paused on the sidewalk at the bottom of the steps, feigning the removal of clumps of snow from under her boots. The DA was the last person she wanted to see before she could put her plan into action. They were well acquainted with each other from her occasional work as a rare-book consultant on a couple of his past cases, but now she didn't want him to get the wrong idea—or, in this case, the *right* idea—about her being there. She didn't want anybody to try to stop her from pleading Nikki's case to anyone with authority and who would listen to her.

When the coast was clear, and the DA and his small

entourage had all entered the police station, Addie hurried up the steps and flung the door open, only to find a packed waiting room. A couple of cameras flashed in her face as she entered. At the collective groans, and with one person mumbling something about her being "*a nobody*," he lowered his camera, and they all moved on. Other gawkers in the waiting room appeared to be focused on the DA, who was heading into what had been Marc's office, the door closing with a *bang* behind him.

Addie took a quick scan of the people behind the cameras. She had a funny feeling that she knew most of them, but couldn't place them. She spotted a local television news crew setting up in the corner and smiled at the young blond reporter she had met once in her shop. Her gut swirled with unease.

"Excuse me," Addie said, shuffling sideways through the crowd, trying to make her way over to the reporter. "Hi. It's Katie Crombie, right?"

The reporter nodded.

"I know you're busy"—Addie gestured to a technician running the reporter's sound check—"and I don't know if you remember me . . ." She thrust her hand out in greeting. "Addie Greyborne."

"Addie, of course, I remember you." Katie smiled. "My favorite bookseller and Greyborne Harbor's very own Nancy Drew."

"I wouldn't say that." Heat crept up Addie's neck and rested uncomfortably on her burning cheeks. "I've just been lucky on a few occasions, that's all."

"You know what? When this press conference—"

"A press conference? For what?"

"The police apparently have already caught the killer in the latest murder."

Addie stared blankly at Katie.

"You of all people haven't heard about the man they found on the rocks below the lighthouse?"

Addie studied the throng of people crowded into the waiting room. Of course, that was why they looked familiar. They were reporters from all over Massachusetts, some of whom had hounded her themselves on one or two occasions.

"I'd have thought," said Katie, lowering her voice and leaning into Addie, "that since the killer is rumored to be the victim's ex-wife—*and* your employee—you'd be knee-deep in this one."

She straightened up and pinned Addie with an intense gaze. "Tell you what, when this is over, how about an exclusive interview with you? It would be great to get the inside scoop from someone who knows the killer well . . . and who could get higher ratings than the Nancy Drew of Greyborne Harbor, right? I tell you, my news director would eat it up, as would our viewers. It would also give your shop a little boost in sales for the holiday season. What do you say?" Katie was nearly breathless as she waved at her cameraman to turn around and get a headshot of Addie.

Addie pulled up her coat collar to block her face and quickly began pushing her way back toward the door. Her mind raced, and panic slithered up her spine. This was all she needed. She had come here with the intention of convincing someone they'd made a mistake about

Nikki's involvement, not to become part of a sensation-alized news story.

But with Nikki's arrest and this madhouse of a press conference, Addie contemplated for the first time the possibility that maybe her employee, housemate, and Marc and Serena's cousin had done what everyone was here to cover. That Nikki really had been pushed far enough to send Chad sailing off a cliff to what would surely be his death.

As Addie inched toward the door, the answer to her mind's overwhelmed musings sent a resounding *no* vibrating through her head, and tears burned at her eyes. All this was stifling and Addie felt for a moment that she couldn't breathe. The reporter—all these reporters—were there to cover the story about the ex-wife who had killed her husband, and for a few moments they'd had her believing it, too, but she knew better. She'd only come today because she thought she could act as a character witness, to convince the powers that be to look elsewhere for a suspect. After all, she knew Nikki. She lived with her, and she knew Chad was a brute. There was no denying that.

What Addie really needed was to put as much space as possible between herself and the overzealous reporters. However, as she neared the exit, she realized there was absolutely no way out unless she created a scene, drawing more unwanted attention. She stared helplessly while more reporters and lookie-loos flooded into the waiting room. The lobby resembled sardines crammed in a can, leaving no space for her to make a run for it.

A burgeoning sense of dread exploded inside her, and she froze. She needed to get out. She needed to be able to breathe. She needed to come up with a real plan, not a knee-jerk response based solely on some delusional sense of self-importance. How could she ever have imagined that she could sway anyone in their thinking? Besides, with this circus going on, it was clearly too late for that, anyway. It was time to face the facts. Her days of running to the police station every time she had ideas to float around with Marc or various scenarios to work through with him in a murder investigation were long gone. All the times they had spent speculating on various suspects were in the past. What was happening now was the perfect example of how much Greyborne Harbor had changed. It was time she did too.

She drew in a deep breath to squelch the unease bubbling up inside her. This . . . she scanned the room; this was, indeed, a circus. It had been arranged for one purpose and one purpose only. There was no doubt that the mayor wanted to offer up his police chief's cousin as a sacrificial lamb—to serve his own needs and announce his reelection bid. Something Addie wanted no part of. Her blood ran cold, and she shivered, put her head down, and frantically pushed her way through the last of the reporters blocking the entrance.

Chapter Fourteen

Just before Addie could make her escape, Marc's office door opened, and a barrage of camera clicks and flashes lit up the waiting room. She held her breath as Jerry stepped out, hands in the air, calling for quiet. She looked longingly past the last of the heads and shoulders barring her from making an escape. It seemed—like it or not—she was stuck. She was going to have to listen to the mayor pat himself on the back for his officers solving the murder so quickly and then use that as fodder to fuel his reelection bid for another term.

"If I may have your attention, please!" bellowed Jerry through a handheld microphone. "Quiet, please, and no questions. Thank you." His pointed glare covered most of the room, then settled on a group of reporters who were shouting questions over each other. "District Attorney Wilson and Mayor Bryant will be with you shortly to answer *any* questions you might have."

"Is it true you have taken the victim's ex-wife into custody and charged her with murder?" shouted Katie from the corner to Addie's left.

"I'm sorry. Can't you hear me in the back there?" Jerry smirked, then tapped the microphone, which squealed.

Addie stood on her tiptoes and searched for any sign of Noah. Her heart sank. He wasn't in sight. The door behind Jerry opened again, and he brought the microphone to his mouth. "Now, I'd like to introduce Mayor Bryant and District Attorney Jeff Wilson, who will be happy to answer some of your questions." Jerry handed the microphone over to the mayor, then stepped back, applauding along with everyone in the room.

One look at the smug expression on the mayor's face was all it took for Addie to feel as though she was going to be sick on the spot. Then she saw Noah hovering behind the DA in the doorway of the office, and the weight in her heart lifted. He was standing there with them, which could only mean his interview had been successful and he was now part of the investigation. It also meant that, with him being the fair and brutally honest detective she knew from her own experience, he wouldn't let the mayor turn Nikki's arrest into a circus. Although, Addie sighed, from the energy and chaos present in the room, she feared it had already become one.

Her gaze focused on Noah, and the mayor's words faded into vague grating sounds in the background. Noah scanned the crowd, making Addie wonder if he was convinced the real killer was here and was looking for any sign that would give him or her away. After all, murderers had been known to show up at events, like court hearings and their victims' funerals, before. Perhaps Noah was hoping this was the case here too.

She shifted on her feet, stood on tiptoe to peer over heads, and checked out the crowd to try to see anything that might help identify the possible murderer. Unfortunately, since she was still at the back by the door, she couldn't see anyone's faces. But when she glanced back over at Noah, his eyes were pinned on her, and he flashed a lopsided smile before quickly diverting his eyes and looking straight ahead. Her heart raced, and butterflies swirled in her chest.

In that moment, one more guardrail slid away from the fortress she had erected around her shattered heart, and she drew in a deep breath, eyeing him closely, but he showed no tells. There was nothing to indicate that what had just passed between them had affected him as much as her.

Deflated, Addie tried to refocus on the mayor, who was grinning and waving as camera clicks and flashes ignited the room. Apparently, he had just made his formal announcement to run again for the mayor's office next spring.

"Tricky little so-and-so," she muttered.

A reporter in front of her glanced over his shoulder and nodded in agreement. "This guy knows there are reporters here from all over the state," he said, waving his camera around. "Maybe even farther away, as he's sure playing to a larger audience than Greyborne Harbor. He's piggybacking his reelection bid on a news conference that was supposed to be about the murder of a sports legend."

"A 'sports legend'?" Addie gasped. "Is that how this was promoted?" She shook her head. "So, you had no idea that he was going to announce his run for another term in the next election, then?"

"Nope, not me. I'm a sports reporter. I don't give a hoot about anyone's political aspirations," he grumbled. "This is nothing but a waste of my time, because so far he hasn't said a word about the murder of Chad Sanders. Now, *that's* news. Not some old has-been windbag running for reelection."

The mayor's high-pitched voice cracked over the microphone as he attempted to be heard over the murmurings. "Are there any questions about the new policies I plan to bring forward during my next term?" He raised his arms in an effort to quiet the increasing grumbling in the crowd.

"Yeah, yeah, congratulations on your next bid for mayor," called someone from near the front, "but what about the apparent murder of two-time Super Bowl offensive lineman Chad Sanders? Do you have any suspects?"

Murmurs of agreement filled the room.

"I heard it was his ex-wife," someone else called out.

"If you will all be patient for a moment, we will answer all your questions." The mayor's voice rose over the rumblings that rippled through the room. "But first, I would like to take this time to outline my policies for—"

Jeers drowned out his voice.

"Do you know if the robbery at the lighthouse museum was linked to the murder of Chad Sanders?" shouted the reporter in front of Addie.

Whispers and mumbling continued to rise up throughout the crowd, and the mayor held up his hands in an attempt to regain their attention, but it was clear they were not there for his campaign launch. They were after the nitty-gritty on the untimely death of a so-called sports hero. Addie scoffed and shook her head. Little did they know the true behavior of their so-called hero. Addie only hoped that when it all finally did come out, the truth would knock Chad right off his public pedestal.

As angry and irritated voices echoed throughout the waiting room, Addie hoped someone would press the mayor again about Chad Sanders's murder and the possible link to the lighthouse robbery. Even though Marc and Jerry had claimed it was merely a coincidence, she wasn't convinced. Two crimes being committed at roughly the same time, only a few hundred yards away from each other, was just too much to be a so-called coincidence. There had to be a link, and as much as she was convinced Nikki wasn't a killer, she was equally as sure Nikki wasn't the elf robber she'd encountered either.

Addie shook her head, bringing her attention back to the hubbub around her. The DA glanced at the mayor and gestured to the mic. Flush-faced, the mayor conceded to the reporters and stepped forward. "Members of the press, I'd like to introduce District Attorney Jeff Wilson, who will be happy to answer all your questions regarding the recent theft at the lighthouse museum and the death of a true sports hero of our time, two-time Super Bowl winner offensive lineman Chad Sanders." He stepped aside as clicks and flashes again erupted throughout the room, his slimy grin still in place as he posed for pictures with his arm around the DA's shoulder in a show of camaraderie.

The DA took the mic, pulled away from the mayor, and raised his arms, garnering quiet. "Ladies and gentlemen, members of the press, if I might have your attention. Please be quiet so I can continue, and we will be able to get to your questions sooner." His commanding voice gradually dispelled the murmurs and rumblings circulating throughout the room.

"As many of you may know, I am the district attorney for Essex County, Massachusetts. It is my great pleasure to introduce you to the newest addition to our investigative team, Detective Inspector Noah Parker, formerly of the Metropolitan Police Department in London, England." Wilson placed his arm on Noah's elbow and not so gently urged him front and center beside him. He then ceremoniously passed Noah the microphone.

Noah looked at the mic, a flash of horror filled his eyes, and he glanced questioningly at the DA. Addie's heart lurched, and she looked at the DA and the mayor both standing there with silly Cheshire grins plastered across their faces.

"Why is a foreign British detective heading up this investigation, and Police Chief Marc Chandler isn't?" shouted Katie, the local television reporter. "Is it true, then, that the murder suspect is a close family member of the chief's, and he can't be involved in the case?"

"Yeah, what's going on?" Other reporters joined in with a barrage of their own questions, piggybacking off Katie's.

Noah appeared flustered for a split second as he tried to make sense of the carnival sideshow that had thrust him onto center stage. "If you'll bear with me . . ." He threw his hand in the air in a shushing motion. "I will attempt to answer all your questions, one at a time. The first one, I believe, was why Police Chief Marc Chandler is not leading this investigation, and why I, a British detective, was brought into the investigation, is that right?" He scanned the audience as reporters murmured their agreement.

He lifted his shoulder in a half shrug. "Well, then, that's simple. Your beloved police chief, Marc Chandler, happened to have his annual leave already prescheduled, and when the body was found right after the robbery was reported, the police department found they were a senior officer short to conduct simultaneous major investigations. As for my attendance here today, and my recent recruitment to the Greyborne Harbor Police Department"—he massaged the back of his neck—"I happened to be in your beloved town on a different matter, and since a murder and a robbery took place on the same evening, I was asked to help out. My chief superintendent at the West Yorkshire Constabulary agreed it would be a good step toward rebuilding US and British policing relations."

He gazed around the room as the reporters appeared to hang on his every word. Addie had to admit he did have a way of seducing a crowd of even seasoned reporters with that BBC-type, clipped, no-nonsense London accent of his. He certainly had their attention for the moment.

"Next question, as I recall," he continued, "was whether we have any suspects in the murder of Mr. Chad Sanders." He pinned the reporter who had shouted out the questions earlier with an equally no-nonsense look. "We are still in the early days of the investigation, and we are following a couple of leads. However, as this is still an ongoing investigation, I can't comment any further. Now, if you will excuse me, I have work to do." Noah passed the mic to the DA, along with a scathing side-eye. Noah then nodded at Jerry, who was hovering by the stairway leading down to various offices and the jail cells. Jerry gestured with a jerk of his head, and he and Noah disappeared down the steps.

A few minutes later, and after her escape from the media circus, Addie sat in her car, dazed, and stared out her windshield. Not that she could see anything, as a thick layer of ice had been deposited on the glass during her time inside the station. While waiting for it to defrost, she racked her brain, trying to piece together what had just happened. When she had unexpectedly become trapped in the waiting room, she certainly hadn't expected to walk away from that circus knowing more than she had before she went in. *Which was absolutely nothing!*

Addie drummed out a beat on the steering wheel and mulled over the situation. Did the police only have enough circumstantial evidence to secure an arrest warrant, but have nothing else to go on? If that was the case, though, why didn't the DA or even Noah make a plea for the public's assistance?

In other cases, both in Greyborne Harbor and back in her old stomping grounds of Boston, the police were always reaching out to the public in a case like this, asking for anyone with information to step forward. Why didn't they ask whether anyone had seen Chad out on the cliff that day? If they had, could they tell if he was alone, or were others with him? The storm had hit, but people had still been around, especially the museum board of directors, volunteers, and heck, even the elf thief. Surely someone must have seen something.

Addie flipped her wipers on in an attempt to dispel the last remains of the ice. She was sure she wasn't alone in her confusion about the media circus. She was convinced the reporters who had come sniffing for information about the death of an ex–football player were as dumbfounded as she was.

That sports reporter she'd talked to earlier had been right. The mayor had called the press conference to announce his candidacy. It was clear he knew the press wouldn't care, based on his not-so-stellar past history as mayor. He'd used the murder investigation as a tantalizing bread crumb to get the coverage he needed to launch another lackluster run for office. On the other hand—and something she hoped she was wrong about—was the assumption that police already had everything they needed to prove their case against Nikki. Was Noah going downstairs for a final interview to wrap it up before the DA took over?

She turned the wipers off and silently cursed the last smear of ice, dead center on her windshield, still blocking her line of sight.

"What to do . . . what to do?" Addie drummed her gloved fingers again on the steering wheel. She had nothing to work with to prove Nikki's innocence. For the first time, she was left with a sense of helplessness and had no idea where to start. It really hadn't hit her until now just how much she missed the insider information Marc and Simon had often provided her— sometimes against their will. A sad smile flitted across her lips. Gone were those days. She was flying solo now.

When the ice finally had completely melted, Addie shifted into reverse and maneuvered her car out onto the slushy road. "Noah, you thought I was like a dog with a bone back in England. Just you wait and see what I'm like at home."

Chapter Fifteen

Her mind whirled with possible scenarios all the way home, but Addie still had no clue where to start. She was used to working with people, but everyone had moved on, including her sounding board, Serena. Even Paige, whom she saw at the bookstore most every day, was too busy with family drama and wedding planning to throw ideas on the wall with her to see what stuck.

But while Addie didn't know where to start, she did know one thing. It had taken only a glance at the eager faces of the reporters with their array of cameras and recording equipment to realize going to the police station today had been a mistake. She'd gone on a whim, with an unhealthy dose of self-importance, in the hope she could say something that would dissuade the DA from pressing murder charges against Nikki.

* * *

Addie shook her head in self-reproach, and her grip on the steering wheel tightened. She knew better than that. It was going to take proof and facts, not gut feelings and blind loyalty—the same kind of hard evidence Marc had always yammered on about—for her to establish Nikki's innocence. Addie needed to find something, anything that provided as much reasonable doubt in the DA's mind as it would for a judge or jury. No, better yet, she needed to discover the identity of the actual killer.

Her hold on the wheel relaxed and a smile tugged at her lips. Then again, if she could combine sniffing out the real killer and destroying the mayor's obvious political smoke-and-mirrors act, meant to give voters the impression that he was tough on crime and worthy of re-election in the spring, she'd consider justice truly served.

However—her grip tightened again—in order to do that, she needed to get her facts straight. Number one: The night of the robbery, when police were questioning her at the museum, Nikki was at home and in her room. Addie made a mental note to tell Noah that, now that he was in charge of the case.

Addie slowed for a crossing pedestrian, which gave her pause. She hadn't arrived home until late that night though, but she was certain Nikki was in bed then, at least in her room. But . . . she smiled at the slow walking pedestrian as she passed, since Addie didn't know the estimated time of Chad's death. She really couldn't be sure Nikki *had* been home all evening.

When the woman reached the curb, she waved her

gratitude, and Addie started off again. In her mind, Nikki had to have been home all evening. It was a stormy night. Where else would she be? A lump grew in the back of Addie's throat. That was the obvious flaw in Addie's alibi for her housemate. Addie wasn't home all night and gut instinct wasn't proof. If she shared this with Noah that was the first thing he'd point out. No, Addie definitely needed more—much, much more—but where did she start?

She was about to head for Serena's house in search of all the inside details about Chad Sanders, but then she glanced at her dash clock. Serena would be getting her baby down for her afternoon nap right about now. A pang of regret stabbed her heart. Another reminder of how the people in her life had moved on. Refusing to dwell on that fact, Addie made a hasty back-end, swerving turn onto Birch and headed to the harbor instead.

She crossed her fingers in the hope that after a night to sleep on it, someone who'd attended the museum board meeting might have a faint memory of seeing someone or something out on the cliff top. Hopefully the shock of the robbery or of finding poor Karl in the closet had faded enough for someone to recall even the smallest, seemingly insignificant detail that might lead somewhere.

She slowed down to make a left-hand turn into the museum parking lot and glanced at the driveway leading to Greyborne Point B&B. She hoped to see Noah's rental car parked in the small guest lot beyond the stone pillar columns of the covered carport. Instead, she spotted what appeared to be Marc's Jeep. She slammed her MINI Cooper into reverse, backed up, and parked behind the Jeep.

She got out and peered through the side window of the Jeep. There was no question about it. The vintage Boston Bruins cap Marc always wore when he was off duty sat on the passenger seat.

A tap from inside one of the bed-and-breakfast's side windows drew her attention, and her gaze flitted over the 1901 Georgian Revival–style building until she saw Marc, arms crossed, scowling down at her through a window.

She smiled—feeling awkward in this new relationship with him—and gave him a timid finger wave. He gestured with his head for her to come in. Addie instinctively glanced around to make certain he meant her. When he rolled his eyes and gestured with bigger hand motions, she gave a half shrug, worked her way around the icy patches on the driveway to the front, and stepped through the door into the ornately decorated foyer.

"Addie!" cried Bin Thomas from behind the reception desk. "It's so nice to see you again," she said sardonically while closing a large ledger. "I suppose you're here to see your English *friend*?" Bin's barbed tone matched her pointed gaze.

Amused by Bin Thomas's attitude, Addie purposely took a moment to admire the foyer's lavish Christmas decorations. Then painstakingly hid a smile as she slowly removed her gloves. Bin had made no secret of being jealous of Addie's past relationship with Dr. Simon

Emerson, and by her demeanor now, it appeared Bin also coveted any friendship Addie might have with her newest guest, Noah Parker, the man whose food she'd cut up for him. "Actually, I'm here to see Marc Chandler."

"Marc? Why would you even think he was here?"

"I know he's not a guest." At least, Addie hoped he wasn't and that Whitney hadn't done something silly, like kick him out because of the whole Nikki fiasco coming between them. He was Nikki's relative, after all, and Whitney was a tenacious reporter. "I was heading to the lighthouse to inquire about the robbery the other night, and I happened to see his Jeep in the drive, and well, he—"

"It's okay, Bin," said Marc from the double-wide doorway of the room across the hall from the desk. "If you don't mind, I asked Addie to come in."

"Yes, yes, of course, it's no problem," Bin said. "Anything I can do to help with the investigation, Chief. After all, I'm certain you have a lot of questions about that robbery she was involved with the other night." She gave Addie one more scathing look, then gave Marc a smile full of saccharine. "Since Bev is going to be setting up the dining room for dinner soon, you may *question* Addie in our office. It's the room just down the hall with the sign on the door that says 'Private.'" She gestured with her hand toward the back of the large house.

"Too bad he's married now, isn't it?" whispered Bin as Addie passed the desk.

"I think it's wonderful, don't you?"

"Do you?" Bin pinned her with a knowing look. "I mean, let's face it, Addie, you and Marc have quite the history." She *tsk*ed and shook her head.

Addie stopped and faced the petite woman. "What do you mean by that?"

"It just seems to everyone that whenever either one of you was between *loves*, you'd fall right back into each other's arms. I just hope his wife is aware of all this." She jerked her head in the direction Marc had gone. "I'd really hate to be the one to tell her you're on the prowl again."

"I am not, and I'm—"

"Don't defend yourself with me. I know you and what happened with Simon. Then I heard that after you ran away to the other side of the world to pout, it didn't take you long to get your claws into the Englishman, but I think I've set him straight about the likes of you. Now that he's set you right, it's clear that you're running back to Marc, as always." She glared at Addie and lifted her chin, a defiant expression on her face.

"Is that what you really think of me?"

"If the shoe fits."

"It doesn't! I—" Addie snapped her mouth shut. There was no use standing there and arguing. The woman was clearly delusional.

Addie shook her head in disbelief that a woman who was the epitome of polite in public could harbor such a catty side when it came to men. What in the world had happened in her past to make her so hateful and jaded?

"Addie, are you coming?" Marc called from the door he held open.

"Yes, sorry," she said, walking quickly toward him with an apologetic smile.

"What was that all about?" he asked with a head jerk toward the front desk.

"Nothing, it's fine." She waved off his question, even though she wasn't fine.

Addie wasn't sure if it was Bin's words, and how others too might perceive her appearance today with Marc, or the fact that her old friend and one-time love was happily married with a baby on the way that bothered her. But one thing she did know was that she would have to keep her physical distance from him in order to keep busy-body tongues, like Bin's, from wagging. With that in mind, she made a wide arc around Marc as she slipped into the office.

Marc closed the door behind them. "Can I ask why you're here today?"

"Most likely for the same reason you are," she said, eyeing the closed door. She was tempted to ask if they could keep it open. Her mind playing into her worst fears about Bin Thomas starting malicious gossip about the two of them meeting at her B&B behind closed doors.

"I doubt it."

"What do you mean? Aren't you here to find out how Noah managed with the DA?"

He shook his head.

Oh no. She glanced at the closed door again. Did that mean Whitney really had tossed him out? After all, he was a cop working on a case involving a close family member, and she was the editor of the local newspaper. Was it a conflict of interest for him not only at work, but also at home? Did Bin know and that's why she said what she did about them running back to each other?

"I'm here following a lead," Marc said.

"What lead?" Addie asked with a bit of mixed surprise and relief about his marriage being intact and his probable reason for closing the door. "I thought you were on forced leave—" Her eyes widened. "Are you working this undercover?" she whispered glancing at the door.

"No, and technically, I am on leave from the Greyborne Harbor Police Department."

Addie eyed him skeptically, crossing her arms over her chest. "In that case, don't you dare give me any of that I-can't-share-police-information-with-you garbage."

"Okay, but what I tell you doesn't leave this room, all right?"

Addie sat on the antique gold-brocade sofa by the ornate mahogany desk and gave him her full attention.

"Well, it seems our victim—"

"Chad Sanders," Addie clarified.

"Yes, good old football star and wife abuser Chad Sanders was a guest here at the B&B."

"You're kidding."

"Nope, apparently a couple of people saw a man coming out of the B&B here on the night the storm set in. They took notice because he headed across the road to the lighthouse, which they thought was strange because the wind was really howling by then."

"And it was Chad for sure?"

"I brought a picture in today and asked the sisters if they had seen the man, and they said yes. He'd been a guest here for over a week."

"He was staying here for a week, and when he suddenly disappeared, they never thought to report him missing?"

"I guess he'd mentioned to Bev that he was expecting a friend to show up and might be gone for a few days, but he'd pay to keep his room."

"Did he say who this friend was?"

"No, but when I asked the sisters about it, they said . . ." His face paled, and his eyes took on a haunted look.

"Said what, Marc?" Addie rose to her feet. "What, what did they say?"

"That the last night they saw him, a woman was seen leaving his room. They thought his friend had arrived and that's where he had gone, like he'd told Bev."

"Did they say what the woman looked like?"

"The woman they just described to me sounds a lot like Nikki."

"That can't be right. Nikki had a restraining order out against him because he'd terrorized her. Why would she seek him out here? Did she even know he was in town?" Addie bit her lip when she recalled Nikki's strange reaction to that same question the other day when Serena had asked her. "What else did the sisters say?"

"According to both Bin and Bev, they were serving dinner in the dining room, and Chad hadn't come down for the meal yet. That's when Bev heard footsteps on the stairs, and a woman wearing a headscarf raced down the steps and out the front door."

"That's it? A woman wearing a scarf in the winter during a snowstorm isn't abnormal. Isn't it a bit of a stretch for Bev to say for certain it's Nikki, don't you think Marc?"

"Normally I would agree, except when I asked her to describe the scarf, it . . . it matched the one Whitney and I gave Nikki last Christmas."

"Phew." Addie sat back down on the sofa. "But surely more women than just Nikki had that same scarf. You say it was a Christmas gift, so half the town—"

"No," he said, shaking his head and leaning back on the desk. "We picked it up in Chicago last fall, when we were there for a convention Whitney had to attend for work." His hands tightened into fists. "To make matters worse, I called . . . a friend at the station to ask if they had followed up with Chad's telephone service provider to get the numbers he had called recently . . ."

"And?"

"The phone records show that Chad had called Nikki a number of times from both his cell and the front desk over the last week, which—"

"Which means, she knew where he was staying." When the significance of his words had sunk in, she locked her gaze on his. "That's not good—and it's definitely not good for Nikki. Does Noah know all of this?"

"I have no idea. I only found out about Chad staying here and the phone calls just now."

"My guess is, the police already know this," said

Addie. "And that's exactly why the mayor is so certain he's going to get his quick conviction."

"Come on, Addie! You can't sit there and tell me you actually think Nikki killed Chad. You live with her. You know she's not capable of killing anyone."

"Marc, first of all, I never said she did it. I said the mayor is hoping for a quick conviction." Addie sighed and hoped he'd forgive her for her next statement. "Secondly, if there is one thing I learned from my father back in New York City, it's that everyone is capable of murder, given the right circumstances."

"Not her—not my cousin. I know what she went through during her marriage to him. If she was going to kill him, she would have done it long ago, but she didn't because she's *not* a killer."

"Those are my thoughts exactly, but how do you explain what Bev told you about the scarf?"

"I don't know, but I'm sure as heck going to find out." Marc's chest rose and fell with rapid breaths. "According to Serena, Noah's smart, so with his help, I'm pretty sure he and I can find the real killer."

Chapter Sixteen

Addie *tsk*ed. "I'm going to tell you the same thing you always told me. You're not a cop right now, so Noah can't share police information with you."

"I'm still a cop. I'm just—"

"You are on a forced leave. That's like a suspension, and you have no badge, no gun, and no authority, so what are you going to do? Noah is certainly not going to share police information with you, a police chief under suspension, because he's a rule follower just like you." She smiled saucily, reveling in finally one-upping him. "Welcome to my world, Marc. Isn't that what you always yammered on about to me when, how did you put it?" She peered at him innocently. "Oh right, 'stop poking my nose into police business' . . ."

His ears reddened, and if he hadn't looked so dejected by her words, she would have laughed. Instead, she straightened her shoulders and met his gaze. "Alright then, let's think. How do we prove Nikki is actually innocent? What do we know so far?"

A sharp knock sounded on the door, and before either of them could answer, Noah opened it and poked his head inside. "I hope I'm not disturbing anything?"

"No, not at all," said Marc, appearing somewhat flustered. "Come in, please."

"I see you're done at the station now," added Addie, smiling. "How does it feel to be leading the investigation team?"

"I have a lot to learn about policing in America, but I think it's going to be all right." He stepped inside the office and closed the door. "However, imagine my surprise when Miss Bin told me Police Chief Marc Chandler was in here questioning a burglary suspect."

"She said that?" Addie asked.

"Yes, both the sisters seem to believe you have turned to the dark side of crime," Noah said. He pinned Marc with a questioning look. "And I certainly hope you are only speaking to Miss Greyborne as a friend and not as a member of any investigation team? Especially not one concerned with the unfortunate mishap a certain football player had with rocks at the base of a cliff?" His reserved smile barely showed on his face as his gaze remained focused on Marc.

Marc's eyes narrowed, but he held Noah's steadfast expression.

Certain these two were going to come to blows, Addie leapt to her feet and stood between them. "I told you, Marc," she said, fighting to keep her tone light, "Noah's as much of a stickler for the rules as you are."

"A rule man, hey?" said Noah stoically before his waggish grin showed his British side. He chuckled and held out his hand to Marc. "I like that. We should get along brilliantly, as long as you remain on your side of this case and let me run my murder inquiry."

"Of course," Marc said, shaking his hand. "You're in charge. I would never do anything that would jeopardize the investigation. I might be suspended, but I'm still an officer of the law, and I'm only interested in getting to the truth."

"No matter what that truth is?" asked Noah guardedly. "Sometimes it's hard to hear the answers to the truth you don't want."

"No matter what the truth is, I'll accept it."

"Brilliant, since at the moment, it's not looking very good for your cousin. All the evidence appears to point to her being the murderer."

Marc appeared more relaxed now than when Addie had insinuated the same thing. She frowned. Probably some weird male camaraderie she didn't understand. One moment they'd looked ready to duke it out, and the next? Addie glared at them. They were brothers in arms. Well, there was no sense in avoiding this odd assortment of crime solvers. She cleared her throat. "It's settled, then. We're going to work together as a team to solve this murder."

"Not *we*," said Noah. "Marc is a trained professional and a close relative of the suspect's. There is no one better than he to assist me, behind the scenes, of course, and provide the investigation with a glimpse into Nikki's behaviors."

"No one except perhaps me," said Addie doggedly. "After all, she's been my employee for nearly two years, and my housemate since I returned from England. Living and working with someone as long as we have, you get to see each other at their worst and best, which gives you a pretty good insight into them."

"She's right," said Marc. "Addie knows Nikki better than I do these days, if for no other reason than she's a woman."

"I hope you can explain what you mean by that?" Addie frowned.

Marc hooked his thumbs into the front pockets of his jeans, and shrugged. "It's a known fact that most women tend to share personal stuff with other women, far more than they do with men—especially a male family member who also happens to be the chief of police."

"I see what you're saying, and you're probably right," she conceded. "I know I share more with Serena and Paige than I ever did with anyone else."

"That's normal, I think," said Marc. "I know Serena doesn't talk to me like she used to when she was a kid, especially since I became a cop, and neither does Nikki. She only comes to me now when she needs help getting something in her life fixed." Marc scowled and jerked his thumb toward Addie. "I'm sorry to say, Noah, that Nikki probably turns to Serena and Addie for everything else."

"Well, *Inspector Parker*," Addie said, an inflection of hope in her voice, "can I help you prove who killed Chad Sanders?"

Noah drew in a deep breath, and his eyes darkened.

"Please? It's like Marc said—who better than her employer and housemate to understand the real Nikki? At least the Nikki she is now. Not the one she used to be before, when they were growing up . . ."

"I don't know, Addie. If the mayor ever gets wind of Marc continuing with the investigation, after he not only took him off the case but put him on leave. Then combine all that with him discovering a civilian is also involved in the inquiry . . ." His shoulders tensed, and he massaged the back of his neck. "It wouldn't go well for international policing relations, and I'd probably be out of a job back in Yorkshire."

"The stakes are high, I know," Addie said thoughtfully. "But, really, if he found out I was involved, it wouldn't be such a big deal. He's used to me 'poking my nose in police business.'" She flashed Marc an impish grin. "And don't forget, the DA has hired me as a consultant in the past. It seemed my involvement was never too much of a problem then, so it—"

Marc coughed, clearing his throat.

"Well," Addie said eyeing him, "at least, not *that* much of a problem. He never had me locked up for being part of closing a case, did he?" She gave Marc a sassy grin. "Anyway, that could be a cover for Marc working in the background. If they found out about his involvement, they'd just think any information he was getting was coming from me, and it would keep you in the clear. That is, at least, until we can serve up the real killer on a platter to him and the DA. The mayor will get the conviction he's looking for to boost his political aspirations, and he won't look twice about looking a gift horse in the mouth."

"Playing devil's advocate here, but why do you believe Nikki is innocent?" asked Noah.

"Because I know her," said Addie, "and I . . . we"—she gestured at Marc—"know what she went through during her marriage. If she didn't kill Chad back then to save her own life, why would she kill him now that she's gotten free of him?"

"As you know," Marc said, "I've grappled with the same question, but we do have to face the fact that Chad was in town for a reason. And if witness accounts are correct, Nikki knew he was here. The phone calls between them substantiate that."

Noah eyed Marc. "How did you know his phone records show calls were made to her?"

"The same way I know Nikki also called him a number of times," added Marc, holding Noah's probing gaze. "I might be on leave, but I still have friends in the force who I can ask for a favor or two when I need it."

Noah nodded, his gaze steady on Marc's, as he began asking questions about the case.

Addie recalled Noah's team throughout the murder investigation and the little bit they'd shared with her about his demotion from the Metropolitan Police Department, and she doubted Noah could say the same thing about loyal colleagues as Marc could. It didn't take much to make a man feel two inches tall when his choices were going to work in Yorkshire or forgetting about policing in the UK forever. On the other hand, from what Addie had heard from her friends in Moorscrag since she'd left, Noah had moved to the village and had become a regular attendee of her friends' Saturday night murder-trivia group.

Addie studied Noah while he talked shop with Marc. Maybe he really had changed, and he wasn't the outsider everyone in England had proclaimed him to be. Yet he was an outsider here, and if it ever came to light that he had broken police protocol, it wouldn't just be job ending. It would be career ending, and as he told her back in England, being a detective inspector was all Noah had left after the tragic death of his wife. His job had become his lifesaver, the one thing tethering him to sanity. Addie knew, too, what it was like to lose yourself in the only thing you had left. For her, it had been her books.

Her career might have changed since David was murdered all those years ago, but after his death had sent her spiraling into the darkened world of grief, books had kept her sane. After finding out last year she wasn't who she thought she was, her world had tilted sideways again, but her books kept her centered. Noah was the same. She studied his chiseled jaw and the ghost of a smile on his lips as he responded to one of Marc's stupid jokes. Yes, being a detective was who Noah was. She wouldn't let him lose that after everything else had been stolen from him.

Addie clapped her hands, interrupting the camaraderie between the two men. "Well, boys, it sounds like we have a plan going forward. Should we start a crime board to jot down what facts we know?"

"We are going to need one," said Marc, sitting perched

on the edge of the desk. "It'll help us keep track of the evidence and keep us all on the same page. The less time we spend chasing our tails, the better."

"I still have the blackboard I used to use at the store," said Addie, from her seat on the sofa. "I use it now to keep track of scheduling, but I can do that on something else. No big deal."

"That would work," Marc said, "but Nikki works for you, and we can't take the chance of her seeing it if she gets out on bail. That drop cloth you used to cover it with won't work to keep our secrets . . . well, secret."

Noah sat on the sofa beside Addie. "Not to mention, it's harder to keep prying eyes off it in a shop. You have other staff members, and we have to keep our involvement hush-hush."

"Which also means we can't keep one here. Too many prying eyes from you know who?" Addie jerked her head toward the door.

"That means my house is out, too, since my wife is the managing editor of the *Greyborne Harbor News*. Talk about giving her a scoop."

"Would she do that?" asked Noah.

Addie looked questioningly at Marc. "Surely you talk shop at home, but she doesn't print everything you tell her, does she?"

"No, we don't talk shop at all. It's a boundary we set when we started dating, and I would hate to test it now, when there is so much at stake—not only for Nikki, but also for Noah's and my careers."

A contemplative silence fell over the room.

Addie snapped her fingers. "How about Serena's?"

"Serena's what? House?" asked Marc.

"Got any better ideas? Besides, she's been a great sleuthing partner for me over the years."

"Yeah," said Marc, "back when she wasn't married and didn't have three children."

"Are you implying she isn't capable of helping us because she got married and had kids? That that somehow makes her incapable of using her brains anymore?" snapped Addie indignantly.

"No." Marc looked at her as if she'd sprouted a second head. "If you're going to be part of this team, you're going to need to keep your temper under your hat. That's not what I said or even implied. She's my sister for goodness' sake. Serena is a busy woman, Addie, and she has a lot on her plate, especially with her wanting to get back to her shop. I don't think she needs us underfoot at her house."

Noah looked from Addie to Marc and cleared his throat. "If I recall, she was involved last year in Moorscrag, wasn't she?"

"Yes"—Marc glowered at Addie—"and Addie knows me better than that, to think that's what I meant. As I just said, things have changed in Serena's life, and I'm sure with a new baby and the twins in preschool, she's not going to want us traipsing into her house at all hours to update the board."

Addie took a deep breath, held it, and exhaled slowly. She smiled apologetically at Marc. "I'm sorry. You're right."

"Okay. We're all under a lot of pressure. No worries." Marc returned her smile, and as if to buy her time to settle her nerves, he began to tell a funny arrest story to Noah.

Why am I so ready to jump at every perceived slight I have with Marc's choice of wording? Addie wondered. Perhaps it was her way of punishing him for moving on and not being the last person left in her old life. As he had most adeptly explained, even Serena's life had changed. As much as Addie was fighting against all the changes thrust on her this past year, it was time to stop all the kicking and screaming and take the next steps into her new life willingly. Like it or not, changes were part of her new reality.

"I have an idea," she said, then waited for Marc to get to the "good" part of his story, to which Noah laughed heartily. After a few moments, and finally noticing her crossed arms and tapping foot, Noah and Marc cleared their throats and gave her their full attention.

"Why don't we make up a shareable electronic spreadsheet? That way we can check it and update it whenever we want. That is, unless either of you is afraid the mayor is going to hack your accounts."

Noah shook his head. "Sorry, I have a UK police–issued mobile phone, and I was just given a Greyborne Harbor Police one for my use in this case. I won't be able to participate in that. It's too risky."

Marc looked from Noah to Addie. "And I don't have my work phone anymore. I'm using a pay-as-you-go one for now. So, that idea won't work for me either."

Addie burst into laughter.

"What's so funny?" asked Marc.

"It's . . . it's not . . ." She waved her hand, trying to catch her breath. "It's just, look at us, this great crime-fighting force, and we can't even figure out a silly crime board."

The two men began to chuckle, as well, when her laughter erupted again.

Chapter Seventeen

"**O**kay." Addie took a deep breath once their laughter had subsided and patted her erratically palpating chest. "I've got it back together now." She sat up straight on the sofa. "We were discussing where to establish a crime board. May I suggest that until a perfect opportunity presents itself, I just keep notes for us for now?"

"I can go with that," said Noah. "Do you have paper and pen?"

"Ah . . . let me look . . ." she said, digging through her handbag.

"If you have a pen, here's a notepad on the desk," said Marc. "I doubt the sisters would mind us tearing one or two pages out of it." He handed the coiled notebook to Addie.

"Thanks," she said and flipped it open. "Oh, it already

has notes in it." She went to flip to the back pages, but as she did, something on the front page caught her eye. She took a closer look, then turned to Noah. "What was that other man's name? The one you said the sisters were paying a lot of attention to?"

"Greg Carpenter, why?"

"This is a handwritten list of the guests, and it's dated the same day you checked in to the B&B. Beside each guest's name, there are notations. Greg Carpenter has '*good match for Bev,*' and beside your name is written '*he's all mine.*'"

"That's kind of creepy," said Marc, going to Addie's side and reading over her shoulder.

"Yes, but look what it says up here about Chad Sanders." Addie pointed to Chad's name on the list.

"'*Rich ex–football player. We'll fight to death over this one,*'" Marc said, reading it aloud.

"Alrighty then." Noah joined them, slipped the notebook out of Addie's hand, and scanned the page. "This is definitely something I'm going to have to look into deeper."

"I don't get it," said Marc. "What does this mean, and why are they writing these notes beside some of the guests' names?"

Addie quickly reminded Marc about how they had treated Simon in the past, as well as Bin's seeming jealousy toward Addie when Addie and Simon became involved. Then she told him about Noah's experience at dinner the other night, when Bin had cut up his food and then tried to feed him. After seeing this list and what was written on it, though, the moment didn't seem as funny as when Noah had first told her and Paige about it. Now it was downright disturbing.

"Noah," said Marc, shaking his head as he continued to read down the page. "You know you can't mention this list when you talk to the sisters. If these comments have any bearing on the murder case, they can't be used in evidence since this list was not lawfully attained."

"I know," said Noah, "but I have to find out whether this comment would translate to this man"—he poked his finger on Chad's name—"ending up at the bottom of a cliff, perhaps out of jealousy by the other sister?"

"I, for one," said Addie, "can't imagine either sister being capable of murder, but when I recall how possessive Bin was when she tried to seduce Simon with her homecooked meals and flattery, and the glaring looks she gave me, perhaps . . ." Addie looked up at the two men towering over her. "Luckily, the one thing this list does do is give us something we didn't have before."

"What's that?" asked Noah.

"Two more suspects to look at besides Nikki." She took the notebook back from Noah, flipped to the back, and tore out a single blank page. "Now, what do we know?" She laid the notebook on top of her purse on her lap to use it as a table, then poised a pen at the top of the lined page.

Marc sheepishly looked at Noah. "There is something the sisters did tell me before you got here that you should be aware of . . ."

Noah eyed him curiously but remained silent.

"Bin told me that the night of the murder, she hadn't

seen Chad come downstairs yet for dinner, and she was about to go up and let him know it was being served. Just then she heard footsteps on the stairs and a woman, wearing a headscarf, raced down and out the front door. Shortly after that, Chad came down, but when Bin called him to come and eat, he waved her off. He said he had to go meet someone and then left."

"But she didn't say who he was meeting?" asked Noah.

"No, she assumed he was meeting up with the woman who'd just left."

"Could she identify this woman?"

"No, but I think I can."

"Who was it?"

"Nikki."

"You're certain?"

"No, he's not certain," interrupted Addie. "He says the scarf Bin described the woman as wearing was the same one he'd given Nikki last Christmas. They bought it when he and Whitney were in Chicago for her work conference last fall."

"Yes," said Marc, staring at Addie, "because it would be highly unlikely that another identical scarf, purchased at such a small boutique—one specializing in handcrafted merchandise, I might add—would have found its way to Greyborne Harbor, Massachusetts, wouldn't it?"

"But not impossible," Addie said weakly.

"No, not impossible," said Noah, lowering his head and pinching the bridge of his nose in thought, then looking back up at Marc. "But highly improbable. No," he said, glancing at Addie, "but I agree with Marc in the sense that it is something else that needs to be investigated."

"Okay, if the two 'experts' in the field feel we need to chase down that rabbit hole, who am I to stand in the way?" She begrudgingly added the words *Chicago purchased scarf* to the list on her lap. "But I'm just saying, if we ever find this woman Bin saw and compare her scarf to Nikki's, I doubt that they would be identical in anything but the color, because that's pretty much the only description you got from Bin, right?"

"No, Addie, she also described the pattern. It is the same scarf."

Addie sat upright, meeting his gaze. "But didn't you say Bin was serving dinner then?"

"She said she was in the dining room, and it was dinnertime, so she might have been serving, I don't know. I just know she described the scarf in detail, pattern, and color."

"If it was dinnertime, and she was worried about Chad not coming down yet and thinking about going upstairs to call him, that means she wasn't focused—especially since she fancied him as the man of her dreams. The dining room would also have been busy then, and—"

"I guess," Marc said, quickly interrupting her.

Addie looked at Noah. "When you're in the dining room, how much of the staircase and front door can you see?"

Noah leaned his head back and closed his eyes. "Not much, really. I guess it all depends where in the dining room one is seated, but from the table Mr. Carpenter and I share, I can only see the bottom of the stairs. I suppose given the angle, Mr. Carpenter would be able to see the door."

"But neither of you could see both?"

"No, and I can't think of any one table that would be able to see both the bottom of the staircase and the door. The angles would be all wrong."

"Okay," said Addie, tucking the list inside her handbag and standing up. "But just to be certain, Noah, why don't you go into the dining room and talk to Bin or Bev, whichever one of them is serving tonight. Follow her around and stand in different areas of the room, then come back and tell us where she would have been to see not only Nikki, but also her scarf in detail, as she came down the steps and rushed out the door."

"I already know what you're getting at, Addie," said Noah.

"Then you agree?"

"If we hadn't found that list in the notebook, I'd be inclined to say no and consider the scarf a good lead, but . . ."

"But what?" asked Marc. "Are you saying Bin Thomas lied about the description of the scarf she gave me?"

Addie and Noah turned and looked at him.

"It is a possibility," said Addie, "that she saw Nikki and Chad talking at some point during his week's stay. Who knows? They talked on the phone, it seems, or maybe Nikki came here to the B&B sometime. But given Bin's notation in the book about Chad, it might be her way of providing evidence against Nikki, whom she viewed as a threat to her plan, not knowing their history, of course."

"That's ridiculous," said Marc. "The sisters are a little, shall we say, *different*, but setting up Nikki based on seeing her talking to Chad, if she even did, is stretching it a little too far, if you ask me. No, I don't buy it. Bin described the scarf to the last detail."

"And you don't find that odd?" asked Noah.

"No, her statement told me that what she saw, combined with her being able to describe it in such detail, makes it even more believable."

"A little too believable," said Addie. "Especially for someone who would only have gotten a quick glance of a woman coming down the stairs and then out the door. Besides, the sisters know Nikki well. They are regular customers in the bookstore, and Nikki wears that scarf all the time. Bin would have seen her wearing it plenty of times, which means she would have been able to describe the pattern in detail. I don't believe Nikki was this mystery woman Bin said she saw coming and going that night—if there was even ever a woman that night."

"I tend to agree with Addie," said Noah. "At least, until we can get an explanation about the notations in the book. If Bin did see anyone leaving, it would likely have been a blur, not someone she could describe in such detail."

"You're right," said Marc, collapsing on the sofa. "I guess I've just known the Thomas sisters so long, and I put so much trust in Bin's words because deep down I do worry that Nikki might be guilty, especially with all the phone call records."

Addie started to place her hand on Marc's shoulder, not sure if she wanted to shake him for doubting his own family member or offer comfort because she knew how stressed he was by this whole situation—but she caught herself and glanced over at Noah. "Unlike Marc, I'm not wobbling on the idea that Nikki could have killed him. I know she didn't, so I'm going to be trying to figure out who did."

"And I have no connection to Nikki, so I'm only interested in the truth," said Noah.

"That's what I want too," croaked Marc. "It looks like the mayor wasn't wrong in taking me off this case, since everything appears to be coloring my ability to reason right now."

"Don't beat yourself up." Noah gave him an understanding smile. "When a family member is involved in a murder inquiry, we can all lose our ability to remain rational."

Addie leaned back against the desk, studying Noah, before turning her gaze on Marc. "Do we have a plan going forward now?"

They both nodded.

"Discovering the truth," Marc said firmly.

"No matter what or who it leads to?" added Noah.

"Yes, even who," Addie said. "But all I know is when I finally got home that night from the museum after being questioned by the police about the robbery, Nikki's car was parked in the garage, and when I went upstairs to bed, the light under her door was on. I thought about knocking to tell her what had happened, but when I raised my hand to the door, I heard Nikki's voice. It sounded like she was on her phone."

"Really? What time was that?" asked Noah, pulling out a pad from the inside pocket of his coat and jotting something down.

"It was late, probably about midnight. I really didn't look at the time."

"Could you tell who she was on the phone with?"

Addie shook her head.

"That's okay. I can check her call records to see what time and get a number for the person she was talking to." He made a notation and then pinned his eyes on Addie. "Did you try to talk to her later?"

Addie shook her head again and glanced over at Marc, who appeared miserable.

"Are you saying you never spoke to her that night?" Noah asked.

"No, I didn't." Addie sighed.

"Then you don't know whether she had been home all evening or not?"

"No, but there is no question in my mind that after Nikki finished wedding shopping with Paige, she went directly home. There was a snowstorm raging outside, remember? Why would she be out in it?"

"You were." Noah gave a half shrug. "Just so we're clear, though, you never did talk to her that night?"

"No, but I did go back downstairs a little later to make some of Serena's sleepy-time tea." Addie looked up at Noah. "I was having a hard time sleeping because of what happened at the museum earlier, and I'm sure Nikki's light was off by then."

"What about the next morning? Did you talk to her then?" Noah asked.

"No!" Addie said, an edge of irritation in her voice

at Noah's unfriendly, overly professional tone. She knew Noah would find the flaw in her alibi for Nikki but she thought, hoped, they were past the blatant cross-examination approach. However, it appeared he had a hard time taking off his detective inspector's hat with the way he was grilling her. "She wasn't up yet, and she wasn't scheduled to come in to work until after lunch." Addie gave a bitter laugh. "Is that all, *Inspector*? Can we get back to making our list now, or do you want to carry on with working this case alone?" She gestured to the notepad he had in his hand.

"Addie!" said Marc sharply. "He is just doing his job."

"I know, but . . ." Her eyes burned with the tears she fought not to shed. Marc was right; even though they had shared information earlier, it was still Noah's job to find the killer. If she could help prove Nikki was innocent, did it really matter? After all, she wasn't his or Marc's equal in the sense of their law enforcement credentials or experience. She was only a concerned friend who knew something felt off and wanted to make certain every avenue had been explored.

She drew in a deep breath. "Okay, then . . ." Addie fished the paper out of her bag, clicked open her pen, and looked up. "Since we've just learned we have two more possible suspects, who is going to look into what? You know, just so we're not tripping over each other and stepping on any toes as we investigate."

Noah crossed his arms over his chest, an amused smile on his face. "You have it all figured out, don't you? Okay then, Agatha Raisin, the first question a seasoned investigator should ask in a murder inquiry is . . . who benefits?"

"That's easy," said Addie. "There was no upside to Nikki killing Chad. He'd severed all business ties to her with the divorce. She has nothing to gain by his death."

"That's not quite true," said Marc.

"What do you mean?" Addie asked.

"I mean, yes, financial payments from Chad to Nikki were stopped with the divorce settlement, but the dissolution of their business partnership hadn't been finalized, as there were other shareholders involved, at least, according to her the last time we spoke."

"I could have sworn the other night she told me and Serena that it was all taken care of, and she didn't have any claim to any profits from his business franchising."

"It sounds like you'd better add *look into Nikki's finances* to that list," said Noah.

"Yes, but you know as well as anyone that money isn't the only benefit to seeing someone dead."

"You're right," Noah said, "but it's a good place to start. I'll leave you two to look into that while I start checking the backgrounds of the other suspects we're considering and making inquiries pertaining to any other reasons a person might want to see Chad dead."

"Jealousy, revenge, love?" asked Addie.

"Or, in this particular case, it could be more like unrequited love." Noah stood. "Well, I'm going to head down to dinner now, because based on the clatter of dishes and cutlery coming from that direction, it's well underway, and I have some inquiries to make of the sisters." He gave Marc and Addie a head nod and a grin, but then paused at the door. "You know, it's been proven in forensic-science studies that there is another driving force behind murder that we haven't mentioned."

"Which one was missed?" asked Marc.

"Fear," Noah said as he closed the door behind him.

Chapter Eighteen

Addie glared at the back steps of the bookshop, covered completely with blown-in snow. No, this would not do. She couldn't just go back to normal after all the information she'd just learned. Nikki needed her. And in order to get to the bottom of the issue, Addie had to go back to the beginning. The museum.

She navigated the snowy back steps, didn't bother brushing off her snowy boots, and rushed into the shop. Paige sat contentedly in a leather chair, reading a book, Pippi curled up in her lap. No customers. In normal circumstances, Addie would have been bothered by the lack of shoppers, but this was not a normal situation.

After arranging to have Paige close up the shop and drop Pippi off at home, Addie kissed the top of her fur baby's head, told her to be a good girl for Auntie Paige, and shouted a thank-you as she rushed out the back-room door to the alleyway. She swished off the fresh layer of wind-blown snow from her windshield, chiding herself for forgetting her gloves. With numb fingers, she scraped off as much ice buildup as possible that had settled on the windshield in the few short minutes she'd been gone, cursing the wintry weather as she did.

A shiver rushed through Addie as she sat in her car, waiting for the heater to catch up to the falling temperature outside. She replayed her conversation with Noah and Marc and couldn't get Noah's parting words out of her mind. Was it possible that Nikki had killed Chad out of fear?

"No," Addie spoke to the ice chunk that fell off her shop roof and now sat in the center of her vision. "If Nikki hadn't killed him during the ten years they were married, why would she kill him now after their divorce? What possibly could have happened that night for Chad to have turned Nikki into a killer? Did he threaten her? Was she afraid, like Noah alluded to?"

Addie shook her head with information overload. She had more questions than answers. If she was going to figure this out, she was going to have to put together her own murder board. A part of her worried that despite Noah's assurances that he was only looking for the truth, he didn't know Nikki and had already bought into the narrative of the mayor and the DA.

"No"—she gripped the wheel—"no. Don't let panic get the better of you, Addison Greyborne. Noah might be a tough nut to crack, but he's an honest man. You wouldn't be attracted to him if he was anything less."

She shook her head, ashamed of her foolishness, but instead of righting her thoughts, it jarred another, more unwelcome thought free. How well *did* she know Nikki? After all, for as long as she had lived with Nikki, Addie knew very little about her previous life, and even less about Chad as a person.

All Addie could safely say she knew was that Chad Sanders had been married to Nikki for ten years. He had been a professional football player, but due to an injury, he'd been forced to retire. According to Serena and Marc, he had started treating Nikki horribly after that. He had blamed Nikki for him having to give up football, or something just as ridiculous. When Addie had tried digging deeper into those years, Nikki hadn't elaborated, claiming it hurt too much to talk about it. Addie had accepted that. All that had mattered was that Nikki was safe and had started a new life in Greyborne Harbor.

"Actually"—Addie drummed her fingers on the steering wheel—"Nikki and I aren't that close, even after living in the same house all this time. But I think I know her well enough to know she's not a murderer."

The last of the ice chunk finally melted, and Addie was about to put her MINI into drive when an idea struck her. "Pippi loves Nikki!" she cried out and sat back in her seat.

Dogs and kids were always the best judges of character, and they often had a sixth sense when it came to the true nature of people. Maybe Addie's instincts were right, after all. Nikki could no more kill anyone than Addie could.

Addie jumped at a tap on the driver's-side window.

Marc grinned at her and motioned for her to roll down the window.

"Have you solved the murder yet?" he asked.

"What?"

"Have you solved Chad's murder yet?"

"Hardly. Have you?"

"Not yet, but the way you stare off into space and talk to yourself when you're replaying evidence usually means you're close to a breakthrough."

"Not yet. Unfortunately, all the evidence leads to Nikki, but I'm not buying it." She stuck her head out the window and looked around. "What are you doing here, anyway?"

"I thought I'd see if I could catch you before you left for home."

"What are your thoughts on the evidence?" Addie asked, shivering at the cold burst of air sailing through the open window.

"I don't like it or trust it," he said, resting his gloved hand on the top of the opened window. "But without Nikki, that only leaves the sisters as suspects, and I find that just as hard to believe."

"So, you don't think that maybe they have finally snapped and taken their rich-man obsession a step too far?"

"Not really, given all the evidence there is pointing to Nikki." He leaned in closer and dropped his voice. "Besides, I learned something new from Bin when I scooted back into the bed-and-breakfast under the pretense of forgetting something."

"What did she say?"

"Apparently, after Chad left, she looked out the window and saw the woman she identified as Nikki meet him on the street. Then they headed across the road toward the museum together."

"'Together'?" Addie asked.

"That's what she just said."

"But this is the first time she told anyone that?"

"Yeah, she said she forgot until now."

"She forgot, did she?" Addie's eyes narrowed. "It sounds like a very convenient memory that Miss Bin Thomas has suddenly recalled, doesn't it?"

"All I know is that Noah has to tell the DA what he's discovered. The evidence mounting up against Nikki is not good. I know DA Wilson, and there is no way he's going to entertain the idea that two lonely elderly ladies killed a guest based on the nonsensical ramblings we found in a notebook." Marc shook his head. "As much as I care about my cousin, whom I practically grew up with and spent every summer on the Cape with when we were kids . . ." He sighed and shrugged. "I just don't know. Chad was absolutely awful to Nikki, even a danger to her, and he did have a way of getting under a person's skin. Nikki could easily have been the one who snapped, not the sisters."

"So much for all that talk about the three of us working together, since it appears I'm on my own with this one," said Addie, scowling at him.

"No, you're not alone, and we *are* working together. I want to get to the truth as much as anyone—maybe even more, because I know what kind of person my cousin is. I'm just preparing myself for the fact that she *might* have committed murder."

"Then let *me* prove she didn't." Addie slammed the

gearshift into reverse, pressed the accelerator, and lurched out of her parking space.

Marc opened his mouth, but Addie shut the window, and his words hit the glass soundlessly. She slammed the car into drive and drove out of the alleyway, leaving Marc standing there alone, his hands in the air.

Marc and Noah might have to follow the evidence because that's what they were trained for and expected to do, but she wasn't. The sisters were clearly suspects, especially since the murder had occurred right across the street from their B&B—and that only strengthened her initial resolve to go back to the museum. Evidence only turned up if one followed the right trail to begin with, and her trail started at the lighthouse museum.

Addie parked her MINI in the museum parking lot and made her way into the deserted lobby.

"Hello, is anyone here?" She checked the time on her phone. There was still an hour left before closing time, but the place appeared empty. "Hello?" she called again and walked farther into the building.

The Santa sleigh came into view, its emptiness serving as a reminder of what had occurred that horrible night. It had changed everything about the upcoming holidays.

"No, it hasn't!" She held her head high, then marched toward the stairs leading up to the office area. There was still Paige and Logan's wedding, which would re-inforce Addie's and everyone else's Christmas spirit, she was certain of it. After all, who couldn't get excited about a wedding on Christmas Day?

An image of Martha's face flashed in her mind. "Go away, Grinch. I won't let you ruin this wedding, like the bad elf who tried to steal Christmas." Addie mentally batted away the thought of Martha as a mere annoyance. On top of everything else, she certainly didn't need images of Martha or the reminder of Paige's frustration haunting her thoughts.

A squeaking cart caught Addie's attention, and instead of heading up the staircase, she turned toward the doorway that led into the museum itself.

A young man wearing earphones bobbed his head to a beat Addie couldn't hear.

"Hello, I'm looking for Deanna," she called to no avail as he bopped on past the doorway, oblivious to her presence. "Great security," she muttered and started up the steps.

Just then, Deanna rounded the corner from the back of the historic building and paused at the bottom of the staircase, a steaming cup of coffee in each hand. "Oh, hello, Addie. If you're looking for Trevor, he's gone for the day."

Addie trotted back down to Deanna's side. "No, actually, I was hoping you'd still be here."

"Me? As I've already told the police, I was busy when the robbery occurred. I only have your word about what happened, and I told them as much. If you're looking at getting information to submit an insurance claim, you'll have to speak to Trevor. He handles all the legals. Now, if you'll excuse me, I'm . . . I'm on my way to a meeting." Deanna made a move for the bottom step.

"I just need one minute, please." Addie reached out a tentative hand.

"All right, one minute," Deanna said impatiently.

"Thank you." Addie weakly smiled. "I was just told that a witness has come forward—"

"A witness to what? The robbery?"

"It could be, but maybe also to the murder."

"Who was murdered?"

"The man they found on the rocks at the base of the cliff."

"That person was murdered? I heard someone had fallen because of the storm."

"No, the autopsy proved it was a homicide."

"Really?" Her face turned ashen. "And you say there was a witness to this?"

"I don't know for sure what they observed, but someone told the police they saw a woman and a man—the victim, actually—walk into the parking lot. I was just wondering if you happened to see anyone outside in the storm that evening."

Deanna shook her head. "I wasn't even thinking about the storm. We always get those this time of year, and up here on the cliff, it constantly blows worse than it does right in town."

"I understand that, but that night, when I was talking to Trevor, I was positive that you came out from the back area, like you did just now. That's where the kitchen is, isn't it?" Addie glanced down at the coffee cups in her hand. "So, I just thought that maybe, when you were in the kitchen, you might have glanced out the window at some point to check out the storm and saw someone on the cliff top."

"You're right, I did visit the kitchen that night. I took a break from the meeting and went to make us a fresh pot of coffee. I ended up tidying up the disaster of a mess the volunteers had left it in. I was furious with them, and the last thing on my mind was to look out the window. So, I'm sorry, I can't help you."

"Was Nikki Harrison one of the volunteers who was working that evening?"

"Hmm, I'm not exactly sure who was here. As I said, I'd been in a board meeting."

"Is there a record or a sign-in sheet the volunteers use to keep track of who's working?"

"Yes, Karl would have that, and maybe Trevor, but I'm sure the police would have requested it, as well, wouldn't they have?"

"Yes, probably." Addie crossed her fingers behind her back. "Then, you never looked outside the whole evening? Even after you were made aware that a huge storm was coming?"

"No, we were busy. I do recall, though, that some-one did leave the meeting. I don't remember who it was. However, he did mention he had gone to the kitchen to refill his water, and said he'd spoken to a couple of the volunteers who were thinking of leaving early on account of the storm."

"Even after that, you carried on with the meeting?"

"Yes, we had a lengthy agenda to get through." Deanna set the two steaming cups of coffee on a nearby table. "Why are you asking me all these questions? Isn't that a job for the police? Besides, Trevor is the one dealing with any inquiries about the theft. I am too busy trying to convince the board not to close down the museum now that all our hope for funding has been stolen." Deanna's voice wobbled as though she was on the verge of tears.

"I'm sorry, but the person who's being accused of murder right now because of one eyewitness's claim is my friend and housemate, Nikki Harrison. I was hoping you could shed some light on the matter is all."

"I understand your frustration. But I was caught up in a meeting that was getting rather heated. Discussions about capital expenses for the upcoming year and all that ensuing drama. When I thought I was going to throttle someone for being so pigheaded, I took myself away for a few minutes and went to make coffee. That's when I found the kitchen in a mess and did some tidying up. It wasn't until I took a trash bag out to the bin that I realized the storm had already blown in. The wind was blowing so hard by then that I really didn't look around. I just hurried back inside."

Deanna bit her lip and rubbed her forehead. "I've just been under so much pressure lately. I'm glad you came by, as it gives me the opportunity to tell you I'm really sorry. I feel so guilty about insisting you bring the donated books by that night. No one had any business being out in that weather." She studied the toes of her high heels. "And then for things to turn out the way they did, and your donation being lost like everything else? Well, it just makes me sick with guilt."

"Thank you," said Addie, "but the theft was going to happen whether I was here or not, and Karl still would have been injured and locked in the cupboard." Addie shuddered at the memory of his body tumbling at her feet. "Actually, I'm glad I was here."

"Yes, of course, it would have—"

"Deanna?" A man's voice echoed down the steps.

"I'm sorry, Peter." Deanna smiled at the lithe, middle-aged gentleman at the top of the stairs. She turned and retrieved the cups of coffee. "As you can see, I did get as far as the coffee. I just got waylaid by Miss Greyborne here. Addie, this is—"

"Miss Greyborne." Peter trotted down the stairs. "Peter Allen," he said, giving her hand a solid shake. "May I say, it's delightful to meet the woman who made such a generous donation to the museum."

"You're welcome." Addie glanced at the gray hair at Peter's temples, which, close up, made him look older than he had moments ago. "It's just too bad it turned out the way it did."

Deanna murmured something about him being a board member and eyed Peter with a look that Addie couldn't quite decipher.

"True, true," he said. "However, we have it on good authority that the police in your little town are on the case and close to making an arrest."

"In the robbery case?" asked Addie.

"Yes, I heard they had a suspect in custody."

"In the murder case, yes, but I hadn't heard—"

"What murder?" Peter asked.

"I'll fill you in later," added Deanna quickly. "Miss Greyborne just dropped by to ask me something, and she told me all about it. I'm sure she wants to get home, so I'll fill you in when we get back upstairs to finish our meeting—and enjoy what now must be luke-warm coffee." She gave a half grin and turned to Addie.

"Thank you for stopping by. If we hear anything more from the police, we'll keep you posted."

Deanna started up the steps, then paused and turned. "And I trust that if you hear anything else, you'll let me know. It would be wonderful to have all this resolved by Christmas. We could hopefully save the gala and make some money to pay for all the capital projects the board just approved."

"Yes, of course," said Addie, "and it was nice to meet you, Peter." Addie waved, but he had already turned to ascend the steps, and in moments he had disappeared from view. "Oh, Deanna, I forgot to tell you that the kid cleaning up tonight is wearing headphones, and when I called to him, he didn't even hear me. I just thought that until Karl is back on as the security guard, you might want to have a word with the young man." Addie winced as she heard herself. She really hated to be a snitch or get anyone into trouble, but after what had happened the other night, the museum staff should all be on guard, especially with no one manning the front desk.

"Yes, I will have a chat with Brady. He's covering for our usual custodian, Frank, who sadly slid his car into the ditch the evening of the storm."

"I'm sorry, I hadn't heard. Is Frank all right?"

"Yes, he's fine, just slightly bruised. He'll be back soon."

"That's a relief. It must be hard having both him and Karl off."

"Yes, and I guess with everything going on, I simply forgot to tell Brady he would also have to be our security as long as the doors are unlocked. I'm so used to

Frank covering for Karl when he's off. He usually automatically steps in and doubles as the security guard."

"It's understandable you forgot with everything that's going on," said Addie.

"It really didn't even cross my mind that Brady might not know what's expected of him aside from general cleaning. However, that's no excuse. The board would never forgive me if any of our museum artifacts went missing on top of the donated prizes." She smiled faintly. "I'll just run this coffee upstairs first. Poor Peter has been waiting forever, and he's had a long travel day. But then I'll go and talk to Brady right away. Thank you for bringing the issue to my attention." Deanna turned and headed upstairs with a bounce in her step.

Addie was usually a fairly good judge of people, and if she was correct, what was going on upstairs in that office was anything but a meeting between a curator and an out-of-town board member. She made a mental note to look up the board of directors for the museum, but her intuition had her on edge.

The elusive way Deanna had introduced Peter, to the look she'd given him and the vague mention of the "meeting" they were having—which, if true, was the tiniest board meeting ever, as it was just those two, it seemed—in Addie's mind, it equaled only one possibility: Deanna and Peter were involved in a secret relationship. They were hiding something—most likely a secret rendezvous—and they used a museum "board meeting" as a cover.

As she walked back to her car, Addie considered the

matter further. Did it even matter? Deanna was a grown woman who had been divorced for a number of years, so who was Addie to judge? She had found out what she wanted to know: Bin's *convenient* claim of seeing Chad and Nikki head off toward the lighthouse during a raging storm couldn't be corroborated. Addie would need to come back to the museum and question Karl, Trevor, and Frank, because Deanna had seemed adamant about not seeing anyone outside that night.

In Addie's mind, Bin's allegations were just that, nothing more than unfounded accusations made by a desperate woman trying to stir the pot . . . "Just like Deanna telling me that she and Peter were in a 'meeting.'" Addie chuckled and shifted into drive. "Although, maybe Peter is married, and they are having an actual affair. That would definitely need to be kept hush-hush." At least it would explain the aura of mystery they perpetuated around their so-called meeting. She slowed down when she passed the driveway to the Thomas sisters' B&B.

Noah's car was nowhere in sight. She contemplated dropping by the station to share with him what Deanna had told her about not seeing anyone on the cliff and leave it up to him to talk to Karl, Frank, and Trevor about what they saw, if anything, that night. There were so many suspicious things that had taken place the night of the robbery and murder, including Bin's sudden recollection of Nikki and Chad heading across the road together. Addie's mind raced, she couldn't shake the feeling that she was missing something.

"Maybe I should call Marc and tell him?"

No, it would seem too suspicious to be caught in Marc's presence again so soon, and she didn't know if he was with Whitney. Getting a call from Addie would probably have Whitney asking questions no one wanted to answer.

It was clear to Addie she needed a crime board, regardless of what Marc and Noah thought about the dangers of exposure in using one. She'd made do with jerry-rigged ones in the past, and she could do it again. There was too much going on. She had to see it written out in black and white if she was ever going to figure out her next steps. For now, she would work her crime board solo, a move she hoped would lessen the danger of exposure.

Chapter Nineteen

Once home, Addie fed herself and Pippi and even went for a little romp in the snow with the dog. After their snow-time play, both were shivering, so Addie started a fire in the fireplace. Once thoroughly heated and with a rejuvenated mind from her exercise, Addie unearthed a roll of brown paper from the bottom cupboard of the large bookcase and taped a large piece to the wall beside the fireplace.

Memories of the last time she'd used this brown paper as a makeshift crime board cascaded over her, crushing her with the weight of that moment. At the time, it had been her own cousin she was defending from murder. Now it was Serena and Marc's. In both cases, though, she'd been a roommate to the suspect. Addie cringed with the realization that two murder cases she'd found herself thrust into the middle of, involved people she lived with. Maybe she was a bad-luck charm.

Marc and Noah's earlier expressed fears about having a crime board rushed back to her and she stared blankly at the paper when she recalled what happened when *her* cousin had accidentally seen the board pertaining to the murder she was accused of committing.

She planted her feet.

Note to self: take this down when I'm finished tonight, then she sucked in a deep breath, and proceeded to draw black vertical lines, dividing the paper into five columns: *Robbery, Murder, Motives, Means, Suspects*.

Her hand hesitated under the *Suspects* column. She hated to write it, but due to all the evidence, she had no choice; she jotted down the name *Nikki*. Then without hesitation, wrote, *Elf*, in the *Robbery* column.

A puppy-dog snore broke the silence.

"Really, Pippi?" She smiled at her furry friend, sound asleep in her bed next to the fireplace, nose tucked into her tail. "I don't think the description of the thief being an elf sounds very promising, does it?"

Another doggy snore was her answer.

Addie laughed. "Okay, okay, now, Marc said they could find no evidence of a link between the crimes, but I'm not convinced. They seem to have identified a suspect based purely on 'obvious' circumstantial evidence, and they aren't looking very hard at anyone else. On the other hand, I think what they have is too neat and tidy, and I don't believe in coincidences, so . . ." Beside *Elf* on the paper, she wrote, *Suspect or witness?*

Under *Murder*, she wrote, *Chad—victim*. Addie then circled back to *Suspects* and added *Elf*, writing *time roughly the same as murder*. She then wrote, *Was Chad an accomplice to robbery or a witness to it? Did the Elf have to kill him, or did the Elf witness the murder when he was loading up the getaway vehicle?*

Addie looked over at the still-sleeping Pippi. "It seems our friendly little elf might be the key to this. What do you think?" Addie chuckled at her sleeping crime-fighting partner. "You're definitely Watson. Anyway, it makes sense. Both crimes were in progress at about the same time. One suspect could have seen the other, and that might have led up to Chad being found at the bottom of the cliff."

Addie stood back and reviewed what she had written. "Yeah, it makes sense. If Chad was an accomplice, maybe he and the Elf had a falling-out, or maybe the Elf got greedy, or maybe in their haste to leave under the cover of the storm, Chad slipped, and over he went. Either way, the Elf has to remain on the board for now until I figure out who he was and what part, if any, he played in the murder." Addie looked at where she had written *Elf* under *Suspect* and added, *Volunteer or frequent guest at museum?*

"The Elf had to have known the layout of the museum to be able to send me on a wild-goose chase for boxes, and he seemed to know a lot about Deanna's comings and goings. Add to that, he knew the location of an out-of-the-way closet to stuff Karl into. I'll ask Nikki if she recalls seeing anyone matching his description."

Addie wrote a note at the bottom of the page, adding, *Ask Jerry if he's found anything that links the Elf to the museum*, to her growing to-do list. Addie didn't believe a random thief would dress up in an elf costume just to empty some indiscriminate Santa sleigh three weeks before Christmas without some connection to it and the museum. That coincidence was a stretch too far in her mind.

"Okay, Pippi, now, what do we know about the murder victim, Chad?" She tapped the tip of her pen on the board, closed her eyes, and tried to picture the only photograph she had ever seen of him. Tall and muscular, with bronze-blond hair cut short. But it was his eyes that had stood out the most. They were such a deep brown color they had appeared black, giving him a mysterious aura.

Nikki had told Addie it had been Chad's eyes that had initially drawn her to him. They'd been so filled with mystery—and the promise of a life so different from what she'd ever known growing up on the East Coast that her move to Chicago hadn't seemed so bleak. Little did Nikki know then that the look she'd admired so much had only held maliciousness and deceit. Addie shook off the memory jolt that rushed through her, and she wrote beside Chad's name, *Nikki's ex, abusive, controlling, manipulative*. She knew she could go on and on, but one review of the evidence against Nikki made the rock in the pit of her stomach drop.

Addie studied the crime board, and that rock sank deeper in her belly. "I've just started, and already there seems to be more than enough of a motive for Nikki to have killed Chad." Addie's heart raced. "You know, Pippi"—she glanced down at her still-sleeping Yorkipoo and rolled her eyes—"never mind. If Chad treated Nikki horribly, there's a good chance he treated other people that way too. Maybe even the Elf. The first thing I have to do is find out more about Chad. There has to be another suspect in his past who would want to see him dead for the same reasons as Nikki might have. Maybe that someone committed murder when he or she was pushed too far."

She added, *Need to find out more about Chad*, and stabbed the tip of the marker at the end for emphasis. She circled *Nikki's ex*, *abusive*, *controlling*, and *manipulative* and drew a line to the *Motives* column with a question mark behind them. Addie started shuffling all the different angles, trying to find other motives for someone wanting Chad dead.

According to Nikki, he was a cruel and vile person. He had to have left a long list of victims in his wake. But who in Greyborne Harbor even knew him besides Nikki? Marc and Serena and their parents did, but none of them could be suspects, could they? Not a chance. Addie knew her people, and not one of them, including Nikki, was capable of killing another human being. The answer was somewhere in whatever puzzle pieces she could find and make sense of to put them all together.

She studied the *Means* column. "What do I know besides the fall off the cliff? Nothing."

But there must have been something else in the autopsy report that showed it was, in fact, murder and not the fall alone that had killed him. Addie placed a large question mark under the column heading and made a note beside the column: *Was Chad poisoned, or hit on the back of the head, which caused him to fall forward over the cliff? Were there odd bruises or markings on his legs showing he might have been tripped? What evidence did the police have that he was murdered?*

She clenched her fist at her side. Not having a direct source to the police investigation or the coroner's office was really impairing her ability to figure out what happened. There was Noah, of course, but he was an outsider and a consulting officer and not really privy to the office politics and inner workings of the police station to be of much help to her. He'd seemed willing to help and have her as part of the team, but what if he slipped back into calling her help "*interference*," as he'd called it back in England? Addie's fist tightened until her fingernails bit into her palms. *Who am I kidding? Marc and Simon called my help that too.*

So much so, it was already a running joke by the time Noah met Marc, and they had bonded over her being like an obnoxious dog with a bone when she became involved in a case. A simple thank-you would have been nice once in a while, because ultimately, she was usually the one to put her life on the line. How many times had Marc reprimanded her for putting herself in danger, reminding her that trained police officers only compromised their safety if it was truly necessary?

What did they know, though? She certainly didn't go looking for trouble, and she couldn't help it if she was in the wrong place—or the right place, depending on how one looked at it. It sometimes turned out for the best if she helped them catch the perpetrator. Noah knew that too.

It was time they started to take her seriously. She could do this. She was resourceful, and she would show both of them that she was right. Nikki was no killer, and she would find the evidence to prove it. Digging into Chad's past was the perfect place to start, right?

Despite her belief in her roommate, as Addie scanned the few leads she had written on her board, queasiness swirled in her stomach, and her hand reluctantly wrote, *Nikki—phone calls to and from victim, Nikki—no alibi for time of death, Nikki—seen at B&B night of murder, Nikki—seen leaving the B&B later, going to lighthouse with victim.* Addie held her breath and added, *A well-documented rocky past marriage between Nikki and victim.*

Blowing out a breath, she also wrote, *Bin and Bev Thomas—strange notes in ledger, Bin—the only witness to seeing Nikki the night of the murder.*

"Pippi, should I add in Bin's fussing over Noah and cutting his meat and trying to feed him?"

Soft snores filled the silence.

Addie stood back and read over what she had written, then shook her head. "I have nothing. There is no actual proof." She tossed the pen on the table. "I need an in at the station." She snapped her fingers. "Jerry! At least he might give me a foot back in the door, and who knows? Maybe I can get some information out of that new desk sergeant too. What do you think, Pippi? Perhaps if we take them some Christmas cookies from Martha's bakery, it will help loosen their tongues?"

With a laugh, Addie added her Christmas cookie caper idea to her to-do list. "If I present my reasons, I'm certain one of them will run a background check on Chad." She grinned and turned to Pippi. "At least we have a starting point now. Marc can't help, and I don't want to put Noah in a more tenuous spot than he's already in. If the DA or mayor gets even the slightest whiff of insubordination from him, he'll be out." Addie's heart dropped, and she caught her breath. No, they were a team, but there were things she—a known tenacious sleuth—could get away with more easily than an officer of the law.

She glanced at the mantel clock. "It's late, Pippi. Let's get to bed and take a second look at this tomorrow."

Pippi opened one eye and then yipped.

"*Now* you have something to say. Where were you an hour ago, when I needed your help?" She laughed, then took down the paper and folded it up. After placing it back in one of the cubbies in her grandmother Anita's desk for safekeeping and away from prying eyes, she picked up her furry little friend, hugged her close, and chuckled as a wet pink tongue lapped across her cheek.

"You always know what I need, don't you, girl?"

Addie nuzzled Pippi's head, and they headed upstairs.

Chapter Twenty

The morning sun streamed through the shop's windows, giving the illusion of warmth. If snow hadn't coated everything again in a light dusting overnight, and if Addie's still-numb fingers weren't tingling with fresh blood flow, she'd have believed the lie that it actually *was* warmer outside.

"I'm telling you, Paige"—Addie crinkled her nose—"Deanna Jackson is having some kind of romantic liaison with this Peter Allen fellow, and it makes me think that you're going to have to extend her wedding invitation to include a plus-one." Addie hit Print to get the previous day's sales report.

"Mom will freak out. I only invited Deanna in the first place because I generally volunteer at the museum a couple of times a year. You know, Christmas and Founders Day and then whenever Emma's school has a field trip there. She has always been really friendly toward me, so I thought it was appropriate." Paige leaned over and scratched Pippi's head. "But now I'm trying to figure out a way to un-invite half the people I did when we had the reception booked at the Grey Gull Inn."

"You know you can't do that."

"I know, it would be social suicide. This is a small town, and something like reneging on a wedding invitation might not only harm our business here, but it could also jeopardize Logan's career with the fire department, and he's worked too hard to get where he has. But now you're telling me I have to inform my mother that even more people might be showing up expecting to be fed? She's going to hit the roof!"

Addie reached over and patted Paige's hand. "I was only joking about the extra guest. I don't really think Deanna would bring an illicit lover to your wedding, not when they're working so hard to keep their relationship a secret." She laughed at Paige's incredulous face. "But about your huge guest list, it's not your fault. It's your mom's, for changing the reception venue three weeks before the wedding, especially after the invitations were already sent out and the RSVP cards returned."

"I know, but to avoid another world war in my family, it seems we have to cope with the repercussions of Mario's being half the size of the Grey Gull Inn." Paige's face reflected none of the joy of a soon-to-be bride. "Mom's going to be furious if people keep showing up expecting a meal." Paige nibbled at a recently manicured nail, then huffed and hung her arms lifelessly at her sides. "Maybe Deanna isn't really dating this guy. Maybe it's just as she said and he's a board member."

"Look, I just don't want you to get into it with your mother again, as you seem to have struck a tenuous truce. If Deanna and Peter are using the museum and the cover of a 'board meeting' to conduct 'business,' then I don't think you have anything to worry about. There'd be no reason to bring their secret out into the light of a well-attended event. However, if my initial impression was wrong, there could be a slight chance she'll bring him." Addie supportively rubbed the top of Paige's arm. "Please don't think too much about it. Whether she brings him or not, to either introduce him to everybody as her boyfriend or to simply show him off, all guests were afforded an initial plus-one, right?"

Paige nodded. "But she only replied it'd be her."

"The truth is, she could still show up with an impromptu date. Just be prepared for another mouth to show up expecting food, that's all I'm saying."

"What should I say to her?"

"Who? Deanna or your mom?"

"Deanna. I'd like to double-check before I tell Mom and face more backlash."

"If it's any comfort," said Addie, "I get the feeling it might be a relatively new relationship, so maybe it won't be a problem if you don't give her the option of bringing a plus-one. Don't worry too much, and I'm sorry I even brought it up. I just thought I'd better play devil's advocate, because I'd hate for you to get any backlash if he does show up and you're short a meal."

"I know, and after work I have to go to the antique

store to pick up the vintage hairpiece they specially sourced for me. Then maybe I'll stop by the museum and talk to Deanna. I can say I noticed she only marked herself for attending, but if she wants to bring a plus-one, she should let me know by next week at the latest. How does that sound?"

"Mm, I don't know," Addie said. "She knows we're friends and that you work here. I'd hate for her to think I put two and two together wrong . . . or right . . ." Addie scowled at the receipts in her hand. "Anyway, maybe just say something like there was an error made in the wording of some of the RSVP return cards, and the box for marking plus-one was omitted. You're just letting her know that if she received one of those, not to worry about it, and that she's welcome to bring a plus-one if she wants. Then leave it at that. To be safe with the meal count, order another one in case she does want to show off Mr. Thousand-Dollar Suit. Or something like that keeping in mind your mother's reaction if Deanna decides to bring him with no notice and there's no meal for him."

"Did you just say Thousand-Dollar Suit?"

"That's what it looked like." Addie shrugged and squinted at the sales receipt from the day before. Her heart sank at the lackluster total.

"Do you know if he's local?" Paige asked.

"Huh?" She looked at Paige's expectant face and dropped the receipt. "Sorry, no. I'd never met or even seen him before, so I don't think so. Then again, she did say he was a new board member, so maybe he just moved to town?" Addie grabbed her laptop from under the counter. "That reminds me, today I was going to check the board of directors list and see if he's on there."

Paige looked curiously at Addie and then at the open laptop. "A background check? Really? It's not that big a deal whether they're dating or not, is it?"

"No, I'm just curious. Every now and then, I like to test my gut instincts to see if they are still working or if I'm completely off base."

"Even if he is just a new board member and not a se- cret lover, chances are, it wouldn't be on the museum webpage. Ever since their computer tech volunteer left a few months ago, I've noticed that nothing except the events page, which is manned by Trevor, has been up- dated."

The overhead bells chimed, and Paige let out a squeal. "Nikki! You're out!" she cried and dashed toward a completely disheveled-looking person who vaguely re- sembled Nikki under a rat's nest of hair and makeup- smeared racoon eyes. "Why are you here?" Paige asked, pulling out of the bear hug she'd just suffocated Nikki with.

"I'm on the schedule to work. Sorry I'm late, Addie, but . . ."

"Goodness!" Addie folded the lost-looking Nikki into a hug. "This is the last place you need to be today."

Nikki pulled from her arms and looked blankly at Addie with tear-filled eyes. "I don't have my car." She sniffled, and her bottom lip quivered.

"And no one at the police station offered to drive you home when you were released?" asked Paige.

Nikki shook her head.

"That is inexcusable," Addie declared, taking Nikki's

cold hand in hers. "You're not even dressed for this weather. Where are your coat and gloves? Who released you? I'm calling to file a complaint."

"No!" cried Nikki. "Please don't. It's not a big deal. I told the young officer that Auntie Janis would drive me home, and I convinced her to drop me off here because I was supposed to work. I knew I needed to stop in and explain what happened and why I was late. So, please don't say anything to her or the police. I just thought if I missed another day of work, you'd be mad—"

"You know me better than that," Addie said and led Nikki over to a leather chair. "I'm not mad at you at all. I'm worried about you. You don't have to be here. Let me drive you home?"

A fat tear rolled down Nikki's cheek. "I know, Addie. I'm sorry. I'm so . . . so . . ." She straightened up and swiped at her nose with the back of her hand. "To be honest, I really need the money right now because I have to hire a lawyer."

"They officially charged you?" asked Paige.

"Yes, and my aunt came and paid my bail, so I'm . . . I just need to earn money and . . ." Nikki looked at her fists tightly clenched in her lap. "I . . . I really don't know what I'm doing right now." Her soft weeping increased to full gut-wrenching sobs.

Paige threw her arms around Nikki, and Addie patted her back until Nikki's sobs subsided.

"Okay," said Addie, "let's get you home so you can have a long soak in the tub, something to eat, and a nap. Trust me, you're in shock now, but you'll feel a whole lot better after you're clean, fed, and rested. Then we can talk about next steps. How does that sound?" Addie removed a clean tissue from her sweater sleeve and handed it to Nikki.

"When you say 'next steps,' do you mean you're letting me go?" Nikki's eyes filled with terror.

"I thought we covered this," Addie said gently. "Your job here is safe, and we'll help where we can. Okay?"

"That's the best news I've had all week." Nikki forced a smile between her sobs, dabbed at her eyes, and wiped her nose. "I feel so . . . grungy after being in that cell."

"I remember that feeling well," said Addie, collecting her purse from under the sales counter.

"You've been arrested before?" Nikki asked, her eyes wide. "I bet it wasn't for murder, was it?"

"Yes, as a matter of fact, it was." Addie waved her hand dismissively. "It was a long time ago. Remind me one day to tell you the sordid details of my background." She gave Nikki a conspiratorial wink and smiled.

"It's clear by you being here now that you got off. How did you prove your innocence?" asked Nikki.

"With the help of my friends." Addie pulled Nikki to her feet and draped her own coat around Nikki's shoulders. "I'll do my best to get the charges against you dropped. I need you to be strong, though, okay?"

Addie shared a smile with Paige and was glad when Paige broke eye contact and began helping Nikki get her arms in the sleeves of Addie's coat. Addie wasn't sure how much longer she could keep up the optimistic charade, and she felt like a fraud.

An overwhelming sensation sloshed in Addie's gut.

She was failing in her mission to identify enough plausible suspects to make the police take a second look at anyone besides Nikki. The evidence against her employee and roommate was too strong in the eyes of the DA and the mayor, who only wanted a sacrificial lamb to boost his political agenda.

"Since I have a few errands to do," chimed in Paige, "why don't I run her home? On my way back, I can stop at the antique shop and the museum."

"Do you think you'll be all right on your own, Nikki, until I get home after the store closes?" asked Addie.

"Yeah, I'll be fine. I'm going to have some coffee, eat a sandwich, then take a bath and a long nap. I'm suddenly exhausted and feel absolutely drained."

"That's the adrenaline leaving your system, so be careful not to fall asleep in the tub. Waking up in cold water is not as refreshing as those spas lead people to believe," Addie said with a chuckle.

"I'll bring your coat back with me," Paige called over her shoulder to Addie as she and Nikki headed for the shop's back door.

"Thank you. Drive safe." Addie waved, then went back to checking the museum's webpage. No mention of a Peter Allen as a board member.

Addie drummed her fingers on the counter. "Something doesn't smell right, Pippi."

Pippi paused chewing at the new toy Paige had bought for her and looked at Addie with puppy annoyance.

"I'm sorry to disturb you, princess." Addie chuckled and rubbed Pippi's ear between her fingers before returning her attention to the Deanna and Peter situation.

"First of all, Pippi, why do I care? I shouldn't. These are two adults. But something doesn't feel right. She introduced him as a board member, I know that, but why isn't he on the board of directors webpage?"

Pippi yipped when she hit the squeaker in the toy squirrel.

"At least someone's hitting their mark." Addie scowled at the museum webpage. "Either my instincts are still intact and there's some funny business going on, or Paige is right in that the webpage is simply out-of-date." Addie closed out the webpage and stared at her screensaver. "No matter how this ends up, though, if that man shows up to Paige's wedding and Martha isn't prepared with an extra meal, the you-know-what is gonna hit the fan." Addie frowned. "And as maid of honor, I'll have to run interference between Paige and her mother. I get the strange sensation that battle won't be the only conflict between the two of them that day."

Pippy yipped, grabbed her new toy squirrel by the head, and shook it.

It was best to head that altercation off at the pass. She couldn't control the mounting evidence against Nikki, but she could control adding an extra meal or two at the reception venue and save Paige from the wrath of the prickly cactus known as her mother. Addie dialed the number for Mario's and spoke to Maria, the restaurant manager, who, with her very strong Italian accent, comforted Addie by telling her they always had extra food and would be able to accommodate any additional guests.

"Now, chairs? That might be a problem"—Maria

chuckled—"but food? Never. No one ever goes hungry at our restaurant."

"You're a lifesaver, Maria. Thank you!" Addie hung up, feeling encouraged that she'd at least gotten one thing right since the night of the robbery.

Confident in that one victory, Addie dialed the police station, hoping that one success would lead to another.

Chapter Twenty-one

So much for Addie's Christmas cookie caper plan. With no one to hold down the fort so she could go in person to distribute Martha's tempting baked goods at the police station, Addie wasn't sure how she was going to sweet-talk the young desk officer out of information, especially since he'd thought she was a criminal upon first meeting her.

Addie rhythmically tapped her fingers as she listened to the elevator music streaming through her phone. She made a mental note to suggest that Marc change the station's musical hold feature to something other than screeching, unrecognizable violin music.

When the violin escalated to an ear-splitting crescendo, Addie winced, held her phone out, glared at it, pressed Speaker, and set it down on the counter. "This is ridiculous Pippi. How much crime can people be reporting in one small town for the phone lines to be this busy?"

Pippi, with toy squirrel firmly entrenched in her jaws, flicked a glance at her before continuing to maul her toy.

"If you destroy that one as quickly as you destroyed the other one Paige bought you, you're not going to get anything for Christmas."

Pippi dragged her toy behind one of the book-shelves, disappearing from Addie's view.

"So, you're pouting now?" Addie asked.

Squeak.

"Addie, is that you? Did you just ask me if I was pout-ing?" Jerry's amused voice echoed through her phone's speaker.

Addie jumped, fumbled her phone, and dropped it back on the counter. "Jerry?" she said loudly, aiming her voice toward the small speaker. "So sorry about the pouting comment and then dropping the phone in your ear . . . I wasn't asking you, I was talking to Pippi . . . Ah, never mind. Say, I was wondering if you had any leads in the museum robbery yet?"

"No."

"What do you mean, no? No one has been able to identify the elf based on the description I gave to the sketch artist?"

"Nope."

"I can't believe no one has seen him before. That doesn't make sense, does it?"

"Now, look, Addie, I know how you get when you're on the hunt, but—"

To heck with it, she was just going to take a deep dive and ask her burning question. "Have you looked into the murder victim's past to see if anyone matching the thief's description pops up?"

"Are you insinuating that I haven't done my job?" Jerry asked, his tone clearly not amused anymore.

"No, I wasn't insinuating that you haven't done your job. But do you honestly think these two crimes happening only yards from each other aren't related?"

Jerry huffed a long-suffering sigh. "Can you come down to the station?"

"No, I can't. I'm by myself in the shop right now. Paige just drove Nikki home and then had some errands to run."

"Well, I'll drop by there when I can. Hold tight and don't go anywhere."

"I'll be here. See you soon." Addie hung up.

"As you probably heard, Pippi," Addie called out, "although you're too busy annihilating your squeaker toy to care, I might've overstepped with Jerry. I think I really put my foot in it this time."

The overhead bells jingled, and a few customers walked in, much to Addie's relief. She'd been scowling at the sales receipts again, showing she'd made nearly zero dollars the day before.

Fifteen minutes later, Jerry walked in. He waited patiently at the back of a line of customers, all on a seniors bus trip from Boston to Pen Hollow and all holding books to purchase in their hands. Since Boston wasn't that far away, she slipped a flyer for the following week's Greyborne Harbor Christmas Festival and

Tree Lighting ceremony and told each one she hoped to see them soon.

Then, as suddenly as they had arrived, they were gone, and she was left face-to-face with an annoyed-appearing Jerry towering over her from across the counter. For a fleeting second, Addie figured he'd make an excellent poker player.

"Hi," she said meekly. "I got the impression on the phone that you took my questioning as—"

He put his hand up, silencing her.

She gaped at him and opened her mouth to protest, but since she couldn't read his emotions, she snapped her mouth shut and studied him warily.

"That. That look on your face now is why I'm here."

"Okay?" Addie eyed him uncertainly.

"I need your help, Addie."

"You do?"

"Yes, and I'm sorry about my reaction on the phone. I'm just at the end of my rope right now."

"Why, what's happening?"

"I'm getting so much pressure from the DA and the mayor to solve this robbery and find the stolen donations. They make it seem that if the lighthouse museum loses out on their biggest charity event of the entire year, it'll be my fault instead of the real bad guy, a greedy little elf."

Addie studied him for a moment, figuring out her next move. She might not have cookies to offer, but she did see an officer hungry for promotion. "You know, I think if we work together to find this elf, then we might also find a couple of leads to the murder case. That would be a big boost to your résumé, wouldn't it?"

"Of course, it would," Jerry said, standing a little taller. "And if I helped crack a murder investigation *and* the robbery, they couldn't overlook me again in a major case, could they?" He gave her a toothy grin, but it quickly faded, and a look of horror filled his eyes. "I didn't mean anything by that. It's just that, to be replaced by an outsider and—"

"It's okay. I wouldn't blame you for feeling a bit resentful at being bypassed at your own station."

"Yeah, I'm embarrassed to say it, but to say I'm a little resentful is right. Do you really think that solving the robbery could also help to solve the murder case?"

"It might, but first, we have to find the connection between the two."

"I ran a background check on the victim and couldn't find any links to the museum, or even recent trips to Greyborne Harbor. When I talked to the Thomas sisters, they said that Chad Sanders had only been in town for a week, and when I showed them each the sketch of the elf, they couldn't identify him." He shrugged. "It doesn't look like the murder victim and the elf even knew each other."

"Maybe they didn't cross paths here, but that doesn't mean they didn't know each other back in Chicago, does it?"

"How did you know the victim was from Chicago?"

"Nikki is my housemate and an employee of the bookshop, remember?"

"Of course, but I've found no evidence that links her ex with the elf robber. Although"—his eyes lit up—"there were a few things that did stand out."

"Like what?"

He glanced over his shoulder, then leaned toward Addie. "Like sealed court documents from Chad's youth and a past court case involving one of his investors who accused Chad of running a franchise scam."

"What happened with that case?"

"Chad had a good lawyer, and he won in court. Chad pointed out a clause in the contract that said the partnership could be dissolved if the investor didn't adhere to the strict guidelines of the franchise agreement. The fellow lost his claim and was left destitute."

"Interesting. That might be a motive for murder, don't you think?"

"I suppose, but that case went back a few years. Why would this fellow take revenge now, and why here, in Greyborne Harbor? Some place Chad wasn't known to frequent?"

"Maybe something in his life changed. Who knows? But it's someplace to start. Do you have this guy's name and address?"

Jerry blushed. "Don't judge me too harshly, but I've been going through so many files and documents that I can't remember it off the top of my head. I'll have to go back through the files to find his name and then run another check on him to find a current address."

"Yes, a name would be great—and so would a photo. It also might not hurt to send the sketch of the elf to any car rental companies within a hundred-mile radius to see if anyone recognizes him. I assume you showed the sketch to the hotels and B&Bs around town, right?"

"I do know how to do my job, Addie." Jerry staunchly hiked up his police utility belt, but a blush blossomed on his cheeks. "But the only car rental companies we checked were the local ones, so expanding our search perimeter is a good idea, especially if I can get a name to match the picture." Jerry cocked his head. "Yeah, the elf couldn't have packed all those donations out on foot, and even though the blowing snow covered up any tire tracks, he must have been driving something. Good thought, Addie."

"Here's another thought and another possibility . . ."

"Shoot."

"Maybe Chad and the elf weren't working together and didn't know each other, but the robbery and the death are still related."

"How's that?"

"Think about it. It was stormy that night, right? The wind was howling, and the snow was blowing. We know the elf took off in a hurry because I'd surprised him. He knew he only had a limited amount of time to get away with his haul. Maybe he accidentally knocked Chad off the cliff top in his hurry to turn around his getaway vehicle. Or"—she tapped the back of Jerry's hand with her finger—"stay with me, here, what if they *did* know each other, and the elf is the man who got bilked in his case against Chad? Could be the elf recognized him, saw an opportunity, and used his vehicle to knock Chad off the edge of the cliff."

Jerry rubbed his chin. "Both scenarios are possible, I guess, but I'd have to read the autopsy report to see if the injuries match a man-meets-motor-vehicle incident."

"You haven't read the report yet?" Her heart sank

with those words. She'd been banking on him telling her what proof they had that Chad was murdered.

"No, it's released only on a need-to-know basis, and since I'm not on that case"—he shrugged—"and we haven't been working on the assumption the two crimes were related because there is no evidence to support it, I didn't 'need to know.' But it's a good theory, so I'll ask to read the autopsy report when I get back to the station."

"Good idea. If you can track down this fellow and prove through the autopsy report that there is a link to the two cases based on that business relationship gone bad . . ." She shrugged nonchalantly.

"I'm pretty sure that if the chief saw the autopsy report before he had to recuse himself from the case, or even if that new English guy, your friend, had seen it, they would have put two and two together if the injuries were consistent with a run-in with a motor vehicle." He shook his head. "No, I don't think his injuries are a match for that. The report must contain something else that's unrelated, which is why Nikki is the main suspect."

"Maybe—it was just a theory, anyway. It still wouldn't hurt to read the report so we know what we're working with to get the crimes solved . . . and for you to get in line for a promotion."

"Yes, I'll read it," he said with a smile, "and I'll let you know what I find out." He started for the door, but then turned and pinned his brown eyes on her. "I trust if you come across any evidence, you'll let *me* know?"

"Yes, sir." She gave him a mock salute, to which he

returned an equally mocking one. Addie then shooed him away, and after Jerry left, she sank on the stool behind the counter and wondered why she didn't feel more optimistic.

It seemed that feasible suspects other than Nikki were in short supply. The only hope she had now in proving Nikki's innocence was Jerry finding a link between the mystery guy who had sued Chad and him being the elf thief and ultimately the murderer.

Pippi trotted around the corner, a limp and torn half squirrel hanging from her jowls.

Addie chuckled when Pippi laid it at her feet and looked up at her with guilty puppy-dog eyes.

"Look what you've done, girl!" Addie gingerly snagged the wet, demolished toy and tossed it in the garbage. "But don't worry. Paige spoils you too much. I'm sure you'll get another one soon."

Pippi yipped, crawled into her bed behind the counter, and promptly fell asleep.

Addie eyed her furry friend, slightly jealous of her life, and rested her chin in her hands. In the past, she'd faced brick walls, but this time it seemed different. Due to the covert nature of her teamwork with Marc and Noah, she felt like she was completely alone. She couldn't even tell Jerry she was working with them, and she felt guilty about it. Jerry was too good of a friend to be deceived like that.

At the beginning, she'd been hopeful to rescue Nikki from a murder charge, but as reality set in, that hope dwindled to a mere flicker. What she needed was a Christmas miracle. It was just too bad they didn't exist. So, it was up to her and her own tenacity to find the elf thief, both to save her friend from a possible prison sentence, and to recover the much-needed donations for the museum.

The shop door opened, sending in a flurry of cold air and customers, and Addie was ripped from her thoughts. For the rest of the afternoon, customers descended on the shop, keeping Addie busy, as books flew off the shelves in what must have been a between-the-storms Christmas shopping frenzy.

During a small window of time when customers were milling around but not in line, Addie called Paige but frowned when it went directly to voice mail. She glanced up at the clock and shook her head. It shouldn't have taken three hours for Paige to drop off Nikki and run a few errands.

Addie closed her eyes as her chest constricted with panic and visions of everything that could have gone wrong rushed through her mind's eye. She gasped when a voice broke through her spiraling thoughts.

"Addie, are you okay?"

She opened her eyes and smiled weakly at Serena. "What did you say?"

"I asked if you were okay, but judging by the worried look in your eyes, I think I have my answer," she said, setting down the two take-out cups of tea from her shop. "What's going on?"

Chapter Twenty-two

"Serena," Addie whispered, "I have no idea what to do." Addie brought one of the to-go cups to her nose and inhaled the rich, earthy aroma of Serena's famous afternoon pick-me-up matcha-tea blend. "I know the British think there is no trouble so great that it can't be resolved with a nice cup of tea, but I'm not sure even this will help much right now." Addie sipped the hot brew and relished the sweet, nutty flavor. As the hot liquid warmed her from the inside out, the tight knot in her stomach loosened slightly. Maybe there was power in tea after all.

"Is it Noah?" Serena said, fixing her fiery gaze on Addie. "If he hurt you, I'll . . . I'll . . ."

"No, it's nothing like that." Addie chuckled and waved off her friend's concern. "The issue is with me."

"You? Why?"

"I'm pretty good at putting puzzle pieces together and figuring out who the murderer is, right?"

Serena nodded.

"But this time I can't help but think . . ." Addie realized what she was about to say and to whom and closed her mouth.

"Can't help but think what?"

Addie couldn't tell her best friend she was starting to believe Serena's cousin *was* a murderer. *Pivot and think fast.* "I can't help but think that . . . that . . ." *Think, Addie, think.* "That I'm struggling so much because I keep getting the murder and the robbery all mixed up and I'm confused as to which clues belong with which crime." Addie hoped Serena didn't suspect there was more behind her rambling confession.

"What was it your father used to tell you about police work?"

Addie grinned. "He used to say the most important thing about solving a crime was patience. The clues in front of you were only part of the story, and it took time and patience for the rest of the puzzle pieces to fall into place."

"There you go." Serena raised her paper cup in a salute. "Have you started a crime board? You know you work best when you can see the evidence laid out in black and white."

Addie beamed with pride, but her thoughts immediately went to her DIY crime board and all the evidence she had on it that pointed to Nikki as the most likely suspect. Her grin turned to a restrained half smile.

"Yes, I have one." Addie took a breath, knowing she

could never show it to Serena. "It doesn't have much on it, though. Since I don't have Marc as a resource for any evidence privy only to the police, or Simon to bounce things off of or for any autopsy information, it's pretty sparse." She bolstered herself up, then delved into a breathless rant, relaying all her difficulties over the past few days of solo crime-solving. Finally she paused and smiled helplessly at Serena. "That's why I'm struggling and feeling frustrated. Yes, that's it." Addie hoped she came off as convincing. "On top of all that, Nikki was just released. Paige took her home, but I have no hope to offer her with her case yet."

Serena squinted at Addie in confusion. Her earlier perplexed expression had morphed into a complete stare, as if Addie had just sprung another head. "Since when did you need Marc or Simon to help you figure out a murder?"

"I meant for inside information. You know, like the little things that help put all the pieces together."

"Tell me, my friend, did you have Marc or Simon with you last year in England, when you figured out who the killer of that woman on the moors was?"

"No," Addie whispered.

"See, you don't need them to help you figure out the puzzle pieces. You're very capable on your own."

"Not this time. I feel like I'm in way over my head. I don't even know what proof they have that Chad was murdered and just didn't fall off the cliff in the storm." She massaged her temples to stave off the headache she felt coming on. "Besides, last year I had you and Paige. Oh, and don't forget Meg, the police constable, and Noah . . . to some extent."

Serena snorted a laugh. "If you really think he was much help, then go ahead and believe it." Serena muffled her continued giggles with her hand.

"Take it from me, in the end he *was* helpful."

"I'd have to see it to believe it, because when Paige and I were there, we never got the impression he was helping us with the case. It seemed exactly the opposite."

"That's the point, Serena. Last year it was the three of us, you know, like the Three Musketeers out there doing the footwork and piecing everything together. Right now . . ." Addie knew she'd have to choose her words carefully. "You're busy with a brand-new baby and little Ollie and Addie, especially with Zach taking over the naturopathic clinic from Doctor Lim, and Paige is getting married in two weeks, and I'm supposed to be the maid-of-honor—"

"Yeah, but it appears Martha has edged you out of that role."

With those words, a sinking sensation in Addie's gut nearly left her breathless. She hated to admit it, but Serena was right. With the distraction of murder and robbery, Addie had definitely dropped the ball in sticking up for Paige with the motherzilla of the bride.

"You see, Serena. Right now, I'm kind of at a loss and feeling torn. I don't want to let Paige down, or *you* either," Addie quickly added. "I guess what I'm trying to say is, no matter how much I want to jump in and prove your cousin is innocent, the police might just have to look into this one. I should be helping Paige out more with her mom so we can all get through this wedding unscathed. I hope you understand." Addie cast her eyes down, wishing the floor would open up and devour her.

"But the police think *she is guilty!*" Serena said, with a shriek that garnered a few gasps from nearby customers. "No, I need you to prove there is no way Nikki killed Chad!"

Addie glanced at the elderly woman standing by the bookcase behind Serena, flashed her an awkward smile, and leaned across the counter toward her friend. "Come by later, and we'll talk more, okay?"

"Addie, you have to promise me that you'll find the evidence that proves she didn't do it. It would kill Mom if Nikki was convicted of murder. She has been like a second mother to Nikki since Nikki's mom passed away. And after nearly losing my dad last year, I sure can't think about losing my mom this year. You have to help my family. Please, I'm begging you. Don't give up."

Addie's face grew hot as she eyed the customers at the front of the shop, who now had turned all their attention on the two of them.

"Serena, I . . ."

"Promise me?"

"I, I promise I'll do my best to find out the truth." She pinned her eyes on Serena's. "Okay?"

"Okay, and what about Noah? If he was as big of a help to you as you say he was after we left last year, and since he's in charge of the case now, can't he be a resource?"

Addie wanted to give a nod, even a reluctant one, but with all her customers staring at her, she knew she had to protect Noah. Instead, she patted Serena's hand

and hoped that all her digging around didn't prove Nikki's guilt and inevitably destroy her best friend's entire family. "I promise I'll find out the . . . truth. That's the best I can do."

Serena nodded. "Thanks. You know I'd help if I could, but some days it's all I can do to get out of bed and feed the twins."

"I know, sweetie. It's a tough time with two little ones and a new baby who keeps you up half the night. Go home while your mom is still there and get some rest. Judging by the circles under your eyes, you haven't had much sleep. So, take the opportunity to get what you need most to carry on and have a nap." Addie smiled reassuringly and squeezed her friend's hand. "I got this. Don't worry, okay?"

"I knew I could count on you. Thanks." Serena appeared to struggle through her exhaustion to muster a weak smile.

As soon as Serena was gone, Addie moved to ring up the elderly woman's book purchase, giving her a limp smile that Addie knew came across more like a grimace.

The woman looked at Addie with pity, accepted her change, and then leaned in and dropped her voice. "Just remember, when you're searching for that truth, my dear, to make certain that what you think of as evidence really is what you think it is. Make sure you're not set on the clues you already have and miss out on the real proof you need. Even Agatha Christie knows"—she gestured to the copy of *Appointment with Death* that Addie had tucked into the woman's shopping bag—"the evidence doesn't lie, but people do." She patted

Addie's hand, picked up her purchase, and tottered out the door.

Addie kept an eye on her as she bustled past her front window. The older woman was right, and Addie knew she'd been too willing to accept what had been presented as evidence to be the only evidence. As she'd told Serena, she didn't even know what the official cause of death was. For a fleeting moment, she thought of calling Simon, but quickly pushed that idea out of her head. So far, in the past year in Greyborne Harbor, she had successfully resisted the thousands of urges she'd had to pick up the phone and call him, by reminding herself that was no longer her life. The repercussions of making that call now, even to help her solve a case involving someone dear to her, was not the answer. There had to be another way.

The weight of everything on her plate pressed down on her, and she feared she couldn't bear the enormity of it all. Tack on trying to fit her new round life into the old square hole of her past self, and she wasn't sure she'd be able to take her next breath. Her grandmother Anita Greyborne's face flickered through her mind's eye, and the crushing weight in her chest eased.

"Anita's journals," she whispered and crouched down beside Pippi asleep in her bed. "Why didn't I think of them before? What better way than reading the continued adventures of an unmarried woman who suffered a similar heartache and loss, to figure out who I am now and how to forge ahead."

She grinned at her furry little friend, whose only response was opening a sleepy eye and nuzzling her head into Addie's hand. "Don't you see, Pippi? Anita figured out a way to return to Greyborne Harbor after building a life in England, and it's clear by all she did for the town after she returned that she made it work for her. Maybe I can too." She mentally reviewed the attic and tried to remember where she'd safely stored the extensive collection of volumes of her grandmother's life-long journaling habit.

The *bang* echoed from the back room, interrupting her thoughts. Addie jumped to her feet and glanced at the back-room door.

Wild-eyed and breathless, Paige raced through the door and toward Addie. "I'm so sorry it took me so long, but you aren't going to believe what I have to tell you."

Addie took a quick glance around for prying eyes and ears, recalling the entertainment her conversation with Serena had just given her customers. She put a finger to her lips and whispered, "Let's go in the back, and you can tell me."

Paige met the gawking looks from the nearby customers and sheepishly smiled. "I never thought . . . Yeah, let's do that."

Addie followed Paige to the back room and stood just inside it, keeping an eye on the customers milling around the bookstore. None looked ready to check out yet, but she knew that could change in seconds.

As Paige hung her coat up on the coatrack, Addie asked, "What in the world has you so excited?"

Paige hung her scarf over her coat. "When we got to your house, Nikki was pretty shaky, so I decided to go in and get her settled with a cup of tea on the sofa, hoping she'd just drift off and sleep for a while. Then you'd be home after she woke up to make sure she had a shower and something to eat."

"That was nice of you, but making a cup of tea shouldn't have taken the entire afternoon. Did something happen?"

"You might say that," Paige said hesitantly, twisting her fingers together in front of her.

"What is it you're not telling me?"

"As soon as I gave her the cup of tea and started to leave, her phone rang . . ."

"Okay?"

"It was a lawyer."

"Good, she's going to need one, according to the police."

"Yeah, but . . ."

"But what?"

"I don't think it was *her* lawyer."

"What are you talking about, Paige?"

"A lawyer called to inform her she was the full beneficiary to her ex's will."

Chapter Twenty-three

Addie stared incredulously at Paige. "Nikki told me and Serena that had all changed when they got divorced."

"That's what she thought, too, so she called her own lawyer, the guy she used for her divorce, and he checked into it."

"And?"

"And it's true. Chad had changed all their business and personal financial arrangements, but he had never changed the beneficiary on some old will or a 401(k) or something he had. It still has Nikki's name on it."

"Nikki had no idea?"

"None."

"Are you certain?"

"That's what she said, and I was there when she called her lawyer to check into it."

"You're certain she didn't know this before Chad's lawyer called to tell her?"

Paige's eyes glimmered with hurt. "As certain as I can be."

"I'm sorry, Paige. I didn't mean to doubt you. It's just that this isn't good news for Nikki."

"Why not? Now she's going to get the money she needs to pay for a high-powered criminal lawyer. With the murder charges hanging over her head, she's going to need one."

"Yes, but don't you see? Now there's a stronger motive for her killing Chad, more than her having the sudden urge to take revenge on him after all these years."

At the tinkling of the doorbells, Addie peeked out the back-room door to see Noah standing in the small entrance alcove, scanning the shop. His eyes lit up when he spotted her, and he mouthed the words, *"Can we talk?"*

Addie nodded, gesturing for him to come to the back room. She smiled at a customer who was perusing the bookcase closest to the door, then as soon as Noah entered, she closed the door and dropped the feigned *all is well* smile that she'd flashed to the customer.

"You're scaring me, Noah. What's up?"

"I have bad news about your housemate's case." He shuffled uncomfortably and glanced at Paige.

"I'll just go man the desk," said Paige, scooting out and giving Addie's shoulder a reassuring squeeze.

"Well, what is it?" asked Addie.

"I know we've been hoping to find more evidence that would point to another suspect, but it's time to face the facts."

"So, you're giving up? Is that what you're saying? Are the mayor and the DA pressuring you to wrap this up before the next polls are out? Is that it?"

"No, Addie. I hope you never think I would put politics before the truth, but as an officer of the law, my job is to present the evidence as we uncover it. The DA determines who to charge—or not—for a crime. Unfortunately, I've recently come across some evidence that can't be ignored, no matter who the suspect is."

"What evidence is that?"

"It seems Nikki was the full beneficiary of Chad Sanders's last will and testament, along with a rather large insurance policy."

"An insurance policy too? Nikki told me and Serena that all their joint financial dealings had been dissolved when they divorced."

"This was an older policy," said Noah, "and the will had apparently been drawn up when they were first married. I guess those details were just overlooked in their divorce proceedings."

"How did you hear about this so quickly? According to Paige, Nikki just learned about the will herself."

"We got a notification from Chad's lawyer requesting information about his death. He needed certain details before he could disperse the funds to Nikki. Of course, she won't receive anything as long as she is the number-one suspect or if she's convicted of his murder. On the other hand, Nikki Harrison stands to be a very wealthy woman if she manages to get off on this murder charge. And where I come from, the ex-wife who stands to inherit millions is far more likely to—"

Addie cut him off by holding up a hand. "Even after

hearing this, I still can't believe she's guilty no matter how much she was going to inherit. She's just not like that."

His eyes flashed with pity, and he reached for her, but dropped his hand at the last moment. "I'm so sorry. I really am. In my job, I see things like this every day. A friend, a neighbor, or a family member says he or she could never have done such a horrible thing, but sometimes we don't know people as well as we think." He paused a moment, then took a step forward, placed his hands on her shoulders, and gave them a calming squeeze. "I'm sorry, Addie, but I'm going to have to take Nikki in again for more questioning, and this time"—his eyes glimmered with remorse—"the DA may rule to revoke her bail, based on this new evidence."

The weight of his hands on her shoulders didn't add to the perpetual crushing sensation pressing her down; it alleviated some of it, and she felt lighter. Still . . . "I can't believe this is happening," Addie said, rubbing her forehead. Straightening her shoulders, she tilted her chin up. "Nikki's at home now, probably sleeping after last night, and she'll need all the rest she can get for the next hurdle."

She looked at Noah, hoping her plea for her friend wasn't falling on deaf ears. Heaven knew, the poor girl needed someone in her corner right about now, and Addie wouldn't allow her own exhaustion to keep her from being Nikki's advocate. "Can you wait at least until she finishes her nap, has something to eat, and takes a shower?"

"I suppose I could give her a couple of hours, but no longer." Noah dropped his hands as he stepped back.

"Good, thanks. I'll head home and make her some soup and be sure she showers. I'll call you and let you know when she's ready."

"She's a lucky lady."

"How can you say that? Everyone's already convicted her of killing Chad in their minds. I think the only thing lucky about that is she hasn't been locked up for life yet."

"I meant Nikki's lucky to have such a loyal friend as you. Even with all the evidence pointing right at her, you still believe she is innocent and you're willing to fight for her."

"I'm loyal to the people I care about, especially when I know in my gut they are getting a raw deal."

"I can see that, not just now, but I noticed it last year, when you went out on a limb for your other friends."

"I guess I'm just not as narrow-minded as *some* other people, who believe the uncovered evidence is the only real evidence there is to follow." Even though she knew she was being unfair, that Noah was an honest and just man caught in the cogs of an oftentimes-unfair justice system, she didn't care. Not when her friend's life was on the line. "So, if you'll excuse me, Inspector Parker, I am heading home to help my friend—and then you can drag away an innocent woman and lock her up as you have been ordered to do."

Addie spun on her heel, marched to the front of the shop, and told Paige she had to leave. She stomped back to the back room, grabbed her coat, and flung the alley door open. She flashed a parting glare at Noah, then smugly stepped out onto the small landing, allowing the door to slam shut behind her. "There, that should

show him how serious I'm taking my friend's innocence."

She gasped as she looked back at the closed door. "I
forgot Pippi! I can't believe . . ." She cursed the rest of
her thought under her breath. "So much for making a
dramatic exit." There was no way she was about to do
a walk of shame in front of Noah, not when she'd made
a perfect ninny of herself, and so she gingerly made
her way down the back steps to her car and slid into the
seat. She whipped her phone out of her pocket and
quickly tapped out a text to Paige, apologizing for her
quick exit and asking her to drop Pippi off at home
after she closed the shop.

"Dumb, dumb, dumb! Noah and Paige are probably
having a good laugh right now about my failed attempt
to make a point." She continued to berate herself as her
fingers tightened around the steering wheel to better
maneuver the MINI through the snow and ice ruts down
the back alley.

She wasn't sure if she should laugh or cry as she replayed her failed dramatic scene over in her head, but
she was giggling by the time she pulled into her driveway. "Oh, Addie. You know by now that trying to play
it cool was never one of your best attributes. It always
backfires. When will you ever learn?" she muttered as
she climbed the front porch steps and opened the door.

Her smile faded, and she stopped short at the sight
of a pair of man's snow boots on the mat just inside the
front door. "Nikki?" she called.

No answer.

She grasped the large silver candlestick on the hall
table. "Nikki? Are you here?"

"In the living room," Nikki cheerfully called.

The tension in Addie's shoulders relaxed, but she was left mystified by the boots. Who was their owner? It was clear by the quality of the leather and the style of the boot that they were a higher-end footwear than anyone in town she knew wore. But Nikki's voice had sounded calm, which put Addie at ease, so she set the candlestick down.

No one in town would wear those boots—no one, that is, except maybe Simon!

She grabbed the candlestick again and allowed her mind to consider the damage it could inflict. After all the sleepless nights she'd endured, the wee hours she'd spent in anguish as their ill-fated past came rolling back at her . . . She shook her head and begrudgingly placed the candlestick back in its place. Bludgeoning him now wouldn't change what had happened between them—it would only result in her and Nikki sharing a cell in prison.

She glanced wistfully at the candlestick one more time, then shored herself up and cautiously peered around the door frame into the living room. She narrowed her eyes at the familiar figure, who sat in a chair beside the fireplace. "Peter? What are you doing here?"

"Do you two know each other?" Nikki asked, rising to her feet.

Peter rested a hand on one knee and stood. "Yes, and—"

"No," chirped in Addie. "We met once." She pinned Peter with her gaze. "How do you know Nikki?"

"He was my divorce lawyer," Nikki added quickly, "and he's the person I called when I found out, as I'm sure you heard from Paige, that I had inherited some money from Chad."

Addie's eyes shifted to Peter. "And you just *happened* to be in town?" That was a moot question, Addie scolded herself, but when a strange man she'd only met recently, and in an entirely different circumstance, suddenly turned up in her living room, she couldn't just stand there and gape at him.

"Yes," he said, brandishing a smile of perfectly white teeth as he retook his seat. "I was here . . ." He paused and refocused on Addie. "Well, I think you know why I'm in town, but when Nikki called me and filled me in on what happened, I couldn't say no to a friend in need."

"Yes"—Nikki reached out and squeezed Peter's extended hand—"he raced right over here when I called him about the inheritance. He's here to discuss my options."

"'Options'?" Addie warily eyed Peter and took a seat on the chair beside the Christmas tree in front of the window. "Does Nikki actually have any options after being charged with murdering the man from whom she stands to inherit this large sum of money?"

"That is what we were starting to discuss. I was just letting her know how the will and the insurance policy could have been missed in the discovery process of their divorce proceedings."

"Please continue, then. I'm curious, too, since this new information provides, at least to the police, a stronger motive for Nikki to have murdered Chad."

"But I've just now found out about the money!" cried Nikki. "I was under the impression all of our joint dealings had been dissolved in the divorce. At least that was the outcome explained to me when we signed the final dissolution-of-marriage papers."

Peter rose from his chair and knelt in front of Nikki, taking her shaking hands into his. "No, my dear. Don't you worry. I'm here now. Leave everything up to me."

"But how am I supposed to prove I didn't know about the will before today?"

"That's a good question, isn't it?" said Addie, shooting a piercing glance at Peter. "Kind of like a person saying they were home alone to prove their alibi."

Peter ignored Addie and focused on Nikki. "Don't worry. I will talk to the police and let them know that throughout your legal proceedings, these documents never came to light, at least not until recently, which means they couldn't have been a motive for you killing a man you had been divorced from for years."

"Well," said Addie, glancing at the clock on the mantel, "you only have about another hour until they arrive to take Nikki back into custody for more questioning."

"What?" cried Nikki, turning panic-stricken eyes on Peter.

"It's okay, my dear. I will represent you until we can find you a good criminal lawyer."

"But I want you to stay my attorney." Nikki's voice took on a higher pitch, and she clutched wildly at Peter's arm.

"I'm not a criminal defense attorney, so I wouldn't be the best one to represent you, Nikki."

"But you're one of the top litigators in Chicago."

"Thank you, but my specialty is family law, so—"

"I want you!"

"*Shhh-shhh*, we'll discuss this later. Right now, let's prepare for the arrival of the police, shall we?" He glanced over at Addie. "If you don't mind, would you give us some privacy? Attorney-client privilege, you understand."

"Oh, right," said Addie, rising to her feet. "I'll go make Nikki a sandwich, so she'll have something in her stomach before the next round of police questioning." Addie smiled awkwardly, then left the room, closing the double pocket doors behind her. After taking a deep breath, she headed down the corridor to the back of the house. As soon as she'd crossed the threshold to the kitchen, she whipped out her phone and dialed Paige's number.

"You aren't going to believe this! . . . No, wait, what? . . . Marc said what? . . . How long after I left did he come in? . . . So, I just missed him? What else did he say? . . . Uh, yeah . . . okay . . . Yeah, I'll call him, thanks, but wait—" Addie took a breath to gather her scattered thoughts. "You know that guy I thought Deanna was going to bring to the wedding as her plus-one? . . . Yeah, Peter something. Well, guess who he is? . . . No, he's Nikki's lawyer from Chicago! . . . I know, it was fast, but I guess he represented Nikki during her divorce from Chad. Peter was her divorce lawyer!" Addie pinched her forehead to refocus. "I know, it is weird timing." Paige's inquisitive voice matched the questions swirling through Addie's mind. "Well, whatever it is, it sure is a small world . . . Okay, go . . . sorry, tell Mrs. Danube hi from me . . . Yeah,

I'll finish filling you in when you drop Pippi off, thanks. I owe you big-time." Addie clicked off the call and looked up to see Peter standing in the doorway.

"Did you have that sandwich for Nikki?" he asked, his piercing blue eyes not wavering from her face as he took a step toward her.

Chapter Twenty-four

"The sandwich. Right." Addie gestured to the phone in her hand. "I was just checking in at the bookshop." Peter's stealth-like, ninja arrival had caught her off guard. She took a step back, eyeing him while she stuffed her phone into the back pocket of her jeans. "Give me a second, and I'll get that for Nikki."

To put more physical space between them, Addie walked around the opposite side of the island to the fridge, pulled out a small bowl of day-old chicken salad, grabbed two slices of bread from the bag on the counter, slapped on some butter and pepper, then put the sandwich on a plate out of the cupboard and smiled sweetly when she handed it to him. "She'll probably need a drink, too, so why don't I put on some water for tea and bring it in?"

"Thank you." He took the plate from her hand and

glanced down at the hastily prepared sandwich. "No mayonnaise?"

Addie stared at the sandwich. "She doesn't like it," she said, hoping that Nikki wouldn't say otherwise.

"Okay?" He gave her a curious glance, then headed back toward the living room.

Addie blew out a deep breath of relief once he was gone. "Gotta tell Marc what's going on." She tapped his number into her phone and waited, but it went directly to voice mail. She shoved her phone back in her pocket and fleetingly thought of calling Noah.

"Nope, he'll be here again soon to take Nikki in. And anyway, since he's gone over to the dark side, he's definitely been put on Santa's *naughty* list—not to mention mine too," she grumbled. She proceeded to add water to the kettle and set it on the stovetop to boil while she filled the tea strainer with an herbal blend Serena had made up—one that was guaranteed to bring on a state of calm. A loud knock on the front door rattled her from her thoughts, and the metal ball strainer flew out of her hand and bounced across the counter. Yes, calm was exactly what she needed right about now. *Breathe, Addie, just breathe.*

"I'll get it!" she called out and scurried off toward the front door, but by the time she reached the hall, Peter had already opened the door and introduced himself to Noah.

Irritated by the fact that Peter, a virtual stranger, had seemingly taken over her home—even answering the door—she went to close it herself, then spotted Marc lurking in the shadows of the porch light and frowned questioningly at him.

He shrugged as he stepped inside behind Noah.

She gaped at Marc and then glared at the back of Noah's head, who, without even a word of acknowledgment to her, had already removed his boots and was standing in the living room doorway beside Peter. But just when she thought he was deliberately ignoring her presence, he turned and flashed her a crooked smile. Despite her anger over his pigheaded stubbornness when it came to following the letter of the law, in that moment, his smile made her heart skip a beat.

Noah turned his attention back to Nikki. "It seems, Miss Harrison, that new evidence has recently come to light."

With his words, Addie closed her eyes tight and held her breath, waiting for him to say out loud the words she dreaded hearing.

Noah cleared his throat and drew in a deep breath. "It seems it won't be necessary to take you to the police station this evening. However, I do have some additional questions to ask you, and since you currently have your lawyer present"—he glanced sideways at Peter—"we can do that here in the comfort of your home if you prefer."

"Did I hear you right? You're not taking me in?" asked Nikki as she sat back down in her chair by the fireplace.

"Not at this time," repeated Noah.

"Good news for a change!" Nikki grinned. "Go ahead, ask me anything."

The tips of Peter's ears reddened, and he cleared his throat and glowered at Nikki.

Her cheeks flared fiery red, and she dropped her gaze. "No comment, that is."

"Please be aware that this is just an informal interview, Miss Harrison," said Noah as he took a seat in the chair beside the Christmas tree. "I only have a few questions about the money you stand to inherit from your ex-husband."

"As Miss Harrison's current legal representative, I will answer any questions you might have pertaining to Mr. Chad Sanders's last will and testament, as well as any other monies allocated to my client here," said Peter, remaining in the doorway.

Noah looked over at Marc and Addie standing beside Peter, then gave Marc a head nod toward the kitchen.

"Addie and I will go and make some coffee. How does that sound?" said Marc, steering a reluctant Addie toward the door.

"Tea, actually," she said. "I was about to make tea when you arrived."

"Tea it is, then," said Noah, giving Addie a smile of gratitude.

The flickering lights of the Christmas tree and the glow of the fireplace glimmered in Noah's eyes, and she let out a soft sigh, momentarily forgetting his place at the top of her naughty list.

Noah signaled to Marc to close the living room doors behind them.

"How are we going to hear what he's saying all the

way down here?" Addie whispered as Marc hastily ushered her down the corridor.

"In a minute. Just keep quiet for now."

"Will you please tell me what's going on?"

"Not now, Addie," he said, steering her into the kitchen and closing the door. "There, now we can talk."

"What is going on? What's this new evidence? Better yet, what happened in the last couple of hours to make Noah change his mind about taking Nikki back in?"

"You haven't changed one iota, have you?"

"What are you talking about?"

"You—you want everything *now*. Well, Addie, take a seat, and I'll tell you what's going on, what the new evidence is, and why Noah isn't taking Nikki back into custody tonight." He gave her a side glance. "Tell me was there a question mark between all your questions, or was it a true run-on sentence like it sounded?"

"Smart aleck." Addie took a seat on a stool as directed.

Marc smiled. "Then you'll be happy to know, there is one answer to all your burning questions."

"Which is . . ."

"Bin Thomas changed her story. She has proven to the DA that she's not a reliable witness."

"I knew it!"

"Yes, you did question her statements. Let's just say, when I reviewed what she'd originally reported, I found enough inconsistencies to ask to speak with her again. I ran it past Noah, and after we talked to her this evening, he ended up taking her in."

"Bin's been arrested?"

"No, but she is cooling off in a cell right now as she

contemplates making false statements in a murder investigation."

"That is a chargeable crime, isn't it?"

"Yes, but she insists it wasn't intentional, that her vision is failing, and she just made a mistake about seeing Chad and Nikki entering the museum parking lot together. She's now decided it could have been someone else, or even a swaying tree branch beside him, that she saw, especially on account of the storm brewing. To charge her, Noah would have to prove that her initial claim had showed an intent to mislead, which is nearly impossible to do. Still, for now he's letting her stay put in the cell to think about what she did, in the hopes she'll learn her lesson."

"But doesn't that journal entry we found, where she scored and commented on her male guests, prove her intent? At least in the sense that it would get a woman she thought of as a rival for Chad's affections out of the picture."

"We can't use that journal, remember? We came across it through an illegal search. Besides, how could we even prove she thought Nikki was a rival?"

"It's not fair." Addie stared down at the countertop. Then an idea struck her. "Maybe it was Bin who went to the cliff top with Chad and then pushed him off." Addie excitedly sat up straight. "Yes, that's it! She was pointing the finger at Nikki because she did it herself. She was trying to frame Nikki, who she thought would make a plausible suspect because she was Chad's ex."

"Except, according to the coroner's estimated time of death, Bin was serving dinner in the dining room when he died."

"Then," Addie said grudgingly, "I guess I have to take Bin off my crime board. Darn it! I really thought we'd found another probable suspect." Addie pinched the bridge of her nose. "I guess my gut was right, and Bin was guilty of something—just not murder." She sighed.

"You started a crime board after all that discussion we had about how risky one would be?"

Addie guiltily bit her lip and turned toward the window.

"Addie . . ."

She smiled uneasily. "I was really careful with it. No one else was here, and I took it down and stored it away as soon as I finished working on it."

"And you're sure Nikki won't stumble across it?"

"No, it's tucked inside one of Anita's hidden cubbies in the desk. It's perfectly safe, I promise."

"Okay," said Marc skeptically, "because several people's careers are at stake if that gets out."

"I know, I know."

Marc and Addie sat side by side, and soon the ticking of the clock on the wall was the only sound in the kitchen as they fell into an uncomfortable silence.

Marc cleared his throat. "It was a nice surprise when we arrived and were greeted by Peter Allen."

Addie looked incredulously at him. "Didn't you find that weird?"

"Why would I?"

"Because it's weird how he just '*happened*' "—Addie hooked air quotes—"to be in Greyborne Harbor when Nikki needed legal advice and representation, don't you think?"

"He's been her lawyer for years. I'd never met him before, but I know he handled all her divorce proceedings. He also worked as her financial advisor after her mom passed and left what she had to Nikki. Lucky is what I'd call it, not weird."

Addie studied him, trying to decide if he was serious or just trying to wind her up, but she didn't see a playful twinkle in his eyes. "I'm not questioning his business dealings with her. What I am questioning is the fact that he just happens to be here at the same time she needs him to defend her when she's charged with Chad's murder. And since Peter had represented Nikki in her divo—" Addie gasped. "Marc, he just happened to be here when Chad was murdered!"

"Did you ask him why?"

"Yes . . . no . . . but he had an explanation, which to me sounded rather—"

"Take a breath. What did he say?"

"I actually first met him a few days ago at the museum."

"What was he doing at the museum?"

"He was introduced to me as a new board of directors member, but I got the sense that there was something off about him and Deanna."

"There you go. It sounds like that's the reason he's in town. But listen, I've been doing some preliminary sniffing around Chad's ex–business partner, the one he screwed over, and I think we should concentrate on him. I've done some digging . . ."

"And have you gotten anywhere?" Addie asked gently.

Marc frowned. "Not really, but like you, I'm a dog

with a bone, and I won't give up until Nikki's free from all this ridiculous speculation. If only I could find some solid evidence that takes the attention off her. I could follow it to its inevitable end, whatever that might be. Evidence doesn't lie."

"Evidence doesn't lie, but people do!" Addie gave the Agatha Christie fan in her shop earlier a mental high five and sat back on her stool, waiting for Marc to react.

"Marc?"

The only response was the ticking of the wall clock.

"Marc, I know you don't find it odd that Peter was here just when Nikki needed him, but I got some funky vibes when they were talking this evening about the money she stands to inherit from Chad's death. It kind of made me feel . . . creepy, like he had ulterior motives or something the way he went on and on, pleading for Nikki not to worry, that he'd take care of everything, and . . . Marc, are you okay?"

"Addie, Peter Allen is Chicago's top family-law litigator, and you're telling me you suspect him of murdering Chad Sanders and framing Chad's ex for the murder. For what? How would he benefit financially from the whole mess?"

"I never said that."

"Not in so many words, but I know how your mind works. You're thinking he set her up for murder so he could swoop in and represent her, and then what? Make off with her inheritance while she rots in a cell?" Marc stood up, scraping the stool on the brick floor. "Don't be ridiculous. She can't inherit the money if she's convicted of Chad's murder, so that throws your whole theory out the window, doesn't it?"

"It was only a theory. We used to sit right here at this very island and throw them around."

Marc threaded his fingers through his hair and sighed. He sat back down on his stool. "I'm sorry. I feel so helpless working outside the lines of the law, nothing on Chad Sanders's ex–business partner is looking solid, and I'm afraid that a family member I love will face a difficult trial because I can't put two and two together. I'm good at my job, Addie. Why do I suddenly find myself so inadequate?"

"You are a good cop, Marc, don't forget that. But you're hampered by not having the information you're used to being able to access. You're in my shoes now, and that's frustrating, isn't it?" She playfully bumped his shoulder with hers. "But I know you—and this is not like you. What's really going on?"

Silence once again hovered between them, and Addie feared he'd clammed up on her for good. Just when she'd begun to wonder if she'd jeopardized their friendship, Marc sighed.

"It's Whitney. She's been so sick lately, and the doctor warned us at our appointment yesterday that if things don't get better, she'll have to go on complete bed rest at home or be hospitalized."

"Oh no! How awful." She rested her hand on his.

"I'm scared, Addie. For the first time in my life, I'm terrified." Tears glimmered in his eyes. "Of losing our baby. Of losing Whitney."

Addie squeezed his hands. "Nothing is going to happen to either of them. All she needs is rest and to do exactly as the doctor tells her. It'll be okay."

Marc smiled sadly. "I hope you're right."

"I always am," she said playfully.

Marc laughed and wiped at his eyes. "If that helps you sleep at night, I'll let you believe it." He straightened his shoulders. "Back to business?"

Addie sensed he needed to change the subject and nodded.

"By the way, Addie, nobody really knows about Whitney and the whole bed rest thing. We don't want to worry the family right now, especially with all this horrible stuff with Nikki going on."

"Of course, your secret is safe with me. That's what friends are for." She gave his hands one final squeeze, then released them. In doing so, she felt as if she'd finally released both of them, giving them permission to move forward separately on the paths life had chosen for them. For the first time, she felt confident in her new steps toward a brand-new Addie.

He searched her face for a moment, and a soft smile touched his lips. "Friends. I'm glad to hear it, Addie, and I apologize for my boorish behavior earlier—and any in the future. In fact, I'll make it up to you and look into Peter's travel activities of late, at least as much as I can. I'll see if there are any discrepancies with the story he told you."

"Well, it really wasn't him who told me all of that. It was Deanna, the lighthouse museum curator."

"Are they friends?"

"That's the thing. I can't peg their relationship. It's

odd, and it has my sleuthing antennae quivering." She scowled at him. "What's that look for?"

He grinned. "No offense, but everything makes your sleuthing antennae quiver."

"Yes, well, they usually quiver for a reason. Maybe for Christmas, I'll buy you a set of them. Anyway, Deanna was the one who introduced me to Peter."

"She is the museum curator. It makes complete sense. Why are you reading so much into that?"

Addie recalled the awkward exchanges between Deanna and Peter that night. "I don't know. I can't put my finger on it. I got the sense they were lying or playing at something they didn't want me to know, but you're probably right. In reality it makes sense, I guess."

"I wouldn't disregard your gut instinct so quickly, but maybe you need to look at their connection in a different light and not as immediate suspects in Chad's death. Could be they're guilty of something, but just not what you think they're guilty of, like Bin was. I wish to all goodness that they were guilty of murder and we'd found proof of it. Having no other suspects except for Nikki, at least in the eyes of our *illustrious* mayor and DA, is taking a toll on everyone, and I have a strange suspicion that all this is exacerbating Whitney's illness." Marc stood quickly and nearly upended his stool.

Addie looked up at Marc and felt a wave of pity at the panic-stricken look in his eyes. "There is another way of looking at it."

"What's that?" Marc asked.

"That Nikki is innocent, no matter the circumstantial evidence against her, and the killer is someone we haven't even considered yet. It could be anyone."

"I am well aware of that, Addie." Marc sighed. "But we have to be realistic about this. If we can't find another reasonable culprit, Nikki will likely be facing trial for a crime she didn't commit." Marc didn't wait for a reply and stalked out of the kitchen.

"Marc, wait!" Addie went after him but stopped when Noah's frame filled the doorway.

"Did I come at a bad time?" Noah asked with a jerk of his thumb in the direction Marc had gone.

"No, it's all right."

"Did you two—"

"Nothing like that. I think he's just stressed about his cousin. All of this has hit his family pretty hard." Addie massaged her temples. She didn't like keeping things from Noah, but she'd promised to keep Marc's secret safe.

"Doesn't surprise me," said Noah. "He's also probably feeling helpless because he's been sidelined and has to investigate without his usual methods."

"Oh, and he's off sniffing around Chad's ex–business partner. I'm not confident it will amount to much, but hopefully it will keep his mind off of—" Addie's face heated.

Noah tilted his head. "Off of what?"

Now she'd gone and done it. *When will I ever learn to think before I speak?* "Life changes. You know, being a father-to-be has to be quite stressful, don't you think?"

Noah hummed low in his throat, but he didn't press her.

Needing to change the subject, Addie forged ahead. "I'm thinking, though, that you dropping the charges against Nikki will lift his spirits."

"We're not dropping the charges against her."

"But I thought—"

He shook his head. "I'm afraid your housemate is still very much at the top of the suspect list, because all the evidence we have points to her." He pressed his lips together, and an apologetic look filled his eyes.

"Any evidence you have is circumstantial at best. And your lead witness, Bin, recanted her testimony. You have nothing concrete to tie the murder to Nikki, and you know it."

"Except for all the phone calls and text messages between her and the victim, that is." He sighed. "If we could only figure out what the murder weapon was, it would go a long way toward solving this case."

"You still don't know what killed him?"

"We haven't got a clue. So far, we can't find anything that matches the pattern left on the victim's skull."

"Did Simon make a mold of it?"

"Yes, and I think that's also a reason Marc is so distressed right now. He's frustrated because the investigation hasn't even identified what weapon was used to inflict the fatal blow at the base of the victim's skull."

Excitement bubbled up in Addie after Noah revealed the information she'd been missing on her crime board. Finally, he was giving her something she could work with. "Was there nothing located in the area of the museum?" she asked, coyly fighting to keep her voice even. No point in letting him know her information pipeline had dried up, and this was all news to her.

He shook his head but didn't elaborate.

"Which means . . . ?" she asked probingly, hoping he would tell her more, but he stood silent, staring down at the brick floor. "Can I see an imprint of the wound?"

"You want to see what?" His head snapped up, and he looked at her. "Did Simon ever share molds of wound patterns found on victims in the past?"

"If it was a wound they couldn't identify, I'd help out sometimes. Remember, I'm a trained antiquities researcher. I helped identify weapons used in crimes a time or two." She pulled him down onto the stool next to hers. "Look," she said, "you haven't been able to identify the murder weapon used. Why not let me help if I can?"

"The fact that we can't find anything at the scene that matches the pattern also means the murderer either took it with them to hide it, or brought the weapon with them, which shows premeditation and not a spur-of-the-moment decision to kill. That leads to a different kind of murderer, Addie." He shook his head. "No, I can't let you be involved in this anymore. It's putting you in too much danger. We could be now dealing with a case of first-degree murder, not second-degree murder or manslaughter."

Chapter Twenty-five

Addie stared at Noah, not believing the words that had just tumbled out of his mouth. "Don't you dare go treating me like I'm some kind of fragile English rose, you, you—" She huffed, but then she bit her tongue and focused on the slow drip, drip, drip from the kitchen faucet to keep her from spewing out all the names she was thinking of calling him. The same ones she'd called him that day he'd overheard her in the stairwell in England describing him and what she thought of him to Paige.

"I can't believe Marc and Simon ever put you in harm's way. Did they not care about what could happen to you?"

"What are you talking about?" She glared at him in disbelief. "Did you ever stop and think that they *knew* I could take care of myself? That my skills can even come in handy sometimes?"

"I'm not questioning your abilities. You have proven yourself to be worthy over and over, but . . ." He reached for Addie's hand, and she pulled it away. "I'm sorry. I meant no offense. It's only that I have come to care about . . . about this town. And in the short while I've been here, I don't want any of its citizens to come to harm, including you." He leaned on the counter and reached across again, waiting until she looked up and their eyes met. "Please believe me when I say I don't believe a man protects a woman because he believes her to be weak—"

"Then how could you say such a thing?"

"It's because . . ." He swallowed hard. "Because she's important to him, and . . . and to be honest, you've become important to me. That's all I meant."

Addie took a few deep breaths. She didn't know if she should punch him or kiss him, but since he didn't expand any further on his explanation or make a move to kiss her, she thought better of initiating the latter—and her other instinct might lead to a charge of assaulting a police officer.

"You know I'm not going to stop trying to prove my friend is innocent," she said.

"Even though I said it, I didn't expect you would. I just hoped." There was a hint of exasperation in his tone, but his eyes were soft as he studied her face. "I also know you're already hatching your next move."

"You really are taking a lot for granted, aren't you?"

"No, I'm just good at reading people, that's all." He smiled knowingly. "Let me see if I'm right." He leaned forward, studying her face. "I have just given you information you didn't know beforehand, and now you're going stir-crazy and can't wait for me to leave so you can get back to nosing around." He sat back and smiled. "How'd I do?"

Addie opened her mouth, snapped it shut, then opened it again. "So you do believe this case isn't as open-and-shut as the mayor and the DA believe, and that there might be another suspect we haven't yet considered? Do you think the proof could still be out there?"

"A well-respected judge told me many years ago that a case wasn't closed until a judge said it was. Remember, Chad's death hadn't been ruled a homicide in the beginning, and by the time it was and the CSI team got to the scene, the weather had erased most of the conclusive evidence. So, yes, Addie, I want another look at the scene before I go making any assumptions."

"How did you know I wanted to go there?"

"Because I learned last year in Yorkshire that we tend to take similar approaches to solving cases."

"But you seemed so convinced Nikki was guilty because of the circumstantial evidence. What changed your mind?"

"I allowed myself to get caught up in the excitement of working with a North American law enforcement agency, and I forgot what that judge had once told me."

"Wise judge."

"Yes, he was."

Addie detected a touch of sorrow in Noah's voice as he pushed his stool back quickly, nearly upending it.

"Given it's coming on half nine," he said, "we should get going." He held his hand out to Addie. "I'll drive."

"Thank you," she said, and smiled gratefully, accepting his gesture in an attempt to keep it light between them. "But can I trust your driving skills? After all, we drive on the *right* side of the road over here."

"I'm well aware," he said, pausing at the kitchen door and waving her past him. "But that doesn't make it the *right* side to drive on." He flashed her a playful wink as she shimmied past him.

Addie hopped out onto the snow-covered parking lot beside the museum lighthouse, then gazed over the roof of the police cruiser and shook her head.

"What?" Noah said with a laugh as he closed the driver's-side door.

"Did you happen to bring a flashlight?"

"As a matter of fact, I happen to have two."

"You just happen to have two?"

"To be honest, ever since we got the autopsy results, I've been curious to get back over here myself and check to make sure the CSI team didn't miss something. Then, when I went to throw my torch in the glove compartment, I discovered one in there already. So, suffice it to say, yes, I have two." He grinned, then eased his way around to the passenger side of the car. He pulled a flashlight out of his pocket and handed it to Addie. "Remember, since the murder weapon hasn't been identified yet, it could be anything. It might have been disregarded that night as not being significant to a slip-and-fall investigation, which is what they thought had happened at that time."

"My thoughts exactly," said Addie, pulling up her

collar as they passed several cars in the parking lot. "Must be a board meeting tonight. We'll have to be careful about not being seen together. I would hate it if your job or Marc's was put in jeopardy because of me—"

"You're not putting my job in jeopardy, Addie." Noah reached for her hand and clasped it in his own. "If something happens to me or my job, it's because of the choices I've made. And I've chosen to be here with you, investigating this crime with you. Understand?"

Something deeper than his need for her understanding burned in his eyes. Addie's chest tightened. "Are you sure?"

"Are you questioning a law enforcement officer, Miss Civilian?" He smiled, brushed a snowflake from her cheek, and stepped back. "Shall we? Before we make ourselves sitting ducks for all to see?"

Addie nodded and followed Noah through the parking lot, then they veered off the path leading to the main door, slogging through the piles of drifted snow that had accumulated.

When they rounded the back corner of the white-washed lighthouse, a gust of blustery wind snatched away Addie's breath. She pulled her jacket over the lower half of her face as much as she could and forged ahead, cautious to watch her footing when they reached the wind-swept cliff top. At the area still cordoned off by wind-frayed strips of plastic police crime-scene tape, Noah stopped, removed a pair of blue rubber gloves from his pocket, pulled his winter gloves off with his teeth, and slipped the rubber ones on.

"Righty then, Miss Greyborne, let's see what fresh eyes can find."

She looked at her woolen winter gloves, then back at him. "Since you had two flashlights, you wouldn't happen to have another pair of rubber gloves in that magic pocket of yours, would you?"

He shook his head and glanced at her fuzzy gloves. "If you happen to spot something, don't touch it in case those shed and contaminate the evidence. Just call me over, okay?"

Note to self, Addison Greyborne, always carry rubber gloves in your pocket.

She gazed out under a moonless sky into the blackness of what she knew was a freezing, frothy, and unforgiving ocean. She mentally crossed her fingers that her inability to see how high she was would keep her vertigo in check as she stood on the cliff top. If only she could also drown out the sound of the waves crashing against the rocky base nearly a hundred feet below her. She stepped back and counted, ". . . eight . . . nine . . . ten," to clear her dizziness. "Noah, I think I'm going to look around closer to the museum for any evidence that the robbery and murder were linked."

"Call me if you find anything," Noah responded, then knelt about fifteen feet to her right and searched through tufts of ground scrub.

Head spinning, Addie walked backward, keeping her focus on the direction she knew would mean certain death if she made one misstep. She took a deep breath to steady her nerves, and when her vertigo resolved, she slowly turned her back on the cliff and clicked on her flashlight. As her eyes adjusted to its glaring beam of light, she made her way across the open space between the cliff and the lighthouse museum. With the flashlight's beam, she scanned the ground for anything that looked out of the norm. Her heart sank the farther she plodded. There didn't appear to be anything left to see. The week's changeable weather patterns had clearly erased any evidence of what actually had occurred that night.

Battered by the blustery cliff-top winds and ready to admit defeat by the time she reached the corner of the museum, Addie glanced back. Noah's flashlight beam still scanned the edge of the cliff top, directly above where Chad's body had been discovered on the rocks below.

"I can't believe it." She shivered, shaking her head. "They must raise a heartier stock in the UK than they do here," she muttered, then turned to forge on toward a space that appeared to be somewhat sheltered from the bitter winds.

"That's better." She pulled her mouth out of her coat collar, took a deep breath, and scanned the flashlight beam around her surroundings. To her right was a wooden fence, which, she assumed, hid the glaring eyesore of the industrial garbage bin off the back of the kitchen. No tourists ever wanted to see the unsightly parts of a historical treasure, and the fence served as an effective barrier between their delight and the garbage bin's pure ugliness.

She trailed her light beam toward the end of the fence and scanned the ground around the bin.

"Who's out there?" a man's voice shouted from the other side of the closed kitchen door. "I'll call the police!" The door flew open, and an antique musket barrel poked out, aimed directly at Addie.

"No, don't do that!" cried Addie, instinctively putting her hands up. She squinted and tried to make out the silhouetted form, but with the glare of the flashlight in the surrounding darkness playing tricks on her eyes, she couldn't quite tell if the voice matched who she thought it was. "Is that you, Trevor?"

"Yes. Is that you, Addie?" Trevor lowered the barrel of the gun and stepped into sight.

"Yes." Addie panicked, and her mind went blank for a second. All she could think about was Noah and the risk to his job if the wrong people talked. "I'm here with a police officer who wanted to check something out on the cliff top, and I just wanted somewhere out of the wind to wait while he searched." *There, not an outright lie.*

"The police want to check on something this late?" Trevor peered around the door frame and glanced in the direction of the beam of light still moving near the edge of the cliff. "Does that mean they have a lead in that fellow's death?"

Addie ignored his question. "What are you doing here this late, especially wandering around with a Revolutionary War musket?"

"A board meeting." He gestured to the unopened package of cigarettes on the floor at his feet and kicked them away. "I'm embarrassed to say that I quit smoking years ago, but tonight I'm meeting-ed to death, and I felt a strong need for one." With the toe of his shoe, he shifted a brick in front of the open door. "Makes a great makeshift doorstop for us smokers, so we don't get locked out." He stepped out onto the top stone slab of the three steps leading up to the back door. "I saw your flashlight beam through the window and . . ." He looked down at the musket in his hand. "I just grabbed the first thing I could find. I thought maybe you were that Christmas elf back for more."

"No, I'm definitely not the Christmas elf," Addie said with a reserved chuckle. "I'm sorry I gave you a scare, but I had no idea the kitchen door led right out to the bin area. I never thought someone would be downstairs this time of night, or I would have come inside and told you we were here."

"Since the robbery, the board has been working a lot of late nights, and everyone is a little jumpy, I guess." He gestured to the musket and set it back inside the door.

"Yes, I imagine you are. I heard that the loss of the donation items has caused a lot of issues with the budget for next year."

"You have no idea."

"Anyway"—Addie smiled, hoping her sincerity came through, then pointed at the pack of cigarettes at his feet—"enjoy your break."

"Nah, I've changed my mind now. It's too hard to quit, so why tempt it and have to start all over, right?"

"Good attitude, but I'd better get back over to the

inspec—" Addie cleared her throat and hoped Trevor hadn't noticed her faux pas. "To the officer I'm with and see if he found anything."

"Sure, let me know if you need anything else," Trevor said, starting back into the kitchen.

"There is one thing I'm curious about," Addie said.

"What's that?" Trevor turned back toward her.

"I was speaking to Deanna about the night of the robbery, and she told me she left the meeting to make coffee. Do you recall what time that was?"

"I remember she arrived a few minutes late for the meeting—because of the storm, I assume, as she lives out on Home Road—and then not long after she had to go get a document we needed that she'd left downstairs in her coat pocket, but I didn't notice the times."

"When she left the meeting, how long was she gone?"

"I really don't recall," he said, stepping back down onto the step. "We were reviewing the capital budget with the board of directors and . . ." He shook his head. "Sorry, I wasn't paying attention. I only know she was gone longer than any of us expected. We all hoped her delay was because she was making coffee. So, I eventually went to look for her, thinking maybe she needed help bringing it and the cream and sugar up. I found you instead, and well, you know the rest." He shivered and clasped his arms around himself. "Look, I'm freezing. If you want any more info from me, we'll have to take it inside."

"Just one more quick question. Do you remember if Peter Allen was at that meeting too?"

"Peter Allen?"

"I think he's also a board member?"

"Are you talking about Peter, Deanna's friend?"

"Yes, he's a board member, isn't he?"

"Not that I'm aware of. When he came by the next day, she introduced him to us as an old friend." Trevor turned back toward the door. "Sorry, gotta run, freezing," he called over his shoulder as he took a step up into the kitchen. Just then, his foot on the edge of the top stone slab slipped, sending him careening to the side, landing on the frozen ground with a *thud*.

Chapter Twenty-six

Addie readjusted her coat, which was covering Trevor's prone body. "I know you're in pain, but please try to stay still, Trevor. The ambulance is on its way," she said as he writhed on the ground, gripping his ankle.

"Until they get here, keep this under your foot to elevate it." Noah removed his coat and bunched it into a ball.

Trevor eyed Noah. "So, you're the police officer who was scanning the cliff top?" His gaze flickered between Noah and Addie, but he didn't say anything.

Addie crossed her fingers that Trevor and the paramedics who would soon show up didn't have wagging tongues. All their best-laid plans of covertly operating together were quickly going out the window. Noah must have sensed her churning thoughts because he